ONCE UPON A CHRISTMAS

Diane Farr

A SIGNET BOOK

SIGNET
Published by New American Library, a division of
Penguin Group (USA) Inc., 375 Hudson Street,
New York, New York 10014, USA
Penguin Group (Canada), 90 Eglinton Avenue East, Suite 700, Toronto,
Ontario M4P 2Y3, Canada (a division of Pearson Penguin Canada Inc.)
Penguin Books Ltd., 80 Strand, London WC2R 0RL, England
Penguin Ireland, 25 St. Stephen's Green, Dublin 2,
Ireland (a division of Penguin Books Ltd.)
Penguin Group (Australia), 250 Camberwell Road, Camberwell, Victoria 3124,
Australia (a division of Pearson Australia Group Pty. Ltd.)
Penguin Books India Pvt. Ltd., 11 Community Centre, Panchsheel Park,
New Delhi - 110 017, India
Penguin Group (NZ), 67 Apollo Drive, Rosedale, North Shore 0632,
New Zealand (a division of Pearson New Zealand Ltd.)
Penguin Books (South Africa) (Pty.) Ltd., 24 Sturdee Avenue,
Rosebank, Johannesburg 2196, South Africa

Penguin Books Ltd., Registered Offices:
80 Strand, London WC2R 0RL, England

Published by Signet, an imprint of New American Library,
a division of Penguin Putnam Inc.

First Printing, October 2000
First Printing ($6.99 Edition), October 2008
10 9 8 7 6 5 4 3 2

PUBLISHER'S NOTE
This is a work of fiction. Names, characters, places, and incidents either are
the product of the author's imagination or are used fictitiously, and any resemblance to actual persons, living or dead, business establishments, events, or
locales is entirely coincidental.
   The publisher does not have any control over and does not assume any
responsibility for author or third-party Web sites or their content.

TO MY FAMILY

God bless us—every one!

The author wishes to thank Laurel Chevlen,
a reader of *The Nobody*, whose letter
to the author sparked the idea for this book.

Chapter 1

The vicarage was small and shabby, and so was the girl. But when Her Grace placed an imperious finger beneath the girl's chin and tilted her face toward the light, the better to see her features, a certain something flashed in the child's expression—a look of astonished reproach—that slightly altered Her Grace's opinion. The girl met the duchess's eyes fearlessly, almost haughtily. *Just so,* thought the duchess, a faint, grim smile briefly disrupting the impassivity of her countenance. This milk-and-water miss may be a true Delacourt after all.

The duchess dropped her hand then, remarking idly, "You are offended by my examination. Do not be. A woman in my position must be careful. I am forever at risk of being imposed upon."

Ah, there it was again. The flash of swiftly suppressed anger, the unconscious stiffening of the spine. She had spirit, this unknown grandchild of the duke's Uncle Richard.

She spoke then. Her voice was sweet and musical. At the moment, however, it was also crisp with annoyance.

"I am sorry, Your Grace, that I must contradict you, but there is little risk of your being imposed upon by me. I have not sought you out in any way. You have come to my home, ostensibly on a visit of condolence, and asked me the most extraordinary questions—

scrutinized me as if I were some sort of insect—all but placed me under a microscope—"

Her Grace's brows lifted. "*Not* sought me out? What can you mean?"

Miss Delacourt's brows also lifted. "I mean what I say. I have not pursued your acquaintance. You came to me. How, then, can you suspect I wish to impose upon you? Forgive me, but the notion is absurd!"

The duchess gazed thoughtfully at the girl. Her confusion seemed sincere. An interesting development.

Her Grace sank, with rustling skirts, onto a nearby chair. "We have evidently been speaking at cross-purposes," she said calmly. "I received a letter, begging me to interest myself in your fate. Were you not its author?"

Miss Delacourt appeared amazed. "A letter! No. No, Your Grace, I have never written to you. I would never presume to— Good Heavens! A letter! And it begged you to—what was it? *Interest* yourself in—in—" She seemed wholly overcome; her voice faltered to a halt as she struggled to suppress her agitation.

The duchess lifted her hand, knowing that Hubbard would be anticipating her need. Sure enough, Hubbard immediately glided forward to place the letter in her mistress's palm, then noiselessly returned to her place near the door. "This is the letter I received," said Her Grace. "Someone has been busy on your behalf, it seems."

She handed the folded sheet to Miss Delacourt and observed the girl closely as she sat and spread the paper open with trembling fingers. Miss Delacourt then bent over the letter, cheating the duchess of a view of her face. Only the top of her head, crowned with a mass of dark brown curls, remained visible.

The duchess took the opportunity to look more closely at the girl's person. Although she lacked height, her figure was pleasing. Her fingers were smooth and finely tapered, the hands of a lady of quality. She kept her back straight and her ankles neatly crossed, even in an extremity of emotion. Despite the ill-fitting black dress, the cheap shawl, and the frayed ribbons on her slippers, there were marks of breeding in the girl. Given enough time, the right surroundings, the right company—and, naturally, the right wardrobe—she might yet prove adequate.

Given enough time. But how much time would be given? These days, the duchess tried not to think about time in general, and the future in particular. *Would there be enough time?* The thought was disquieting, but Her Grace had a lifelong habit of steely self-control. This rigidity of mind enabled her to banish unpleasant thoughts—a skill that was proving useful of late.

She turned her thoughts away from the fearsome future, therefore, and studied the room about her. She required information about Miss Delacourt. Obtaining it firsthand was the whole purpose of her visit. What might the vicarage tell her about its occupant?

One assumed that a person of rank would be entertained in the best room in the house. If this was the best room in the house, it spoke volumes for what the other rooms must be like. The parlor, or whatever this was, was spotless, but oppressively small and low-ceilinged. Blackened plaster over the fireplace gave mute testimony that the chimney smoked. Those old-fashioned casement windows were completely inadequate; it was growing quite dark in here as the afternoon closed in. The single candle that was burning was tallow, not wax. And the furniture! Someone had polished all the wood until it gleamed, but the duchess's sharp eyes were not deceived. All of it was old, most of it fairly worn, and several pieces were visibly scarred.

Quite a comedown for a branch of the illustrious

Delacourt family! Her Grace wished for a moment that her sole surviving son could see it. It might give him pause. This, *this* is what lies in store for those who defy the head of the house and indulge themselves in foolish rebellion! Poverty and ostracism, banishment from all the elegancies of life—not only for oneself but for one's descendants. It was a lesson in filial obedience just to see the place.

But the girl's face was lifting from her perusal of the letter. It seemed to the duchess that she had turned quite pale. "Do I understand you correctly, Your Grace? You have come here in answer to this?"

"Certainly I have. Quite an affecting letter, I thought. Do not be offended by my arrival so many weeks after its date. I am sure you will understand that the assertions it contained required investigation before I permitted myself to reply in any way. In my position, I receive appeals of this nature on a regular basis. One grows quite tired of them. But this one contained the ring of truth. I thought it my duty, as a Christian and a Delacourt, to investigate—and eventually, as you see, to respond. Our connection may be distant, but it is not so distant that I could, in good conscience, ignore it. The tale related in that missive is factual, is it not?"

Miss Delacourt pressed her fingertips against her forehead, as if trying to make sense of all this by main force. "Yes. But—why did you think I sent this letter? It is written entirely in the third person."

"I assumed, naturally, that that was merely a convention on your part."

Miss Delacourt gave a shaky laugh. "Oh! Naturally. As if I had my secretary write it! You will be astonished to learn, ma'am, that I have no secretary in my employ. I suppose that must seem strange to you."

"On the contrary, I did not expect that a girl enduring the circumstances described in that letter would keep a staff of any kind." The duchess glanced fleetingly at the nondescript female who was trying to make herself invisible in the darkest corner of the room. "It is not unheard of, however, for the author of such a letter—which is, if you will pardon my frankness, nothing more than a bald appeal for charity—to phrase the message in such a way that it gives the impression it has come from a third party when it has not. The signature is quite illegible."

The girl glanced briefly back at the letter in her hand. "Yes, I suppose it is. I recognize it, however. It is Dr. Hinshaw's signature." She sighed, rubbing her forehead again. "I am sure he meant well. His conscience must have pricked him when he engaged the new vicar. I don't know why it should. What else could he do? He had a duty to the parish. It was kind of him to allow me to stay so long in a house that does not belong to me."

The girl's eyes traveled around the ugly room, her expression one of naked sorrow. She even seemed to be fighting back tears. Was it possible she was mourning the loss of this insignificant little house? Her Grace devoutly hoped that Miss Delacourt did not suffer from an excess of sensibility. There were few things more tiresome than to be subjected to continual displays of sentiment, particularly the sentiments of one's inferiors. True, the child had just suffered a series of tragic misfortunes, but it was high time she recovered the tone of her mind. Her Grace did not approve of persons who unduly indulged their emotions.

The duchess was not, by nature, playful, but in an attempt to lighten Miss Delacourt's mood she offered her a thin smile. "I am glad to hear that you are accustomed to dwelling in a house that is not your own. You will not find it objectionable, I trust, to remove to another house that is not your own."

The girl did not laugh, but Her Grace did not resent

Miss Delacourt's lack of comprehension. She, herself, frequently misunderstood when those around her were joking. Miss Delacourt would understand the duchess's modest jest when she saw her new home. The absurdity lay in speaking of such a drastic change for the better as *objectionable.*

The duchess rose, shaking out her cloak. "I shall send members of my personal staff to assist you in packing. You will find them most efficient. I expect, therefore, to receive you at Delacourt this Thursday week. Henceforward, you may address me as Aunt Gladys, and I shall address you as Celia. I am neither your aunt nor your great-aunt, of course; I am the wife of your father's cousin, but that is neither here nor there. The disparity in our rank renders it disrespectful for you to address me as cousin."

Silence greeted this pronouncement. The duchess glanced at Celia, her brows lifting in frosty disapproval. "Well? Have you some objection?"

Celia had automatically risen when the duchess did, but she appeared to have lost the power of speech. Her mouth worked soundlessly for a moment before she managed to say, "I'm afraid I do not understand you, Your Grace. Are you really inviting me to Delacourt? What of the bad blood that existed between— between my grandfather and his family?"

The duchess waved a hand in languid dismissal. "You need not consider that. We shall be pleased to let bygones be bygones. The present duke has no interest in prolonging the estrangement. In fact, I am told that your grandfather was quite my husband's favorite uncle before the . . . unpleasantness. Do not fear that he will object to your presence. I can promise you that he will not."

Celia flushed prettily. "Why, then, I suppose I—I have to thank you. Pray do not think me ungrateful, ma'am! I am just so surprised that I—I suppose I was taken aback for a moment. My grandfather always spoke of Delacourt with great affection, but I never thought to see it with my own eyes. Thank you! I shall look forward to my visit with pleasure."

The duchess eyed Celia for a moment, considering whether she ought to correct the child. She decided against it. Let the girl think she was coming for a visit. Once she saw Delacourt, she would naturally be loath to leave. It would be an easy matter, once she was actually on the premises, to extend Celia an invitation to make her home there—and once she had seen Delacourt, Celia would understand the enormity of the gesture and be properly grateful.

It was extremely important that Celia be properly grateful. Nothing could be accomplished unless Celia was properly grateful. She seemed to have little understanding, at the moment, of the generosity being extended to her, nor any appreciation of Her Grace's condescension. Her Grace found this vaguely irritating, and had to remind herself that Celia's ingratitude arose from ignorance. That was easily mended. All in good time, she promised herself.

Time. There was that word again. The ghastly specter she must face, and face soon, immediately clamored for her attention. It was, again, swiftly banished. Pish-tosh! She would cross the bridge when she came to it, and not an instant before.

She bade Celia Delacourt a gracious farewell and was pleased to see the degree of deference in the girl's curtsey. She may have sprung from the black sheep of the family, and she might be ignorant of the glories in store for her, but at least she was not one of those brass-faced young women one encountered so lamentably often these days.

The nondescript female who had admitted them emerged from the shadows, showed Hubbard and the duchess to the door, and quickly effaced herself. Hubbard adjusted Her Grace's cloak and tightened the wrap round her throat. The duchess avoided Hubbard's sharp, worried eyes and placidly smoothed the creases on her gloves.

But the more devoted one's servants were, the more impossible it was to hide anything from them. As usual, Hubbard read her thoughts. "Will she do, Your Grace?" she asked gruffly.

It was a fortunate circumstance that Hubbard was so completely loyal. Her uncanny percipience would be embarrassing otherwise. The duchess smiled serenely. "Oh, I think so. She seems a trifle strong-minded, of course, but I daresay that's the Delacourt in her." Her smile faded as she voiced the unpleasant fact possessing both their minds. "She'll have to do. There's no time to find another."

When Celia heard the door closing behind her visitors, she let her breath go in a whooshing sigh of relief and collapsed nervelessly onto the settee. "What a terrifying woman!" she exclaimed. "Why do you suppose she asked me all those impertinent questions? My heart is hammering as if I have just run a race."

Elizabeth Floyd emerged from the shadows to flick the curtain aside. "Be careful, my dear!" she urged in an agitated whisper. "They have not yet gone."

Celia rolled her eyes. "Well, what of that? Even if she could hear me, which I sincerely doubt, I cannot picture the duchess unbending far enough to come back and ring a peal over me."

"I can," asserted Mrs. Floyd nervously. "There! The coach is moving off, and we may be easy. Well! I don't know what she meant by putting you through such a catechism, but it seems you passed the test. Oh, my dear little Celia! What an astonishing stroke of good fortune for you! At last!"

Celia did not move from her collapsed position on

the settee, but turned her head far enough to peer at her former governess with a skeptical eye. "Are you serious, Liz?"

Mrs. Floyd's round eyes grew rounder. "Quite, quite serious! Why, how could I not be? I think it amazing, and really quite affecting, that you should come to such a delightful end after all your travails."

"I am not sure this is any sort of end, let alone a delightful one," Celia pointed out. "I own, it will be interesting to visit Delacourt—which I never expected to see—but do not forget that the duchess is in residence there! How am I to face her on a daily basis? I hope she does not mean to pepper me with personal questions every time we meet, for I am likely to say something rude to her if she does." Indignation kindled in Celia's brown eyes and she suddenly sat upright again. "How dared she question me on my religious beliefs? As if Papa might have neglected his duties! And why do you suppose she wanted to know my medical history? I almost offered to let her examine my head for lice. Do you think that would have satisfied her?"

"Oh, dear. Oh, dearie dear. I am so glad you did not. Think how affronted she would have been!"

"Yes, but what was her *purpose*? I don't believe she was worried about . . . what happened to my family. Nothing contagious was responsible for—"

Mrs. Floyd interrupted quickly when she heard the catch in Celia's voice. "No, certainly not. Not a contagion at all. No question of that. Very odd of her, very odd, indeed! But many people are nervous about illness, you know. I daresay she wished to feel quite, quite sure that you would not communicate some dread disease to her household. Smallpox, or typhus, or something of that nature."

"Well, I like that! Of all the—"

"Now, Celia, *pray*! You should be blessing your

good fortune, and instead you are looking a gift horse in the mouth! She has invited you to Delacourt— *Delacourt,* my dear! Nothing could be more exciting. I declare, I am in transports! You shall have a family again, for they *are* your very own relatives, however grand and strange they may be. And you shall be surrounded by luxury—which I'm sure is no more than you deserve—and *I* shall be able to go home for Christmas, something I had not thought possible a quarter of an hour ago. Oh, I am so happy!" She whipped a handkerchief from her sleeve and dabbed briskly at her eyes.

Celia saw that her old friend was really beaming with joy. "Oh, Liz, what a wretched friend I have been to you!" she exclaimed remorsefully. "I have been so taken up with my own troubles, I never gave a thought to yours. Of course you would rather be home for Christmas than cooped up here, bearing me company for propriety's sake."

"For friendship's sake," said Mrs. Floyd firmly, perching her plump form on a nearby chair. "I have not begrudged a single moment of my time here, and well you know it. Why, Celia, you are like a daughter to me! I would no more think of abandoning you than—than anything."

The cap on the little governess's head fairly quivered with indignation. Celia smiled affectionately at her. "Even friendship has its boundaries, however. Am I to keep you from your family forever? You ought to have told me you wanted to go home for Christmas."

"I will be glad to go home, there is no denying it, but my brother's wife takes better care of him than ever I can, and I am only Aunt Liz there. Had you needed me for another month or so, they could easily have spared me. But, my dear, now that the crisis is past, I do not hesitate to tell you how worried I have been—for I was at my wits' end imagining what would become of you when the new vicar arrives. I could not offer you a place with me, since I do not have a home of my own. There was no possibility of the new vicar being able to spare you a room, with such a large family as he has. And if he could only think how difficult it would be to see another family move into the house where you have lived all your life—the house where you were born! After everything else you have been through, I feared for you, my dear, I really did. How unfortunate, that both your mother and your father had no siblings! With no aunts, no uncles, no cousins—where were you to go?"

Celia tried to smile but failed. "I suppose I would have found myself thrown on the parish. Although I do have four hundred pounds safely invested in the Funds, which will bring me the princely sum of—what is it?—about twelve pounds per annum, I think. And I might double that income if I hire myself out as a scullery maid."

Mrs. Floyd shuddered. "Do not even jest about such a thing. I have been so anxious! And when we received that message from the duchess informing you that she intended to pay you a visit, I was thrown into such a fever of hope it was almost worse than the fear! And then she asked you so many questions, just as if you were being interviewed for a position of some sort, which struck me as so very—but now everything is settled, and quite comfortably. Celia, I congratulate you!"

Celia frowned. "Settled? Surely you do not think that dragon of a female means to offer me permanent residence at Delacourt?"

Mrs. Floyd nodded vigorously. "Oh, yes! Yes, indeed! That is what I understood her to say. Did not you?"

"Certainly not! What an idea! After all—why

should she? Her Grace did not strike me as the benevolent sort. In fact, I thought her the coldest fish ever I met."

"Well, she is, perhaps, a little high in the instep—"

"High in the instep! That woman has held her nose in the air for so many years, it's my belief she can no longer bend at the waist."

Mrs. Floyd fluttered agitatedly. "Celia, *really*! You mustn't be disrespectful. After all, she *is* a duchess. It would be wonderful if she did *not* acquire a great opinion of her own importance, the way everyone round her must bow and scrape. Such a handsome woman, too! I daresay she is accustomed to an extraordinary degree of deference."

Celia's eyes sparkled dangerously, and Mrs. Floyd hurried to forestall whatever remark her former charge was about to make. "Do not forget she is your aunt! Or something like it. And she will be showing you a great kindness."

"Aunt." Celia shivered dramatically. "I shall never be able to address her as 'Aunt Gladys,' try as I might."

"Oh, pooh. I daresay she is perfectly amiable when one comes to know her. And they do say blood is thicker than water."

Celia chuckled. "Yes, they do, but she's no more related to me than you are. She simply married my father's cousin—whom he never met, by the by! The old duke booted my grandfather out of the house without a farthing, cut him out of his will, and never spoke to him again after he married my grandmother. We never encountered anyone from that branch of the family, and never cared to. And now I know why! If that stiff-rumped Tartar is the present duke's choice for his life's companion, only think what *he* must be like! After a se'nnight in their house, I daresay it will be a relief to hire myself out as a scullery maid."

"I wish you would not talk in that flippant way, my dear, about matters that are quite, quite serious! And besides, Delacourt is not a house," said Mrs. Floyd severely. "I would own myself astonished if you encountered the duchess above once a month in that great sprawl of a place. Apart from dinner, that is."

"Gracious. Will it be so very splendid, do you think?"

"My dear Celia—! Delacourt is *famous*!"

"I suppose it is." Celia rubbed her cheek tiredly. "In that case, I've nothing suitable to wear. It is a bit much, I think, to have to take something so trivial into consideration just now."

Mrs. Floyd reached out and patted her young friend's knee consolingly. "Depend upon it, my dear, they will understand that you are in mourning."

"They will have to," said Celia defiantly, "for even if I had the inclination to purchase a new wardrobe right now, I haven't the funds." Her eyes widened in alarm as another thought struck. "What about Christmas? I hope I am not expected to arrive bearing gifts for a houseful of persons I have never met. And I cannot afford anything remotely fine enough!"

"Oh, they don't keep Christmas in the great houses the way we humbler folk do. A pity, I always thought—as if Christmas could go out of fashion! But that's what one hears."

"Yes, but we don't *know*. The way my luck has been running, I shall arrive to find every room decked with holly and mistletoe, and discover that I must give expensive presents to all my unknown relatives—and their servants! Well, that's that. The instant I step through the door I shall tell the duchess that I have other plans for the holidays."

Mrs. Floyd looked uneasy. "But you don't, my dear. They will think it odd when Christmas approaches and no one sends a carriage for you."

"Perhaps they will offer me the use of one. They doubtless have a dozen."

"How will that mend matters? You will have to direct the coachman to take you somewhere. Where will you go?"

Celia bit her lip. "I think I feel an attack of influenza coming on," she said mendaciously, pressing a hand to her forehead and falling back on the sofa cushions. "What a pity! I fear I shall not be able to visit Delacourt until the second week of January. At the earliest."

Mrs. Floyd's face fell. "Well, of course, you *could* plead illness," she admitted. "And Dr. Hinshaw has promised us a goose," she added valiantly, "so I'm sure we will have a very merry Christmas here at the vicarage, just the two of us."

Celia's conscience immediately pricked her. She sat up. "No, no, I was only funning," she said hastily, and forced a smile. "The duchess is expecting me next Thursday week, and Thursday week it shall be. I would not dare to gainsay her."

Mrs. Floyd's relief was palpable. She immediately brightened and began chattering of her nieces and nephews, and how pleasant it would be to give them their little gifts in person rather than sending them through the post, and how there had never been a figgy pudding to equal the figgy pudding her sister-in-law made every year.

Listening to her, Celia felt ashamed. Her grief had made her selfish. It hurt to see how much her friend was looking forward to leaving her. But it was only natural, after all. Anyone who had a home would want to be home for Christmas.

Celia had not given Christmas a thought. Now she realized that she simply had not wanted to think about Christmas, any more than she had wanted to think about Mrs. Floyd leaving. Both thoughts gave her a painful, even panicky, sensation. But she would make an effort to hide that. She owed it to her friend, to let her leave for home with a happy heart, untroubled by the notion that Celia still needed her.

But she did. Oh, she did indeed.

Mrs. Floyd was the last person left alive whom Celia loved. The thought of Liz going back to Wiltshire and leaving her alone, completely and utterly alone, filled Celia with a blind and brainless terror.

It was useless to tell herself how silly she was being. She knew there was no logical reason to fear that Liz, too, would die if she let her out of her sight. But logic had no power over the formless dread, monstrous and paralyzing, that seized her every time Mrs. Floyd left the room. Since the first week of September she had been all but glued to Liz's side, following her about like a baby chick. How would she feel when Liz left the county? Could she smile and wave her handkerchief as the coach bore her only friend away? Or would she make a spectacle of herself, weeping and screaming like a child?

This surely was going to be the worst Christmas of her life.

Chapter 2

The flat in Conduit Street rang, as it did most evenings, with boisterous male laughter. Notwithstanding the lateness of the hour and the quantity of brandy that had been consumed in the course of the evening, a rather haphazard game of darts was in progress.

The target was centered upon a wall dotted with small holes—evidence that this game was not the first to be played in this room, nor the first to be played in the wee hours of the morning by friends who were less than serious in their attempts to best one another. Winning was never the point of any game played in Jack's flat. One was expected to instantly and enthusiastically join whatever game was under way at the moment, but actually *winning* was viewed as a rather unfortunate breach of etiquette.

The contestants were an eclectic lot. It might be assumed, from the fashionable address of the flat, and the fact that it had been home to the Marquess of Lynden for the past several years, that the gentlemen who gathered there would be the scions of distinguished families. Lord Lynden, however, was easygoing to a fault. He made friends easily, and wherever he went. The only prerequisite for becoming one of Jack's intimates was to be a thoroughly decent chap. A great gun. Sound as a roast. So long as there was something admirable about you, Jack Delacourt didn't care who your antecedents were. He also didn't care whether you were full of juice or poor as a church mouse. One could always drop by his flat unannounced and be sure of a welcome; there was generally a stream of idle, but good-natured, company ebbing and flowing at various times of the day and night. Since the company was almost exclusively male, and almost exclusively young, one was certain of finding an abundance of food and drink there as well.

Tonight's impromptu party was small, but fairly typical. Jack himself was present, his tall person flung sideways across an easy chair in a posture chosen for comfort rather than propriety. Dwight Thornburg, an earnest and rather threadbare young man whom Jack had met at school and whose intelligence and loyalty had earned him a permanent place in Jack's world, sat across from him. They occasionally interrupted their conversation to toss a desultory dart or two, but the game was being pursued with more zeal by the other two gentlemen in attendance.

John Emerson, who had a lamentable tendency to throw wide, had hurled a dart with so much vigor and so little skill that it stuck, quivering, in the wall fully six inches from the target. His friend Dick Hart whooped with laughter.

"What a clumsy fellow you are! No precision of eye, Emerson—none at all. And to think I let you drive me here from Worcester! I'd no idea I was taking my life in my hands."

"Well, don't choke to death," Emerson gloomily advised his friend, as Hart's laughter sent him into a coughing fit. He strolled over to pry his dart out of Jack's wall. "I say, it's dead center after all!"

"Eh?"

Emerson pointed with pride at the dart, neatly centered on a wallpaper rosebud. "I was aiming at the rose," he announced.

Hoots and catcalls greeted this pronouncement. Emerson waved them aside with great stateliness and yanked briskly at the dart. It popped out of the wall with sufficient force to send Emerson staggering back a pace, and the unfortunate lad's elbow struck a ceramic jar atop Jack's mantelpiece. It promptly crashed to the floor. A brief silence fell, during which Emerson flushed scarlet.

"Oh, Jack, I *am* sorry, dear chap—I'll buy you another, of course—" stammered the luckless Emerson.

Jack grinned. "On the contrary, old man, I am in your debt." He indicated the papers lying amid the wreckage. "I wonder what urgent communications I have overlooked by stowing them in that pot?"

Jack uncoiled himself from his contorted position in the chair and strolled over to take the papers, which Emerson had hurriedly retrieved from the shards of broken pottery. Then, lightly shrugging off Emerson's attempts to apologize, he returned with the small collection of correspondence to his favorite chair and began leafing through it. The game resumed behind him. By the time it reached its former pitch of hilarity, Jack had gone through several letters, including two that made him smile and shake his head, one that made him wince and pitch it into the fire, and another that caused him to frown in puzzlement. He read this one a second time.

"Here, Thornburg," he said at last, tossing the elegant sheet of hot-pressed paper to the most sober of his friends. "You fancy yourself a knowing 'un. What do you make of that?"

Thornburg caught it deftly, arched his brows in amused inquiry, and perused the letter. "Very proper," he said when he had finished. "What's wrong with it?"

"It's from my mother."

"Yes, thanks, so I see! Nothing mysterious about

that, is there? Why shouldn't it be from your mother?"

Jack gazed meditatively at him. "Have you ever *met* my mother?"

"I have," asserted Hart, unexpectedly joining the debate. "Let me see it."

Thornburg obligingly handed the letter to him and he read it. Emerson, abandoning the darts, crowded up behind Hart and read it over his shoulder. Both Hart and Emerson were well-connected, if impecunious, young men, and both were at least slightly acquainted with the Duchess of Arnsford. Dick Hart, in fact, was related to her on his mother's side, and was therefore rather better acquainted with her than he cared to be. By the time he had finished the missive his eyes had narrowed in suspicion.

"Smoky," was his opinion. "Too smoky by half."

"Yes, that's what I thought," agreed Jack.

Thornburg gave a snort of laughter. "What the deuce is *smoky* about it? It's a perfectly civil letter, inviting you to Delacourt for Christmas. Don't you want to spend Christmas with your family?"

"Well, that's just it," explained Jack, moodily crossing one leg over the other. "I always go home for Christmas. I've never spent Christmas anywhere else."

"Well, then?"

"I don't need to be invited to my *own home* for Christmas! It's really most peculiar."

Hart nodded wisely. "Something's afoot."

Emerson's eyes grew round with conjecture. "I say, perhaps the duke has received notice to quit."

"That did occur to me," admitted Jack. "But I think it unlikely."

"Pho! Arnsford will outlive us all," scoffed Hart. "Besides, if your father were on his deathbed, Her Grace would have summoned you home immediately and permanently. Not just for Christmas."

"Let me see it again," said Thornburg. He read the letter more methodically this time, and finally looked up with a more thoughtful expression. "I see what you mean. On the surface it's a perfectly ordinary, cordial letter, but—"

"But there's no precedent for it," interrupted Jack, shaking his head. "No need for it, no precedent for it, and what's more, although it doesn't sound like her in the least, it's in her own handwriting. What the devil is happening out there in Oxfordshire? It can't be *me* she wants, for I would have come anyway. I read it twice through, looking for the name of the friend she wants me to bring. But she doesn't mention anyone."

"Perhaps she meant to, but accidentally left that part out," suggested Emerson.

Hart snorted at this, and Jack looked skeptical. Thornburg knit his brows. "Would it really explain matters, had she mentioned your bringing a friend? I don't see why she should particularly want you to do so."

The other three men yelped with laughter. Thornburg gazed at them in mild surprise.

"Sorry!" gasped Jack. "I thought you knew. I thought *everyone* knew. My mother has been trying to marry my eldest sister off for years. Very nearly brought the thing off, last Season, but it all came to naught. Caused the devil of an uproar at the time."

Light dawned, and Thornburg's cheeks reddened. "Of course! Lady Elizabeth. You're right; the tale had reached even my ears. Sorry. I've always been a little dense on such matters."

"I've got it!" exclaimed Emerson, and began excitedly ticking the points off on his fingers. "Jack is right that the duchess assumes he will bring a friend. And why not? He's got more friends than any man in London. So she writes him a letter, even though she knows he will come home for Christmas, because she wishes to *remind* him of it, supposing that he will need to extend the invitation before everyone's plans are made." Emerson beamed at the group, evidently awaiting their approbation.

"Yes? Go on," urged Jack. "Why doesn't she tell me whom to bring?"

"Oh, she does not care which of us you bring. She trusts you to bring whomever you choose."

Hart groaned and punched Emerson in the shoulder. Jack dropped his head in his hands, choking back laughter. "My mother and Elizabeth may be desperate, but they will never be *that* desperate! Not *care* who I bring home? You silly young chuff, I am the despair of my family! They live in daily terror that I will arrive on their doorstep with an opera dancer on my arm."

"Well, I don't see the danger in that, old man," said Emerson, aggrievedly rubbing his shoulder. "Lady Elizabeth can't marry an opera dancer."

"No, but—" Jack suddenly broke off, an arrested expression in his eyes. "That's it!" he exclaimed, snapping his fingers. His friends looked at him expectantly. He snatched the letter out of Thornburg's hand and stared intently at it. "That *must* be it."

"What?" chorused Emerson and Hart.

Jack took a deep breath. "She's found a girl."

"A girl? For you, you mean?" asked Hart.

"No, for you!" said Jack rudely. "Of course for me, chucklehead! She's found a girl, and means to supervise our meeting."

Thornburg did not join in the general shout of laughter and spurious congratulations. He merely grinned and shook his head. "Forgive me, old chap, but I don't think you have *quite* reached the age where a man's parents push him toward the altar willy-nilly."

Jack cocked a knowing eye at him. "Ah, Thornburg,

you don't know my family! I'm three-and-twenty now, you know. A very dangerous age."

"Oh, do the Delacourts fall in love at three-and-twenty?"

Dick Hart threw up his hands in mock horror. "My dear Thornburg! Delacourts don't fall in love at any age. How dare you insinuate that our own Jack might be guilty of such a vulgarity? Jack, I say, call him out! Emerson and I will act as seconds."

"Well, Delacourts don't fall in love as a general rule," admitted Jack. "But there have been exceptions to that rule, and the exceptions have formed a certain—er—pattern. The family has grown rather superstitious about it, actually."

"Oh? What's the tale?" asked Hart, dropping into a nearby chair.

As there were no more chairs near the fire, Emerson pulled one over from the breakfast table. "I can't imagine the duchess, of all people, crediting a superstition," he remarked.

"Yes, but this one has an extraordinarily consistent history," said Jack, his eyes twinkling. "I daresay I am committing a solecism by divulging family secrets in this way, but after all, everything I am about to tell you is a matter of public record. Anyone might look it up and put two and two together."

"Well?" prompted Thornburg. "Let's hear it."

Jack assumed a melancholy and impressive air. " 'Tis the curse of the Delacourts," he intoned in a hollow voice. "Although it took us a while to notice it," he added, his voice resuming its normal pitch. He stretched his long legs out before him and crossed them comfortably at the ankle. "Ever since Henry VII carved out a duchy to bestow upon my grateful ancestors, marrying well has been the aim and ambition of the family. Advantageous marriage, my friends, *consistently* advantageous marriage, has been the key to our continued prestige, our awesome political power, our repetitive mentions in the history books, and our increasingly obscene wealth. As Hart so sapiently pointed out a moment ago, we have left 'falling in love' to the lower social orders. Delacourts *never* marry to disoblige the family, as the saying goes."

He looked round the circle of young men, who were all regarding him raptly, and chuckled. Then he held up one finger and wagged it. *"Except,"* he said impressively, "the second sons."

Hart looked surprised. "Really?"

Jack nodded. "They marry beneath themselves. Every last one of 'em. As I say, it took a few generations for the pattern to be noticed. The first duke had only one son, so the question never came up. The fourth duke's second son died at the age of twelve. And so on. There have been several dukes who either had no second son to embarrass them or had second sons who died mercifully young. But the ones that survive—ah, they are nothing but trouble!" He shook his head mournfully. "They invariably fall in love—irretrievably and insanely in love—always before their twenty-fifth birthday, and always with someone unsuitable. During the past century or so, it has caused increasing alarm and annoyance to the head of the family. Became a real thorn in the side, you know. Sterner measures have been taken with every generation, in an effort to stamp out the fatal tendency. Alas, to no avail! My father's favorite uncle, the second son of the fifteenth duke, became enamored of a humble vicar's daughter. He was given an ultimatum: choose her or choose your family. He chose her, and was never heard from again."

Emerson appeared enthralled. "And what of your father's younger brother?"

"He wisely chose to remain unborn. The sixteenth duke had no second son. The seventeenth duke was less fortunate. He had me."

Thornburg looked puzzled. "But, Jack, old chap,

you're the heir. I've known you forever, and you've always been the heir."

"Yes, you'd think that would mend matters, wouldn't you? Being reared as the duke-in-waiting, I ought to have absorbed all the reverence for duty and infatuation with my own consequence that have characterized the dukes of Arnsford since time immemorial. Well, I haven't. I exhibit all the classic characteristics of a Delacourt second son. In fact, I'm the worst one yet. I couldn't wait to shake the dust of my ancestral home from my shoes. I despise all that silly ducal bowing and scraping and protocol and formality. And—prepare to be shocked, my friends—I think my father a fool."

"Never mind, old chap," said Hart soothingly. "Most people think your father a fool."

"Yes, but *I* ought not to think it," Jack pointed out. "Most unfilial of me!"

"You had an older brother, then," said Thornburg, still wrestling with this new information.

"Yes. Henry died when I was a year old. So, you see, I've been the heir for as long as I remember—but all my careful training has had no effect whatsoever. I'm telling you, it's a curse. No one has mentioned it—to me, at least, though for all I know it has been the central topic of conversation at Delacourt ever since I left my father's roof—but I am well aware that everyone is on tenterhooks, dreading the day when I announce my betrothal to a brewer's daughter, or a shepherdess, or some such thing."

Thornburg choked. "You won't meet one in London. Perhaps you'll bring home that opera dancer after all."

"The landlord's daughter," suggested Emerson.

"Your washerwoman," cried Hart, and they all shouted with laughter.

"It's all very amusing, I'm sure," said Jack aggrievedly, "but if this summons means my mother has chosen a bride for me, she's bound to be a fright. What female would agree to marry a man sight unseen? A mercenary female, that's who! Since she doesn't know Jack Delacourt, she could only be interested in the Marquess of Lynden. My mother has found some simpering, well-bred, humorless shrew who means to be a duchess one day, whatever the cost." He shuddered. "If there really is a girl lying in wait for me, and if she's half as skillful as my mother is at manipulating everyone around her into doing her bidding, a mild-mannered chap like Yours Truly won't stand a chance. I shall have to handicap myself in some way."

"Handicap yourself? What do you mean?" asked Emerson.

"I must make myself unattractive to the wench. Come, help me think! What would make a girl like that run in horror?"

Thornburg eyed him doubtfully. "A marquess, young, reasonably good-looking, rich as Croesus, and Arnsford's heir? My dear chap! There's nothing you can do to make yourself unattractive."

"Very well, *less* attractive. What if I played imbecile?"

"No good," said Hart firmly. "Idiocy would make you more attractive than you are now."

"Why, *thank* you—" began Jack, his voice quivering with laughter.

"Oh, no offense, old man! But the sort of female who would fall in with Her Grace's plans is the very sort of female who likes to rule the roost. The more foolish her husband is, the better she will like it."

"That's true," said Jack, much struck. "Only look at my parents. It wouldn't have suited my mother at all, had my father possessed a brain."

Hart grinned. "I'm glad you said that, rather than I."

"Yes, but perhaps it all depends upon the *sort* of idiocy," suggested Emerson. "No, now hear me out! What if Jack were to behave like a despotic sort of fool?"

"Beat her, do you mean?" inquired Jack. "I don't think I have it in me. Besides, it must be difficult to accomplish a really sound beating on short acquaintance. One would have to be on a first-name basis with the victim, I should think, before one could properly begin."

Hart burst out laughing as Jack continued plaintively. "Yes, only think how awkward it must be to strike a lady one has just met. I would be wearing gloves, too! Even if I somehow worked a few blows into the conversation, I don't think they would be effective."

"Oh, no need to actually *strike* the wench. Just bully her a little," advised Thornburg, grinning.

"Bully her a lot," corrected Emerson. "Shout her down. Order her about. That sort of thing."

Jack blanched. "Now, really, dear chap—can you picture me doing that? I wouldn't have the first idea how to go about it. And only think how exhausting!"

"Oh, if you're going to begrudge the *effort*—"

"No, no! I am willing to stir myself a little. But within reason, man, within reason!"

"Yes, but I do think Emerson is on the right track," said Thornburg. "There are any number of behaviors that females find repellent. You merely choose one and adopt it as a habit."

"That's the dandy!" said Jack approvingly. "What shall I do? Short of actual violence, that is."

"Stop bathing," suggested Thornburg.

Jack pulled a face. "I couldn't bear it."

"Belch at the dinner table," offered Hart.

"Belch whenever you begin a sentence!" cried Emerson, inspired.

Hart leaped to his feet. "Drool!" he shouted. The entire company roared with laughter.

Eventually Jack wiped his streaming eyes and managed to utter, "So which of you is going to invite me for Christmas? I can't go home this year, that's certain!"

"Courage, man," said Thornburg, reaching out to give Jack's knee a friendly shake. "We are all being even sillier than usual. Even if it's true and there is a girl, your family can't force you to marry against your will. This is the nineteenth century, not the Middle Ages."

"Never mind Thornburg," interrupted Hart. "He hasn't met the duchess. I, for one, will wager a pony that if Jack goes home for Christmas, he comes back engaged."

"Done," said Jack promptly.

"And I'll bet a monkey he not only comes back engaged, but engaged to the chit Her Grace picked out for him," added Emerson. He grinned. "I've met the duchess, too."

Jack groaned. "Now I shall have to go home for Christmas, just to prove my own mettle!"

Thornburg laughed. "It's my belief you'll win your bet, Jack, and come back after the New Year as unshackled as you are today."

"I don't notice you risking any blunt on it," Jack pointed out. "Still, I shall not despair. My dependence is on the strength of the Delacourt curse. It's never yet failed a second son."

Hart winked. "The curse hasn't met the duchess, either."

Chapter 3

Celia closed the massive door to her new bedchamber behind her—not without difficulty—and leaned her back against it for support. The shock, she felt sure, was killing her. Dear saints in heaven, what a place.

Her eyes traveled fearfully round the room, confirming, to her relief, that she was finally alone. No servants hovered respectfully in the corners. No new faces peered curiously at her. No strangers with unsettlingly familiar features were present to stare with ill-concealed contempt at their drab and poverty-stricken relative.

When the housekeeper had shown her this apartment earlier, she had been in too much of a daze to really look at it. Now she realized that this was the smallest and least prepossessing room she had seen at Delacourt. That was not saying much, however. It was easily six times the size of her bedchamber at home. How could anyone afford to heat such a space through the winter? It would cost a fortune.

Well, a fortune was clearly what they had. A brisk fire burned in the grate, and the room was, in fact, tolerably warm.

Celia moved forward like a sleepwalker and began slowly unbuttoning her redingote. She could just kick herself for her own stupidity. What had she been expecting? She had known all her life that she was a

Delacourt, and that the head of her family was Henry Fitzwilliam Delacourt, the seventeenth Duke of Arnsford. It was no secret that dukes were rich, and that the Duke of Arnsford was spectacularly rich. As the descendant of a disinherited black sheep, the Delacourt wealth had been no concern of hers. She had never given it a thought. Now she was mortified to find herself here, utterly unprepared for Delacourt's magnificence, its gargantuan proportions, and its overwhelming grandeur.

What must they all have thought of her! What a fool she must have looked, arriving at a ducal palace in her rusty black traveling dress and her mother's old redingote, too frightened to say more than two words together—and staring at everything, eyes wide and mouth agape, like a bumpkin at the fair!

She had been in such a daze, she had received only blurred and fleeting impressions of the family she had just met. The duchess was every bit as formidable as she remembered: impressive, ageless, and rather frightening. With a different expression, Celia thought, she might have been beautiful. But long years of self-consequence had hardened Her Grace's features into a permanent mold of finely-etched hauteur. The eldest daughter, Lady Elizabeth, was a striking creature. Her black hair and pale skin had struck instant envy into Celia's heart, but she seemed to have inherited her mother's arrogance as well as her coloring. Lady Augusta put Celia eerily in mind of Fanny, with her willful, discontented face and slanting brows. Lady Winifred suffered from a spotty complexion that one could only hope she would outgrow, and Lady Caroline, despite a disturbing resemblance to Papa—of all things!—was plump and graceless.

The duke was so unlike Celia's mental picture of a duke, she feared she had stared rather rudely when presented to him. He seemed much older than the duchess, spoke ungrammatically, and looked more like a country squire than a fine gentleman. His Grace, the Duke of Arnsford, was fat, red-faced, goggle-eyed, and wheezy, and Celia thought him one of the most unattractive persons she had ever met.

She glanced in the mirror as she untied her bonnet strings, and the reflection of the room around her made her wonder, fleetingly, if her placement here was meant for an insult. It was, by Delacourt's standards, a small chamber, and far from the apartments of the other family members. She walked to the tall windows, half expecting her room to have a view of the kitchens or some such thing.

It did not. "Oh, my," murmured Celia, gazing at the pretty vista of seemingly endless parkland. Delacourt was not a modern seat, but the only remaining vestige of its Tudor beginnings was the vast park that had been the first duke's hunting grounds. The original house had been razed, and Celia looked out from one of hundreds of windows in a gigantic palace of golden limestone erected, perhaps, a hundred years ago. The palace graced the top of a slight rise, from which vantage point, Celia now realized, the Delacourts could view their surrounding domain as masters of all they surveyed. The vast lawns and woods and lakes and gardens belonged to them, and them alone, all the way to the horizon. The situation was perfect; the view breathtaking, even in winter.

Of course, Celia thought cynically, if the rise were any higher one might have caught a glimpse of a village, or someone else's farm. As it was, however, reality did not intrude. Delacourt dreamed in splendid isolation, the self-contained and perfect center of its world.

So much for her idea that this bedchamber was substandard. Delacourt obviously did not contain substandard accommodations. The servants' quarters were probably finer than the vicarage Celia had grown up in.

With a sigh, she dropped the edge of the heavy drapery she had been holding and turned back to survey the room again. It lacked magnificence—thank goodness—but it certainly contained its fair share of luxury. The bed was enormous. She'd never before slept in a bed that had its own little flight of stairs. The sight made her chuckle. She climbed them, sat on the edge of the bed, and instantly sank up to her waist in goose down.

She bounced experimentally. Yes, there was a mattress beneath all those feathers, and a good one, too. It did seem a long way to the ground, however—for a bed. It would be like sleeping atop a great table on a dais. If she managed to get through the night without falling off the edge of it, it would probably prove to be comfortable beyond her wildest imaginings.

Oh, dear. No wonder those hoity-toity servants the duchess had sent to help her pack had looked askance at her few sticks of furniture. They must have thought her a madwoman, insisting so mulishly on bringing her narrow bed and battered chiffonier! But the duchess's instructions were to bring everything, absolutely everything, that belonged to her, and bring it she had. It was a little embarrassing that the sum total of her belongings did not even half fill the enormous wagon the duchess had sent. But most of the furniture belonged to the vicarage and would be passed to the new vicar and his family.

Celia had been too proud to let the duchess's supercilious staff see how much it pained her to leave those things behind. She supposed it had been helpful, in a way, to have their cold eyes upon her at the last. Otherwise she might have broken down. She could not weep before strangers, and had thus survived the experience without disgracing herself.

Sitting on her new bed at Delacourt, cradled in eiderdown, she thought of those last moments and felt her throat tighten with unshed tears. The worst, somehow, had been parting with the dining room table. Odd that that would hurt so much. But the strange thing about grief is, the things one *expects* to find oversetting are bearable. One is prepared to face them. She had sat stone-faced and stoic through the funerals. But the little things, the things that catch you off guard—those are the things that blindside you.

The last thing Celia had done before vacating the only home she had ever known was take the leaves out of the dining room table. As her father's family had grown, the table had grown with it, adding leaf after leaf until it was really too big for the vicarage's tiny dining room. It had occurred to Celia that taking the extra leaves out would make the room seem larger when the new vicar saw it for the first time. So she went, alone, to the dining room and tugged at the heavy table. It rocked and creaked and then, with a final sigh of protest, gave in to her insistence and pulled apart.

It was then, unexpectedly, that grief had struck. Lifting the heavy wooden panels out of the dining room table, Celia was vividly reminded of the faces that had sat around it every day of her life. Faces she loved without thinking, saw without noticing, assuming they would always be there. As she removed the first leaf, her eyes did not see the pitted wooden surface before her.

They saw Benjy.

Benjy had sat here, next to Mama, within reach so she could cut his meat for him, catch his kicking feet in her hand beneath the table, and make sure he did not slip his porridge into his milk cup when no one was looking. And across from him, at the other end of the leaf, had sat Jane, the quiet one, who never gave anyone any trouble at all.

Celia was shaking when she placed the first panel neatly against the wall and returned for the next. She had sat here, next to Jane. It was her own place she was removing now. Hers and Fanny's. They had bickered constantly as children; now she would give anything to have Fanny back again, temper and all.

And the last panel. George, as the elder son, had always sat next to Papa. They had been so alike. George's laugh had been just like Papa's, and his walk, and his kind and studious ways. Papa had been a good and decent man. George would have been just such another, had he lived. And across from George's place, Margery's. Dear, sweet, loyal Margery, who had laughed at all her jokes and kept all her secrets.

Margery was, to Celia, the biggest loss of all. She had embodied everything bright and precious in the word "sister." They had been friends always, playmates as children and confidantes as they grew older, but bonded closer than other friends or confidantes could ever be, through common blood and shared experience. It was not Mama's name Celia woke up crying, these past weeks. It was Margery's.

How sad and empty the table looked with a gaping wound where its leaves should be. She pushed the two ends toward each other and felt them lock together with a soft, final click.

Only Papa's and Mama's places remained. This must have been the way the table had looked in the early days of their marriage, when the other bright faces round the table were only dreamed of. Now the faces that their love had brought into being were gone, and they had gone with them. Celia alone was left behind. And, deep within her, some part of her was sure that a terrible mistake had been made. She ought to have gone, too. Had she been home when the angel of death touched this house, she would even now be sleeping in the churchyard between Margery and Jane.

The dining room did look bigger with the table leaves removed. Less crowded. But, to Celia's taste, the room had looked better after all with the table filling it. What did people find so attractive about empty space? She was intimately acquainted with emptiness now, and saw nothing good about it. Nothing at all.

A traveling chaise with the Arnsford arms emblazoned on its side had taken Celia away, and she had not looked back. She had not dared. She had occupied her mind, instead, by looking ahead and repeating to herself the names of her newfound relatives. She had gleaned the bare facts of their names and birth dates from her father's dusty copy of the *Peerage,* and had idiotically supposed that knowing their names in advance would somehow prepare her for a stay at Delacourt.

Nothing, however, could prepare a country vicar's daughter for a stay at Delacourt. She was the proverbial fish out of water. What a shock it had been, when the carriage had swept round that last bend and she had caught her first glimpse of the place! She'd been gasping like a landed trout ever since.

Delacourt would be a wonderful spot to come for a day of picnicking and gawking, but Celia's imagination failed her when she tried to picture people actually *living* here. What would it be like, to hear one's footsteps echoing on a marble floor and bouncing off a forty-foot ceiling on the way to breakfast every morning? What would it be like, to think nothing of a fifteen-minute hike through one's own home—and without ever stepping outdoors or walking through the same room twice?

It seemed that Celia was about to find out.

At least temporarily.

It was all very awkward; she had no firm idea how long she would be staying here. One could scarcely buttonhole the Duchess of Arnsford and demand particulars. She wasn't sure if the duchess had insisted on her bringing everything she owned merely as a courtesy, since she knew Celia would be supplanted by the new vicar's family in her absence, or whether Mrs. Floyd had been right and her intent was for Celia to actually stop at Delacourt indefinitely. What had become of her furniture and packing crates? Celia didn't know. It made her feel uneasy, as if she were losing control of her destiny. She felt very small and powerless since the duchess had pulled her into her orbit. But when the time came for her to leave, she promised herself firmly, she would not feel the least bit shy about asking these wealthy Delacourts to transport her belongings to her new home. Wherever that might be.

But she would not think about her uncertain future—she had enough anxieties in her dish at the moment. The most pressing of these was that she faced an audience with the duchess in half an hour. And, later, dinner. *Dinner!* Her heart quailed at the thought. This was exactly the sort of household where everyone would stare if she came down to dinner in her morning dress. Well, she would have to contrive something.

She slid off the bed, feeling vaguely guilty for having mussed it, and prowled through the room in search of her baggage. Her battered trunks were nowhere to be found. What a nuisance. She hated to call for a servant, just to find out where her things had been taken. Then she realized her reluctance stemmed from embarrassment: she didn't want a servant to see the imprint she had made, bouncing on the bed like a child. Celia blushed for her foolishness. Silly! she told herself. You must not care what the servants think.

While she was scolding herself for her nervousness, she moved to put her discarded redingote and bonnet away in an ornate wardrobe against the wall. But when she opened the wardrobe door, she froze in startled dismay: *it contained her clothes.* There they were. Her frocks had been neatly hung on pegs, and everything else crisply folded and placed in orderly stacks on the wooden shelves.

Celia's cheeks burned. Foolish or not, she was embarrassed. She couldn't help it. Some unknown person had gone through her things. Whoever had done so was probably regaling the staff below stairs with tales of her meager collection of inexpensive garments, her home-dyed mourning attire, her mended stockings and plain petticoats, the pelisse with mismatched buttons, and the holes in her shoes that she had patched with paperboard.

She looked with new eyes at the dressing table. Sure enough, those were her combs laid in perfect rows atop its highly polished surface. She hadn't recognized them in their new surroundings. She crossed to the table and lifted the top of the elegant porcelain box that sat beside her cheap combs. Yes, there were her pins. How mortifying. Now she had to picture some curious housemaid pawing through her comb case. Thank goodness she had thrown out the comb with the two missing teeth; she had very nearly brought it "just in case."

Twenty minutes later, Celia supposed, despairingly, that she was as ready as she would ever be. She had tried, and discarded, virtually every garment she owned, finally settling on a high-necked, long-sleeved gray broadcloth. It was not meant to be gray. At one time it had been a sort of salmon color, and rather pretty. Her attempt to dye it black had resulted in its present nondescript and muddy hue. It was dreadfully ugly, but it fit her well and there was nothing glaringly deficient in its workmanship or the quality of the fabric. Most of her clothing suddenly looked cheap, unfashionable, and poorly made. She supposed her attire had always been cheap, unfashionable, and poorly made. She simply hadn't known it. Or cared twopence, for that matter.

She cast a last, anxious look at herself in the pier glass. It wasn't just her clothes. She wished her hair and eyes were any color other than plain brown. She wished she were tall. She wished her hair were straight, or longer, or shorter, or at least more fashionably cut. She felt inadequate in every area. Celia drew a deep and shaky breath. Then she lifted her chin, straightened her shoulders, and, trembling, went forth to seek the duchess.

It unnerved her further to be met in the passage by a footman who was waiting there to escort her to Her Grace's apartments. Evidently Celia's summons was known to the staff. She supposed anyone living in this style thought nothing of having her comings and goings tracked and anticipated, but it gave Celia a most uncomfortable sensation.

Her Grace received Celia in her private sitting room, offering two fingers and a thin smile. She did not rise. Celia curtseyed deeply, thinking that it was exactly like having an audience with the queen.

"I am glad to see that you are punctual," remarked Her Grace. She inclined her head graciously when Celia rose from her curtsey. "Pray sit down, my dear. Is your room to your liking?"

"It's splendid," Celia assured her, perching nervously on the edge of a spindle-legged chair. The duchess's keen eyes had flicked over her, reminding her painfully of her deficiencies, but Her Grace gave no indication of her thoughts. The same servant who had accompanied the duchess to the vicarage hovered behind Her Grace's chair. Celia stole a glance at her. She was one of the strangest-looking persons Celia had ever seen—extremely tall for a woman, gaunt and big-boned, with tiny, close-set eyes bracketing a large and crooked nose. Celia's fingers itched with the desire to sketch her.

"And what do you make of Delacourt thus far?"

Celia tore her eyes from the fascinating features of Her Grace's tirewoman. The duchess was regarding her with a proud smile, plainly expecting Celia to fall into raptures. She swallowed and tried to oblige. "It is pretty, of course. Lovely. A lovely place." More was clearly expected of her. She tried again. "It's very large, isn't it? Immense. I mean—I mean—it is a bit overwhelming, you know. Just at first."

Her Grace's smile froze. Oh, dear. Celia simply could not think how to describe her impressions of Delacourt without giving offense. Perfection was all very well in its way, but the thought of living with it on a daily basis was horrid. One could not say so, of course.

Celia took a deep breath. "I'm not expressing myself well, am I?" She sighed and spread her hands apologetically. "You saw my home, Your Grace, so I am sure you can imagine—well, perhaps you can't. Delacourt takes a little getting used to, for a girl who has lived in a country vicarage all her life. I've never seen anything to equal it. Never imagined anything so—so—huge. So flawless. So much space! And so many servants. And so many—well, *things*. Beautiful things. Expensive things! You will think me foolish, I daresay, but I'm almost afraid to touch anything for fear I might break something valuable."

Her Grace relaxed infinitesimally. "Interesting," she commented. Her eyes rested on Celia, their expression unfathomable. "My first impression of you is confirmed. Your manners are direct. You have a tendency to speak your mind with, perhaps, a little too much frankness. We must strive to rid you of the habit. There is no need for a girl of nineteen to be quite so forthright. Indeed, it is generally considered undesirable. You will not wish to seem froward, or disagreeably pert." She smiled gently, but her eyes held no warmth. "When you are older, my dear, your opinions may be deemed to be of interest. At the moment, however, they are not. You will do better to say what is *expected,* rather than what you actually think."

Celia felt her jaw dropping, and took care to close her mouth. The duchess continued blandly, "I understand that your education has not included instruction in the behavior that is expected of young ladies of birth. Indeed, there is no reason why it should have. Your position has altered, however, and you will now need to apply yourself to such lessons. I shall undertake your instruction myself."

Celia nearly choked on all the things she wished to say. She struggled for a moment, then finally took the duchess's advice. She uttered only the phrase that was expected. "Thank you, Your Grace," she said woodenly.

"You may be wondering what your status is here at Delacourt." The duchess bent an inquiring look upon her visitor. Celia did not trust her voice, but managed a brief nod. The duchess seemed satisfied. "I have instructed my daughters to think of you as a cousin. You have my permission to address them as such. Pray remember that you may call me 'Aunt Gladys.' You may also refer to my husband as 'Uncle Henry'—I have prepared him to expect it."

Celia cleared her throat. "Very thoughtful of you, Your G— Aunt Gladys."

"You will have guessed, I think, that I intend for you to stay indefinitely. You may consider Delacourt your permanent home. Ah. Perhaps I mistake, and you did not guess?"

Since Celia's jaw had definitely dropped this time, she saw no point in polite prevarication. "No, I did not guess. Mrs. Floyd tried to tell me, but—no, I had no idea. Or certainly no *expectation* that you would— that is—"

Her Grace's brows lifted. "Are you displeased?"

"Displeased! No, how should I be? I am—I am grateful. It is just that—" Celia broke off. She could not continue without voicing her *thoughts,* and the duchess had already expressed a disinclination to hear them. Still, she could not help blurting out her most pressing question. *"Why?"*

Celia flushed scarlet as the duchess's eyes bored into her. But however much Her Grace deplored bluntness, she did not seem to be actually offended by it. She was tapping her fingers meditatively on the arm of her chair, as if considering how best to reply.

The odd-looking henchwoman standing motionless behind the duchess's chair suddenly coughed. It was a small cough, and quiet, but Celia heard it. She also saw Her Grace's reaction, which was to send a swift, searching look at the servant's face. Whatever she read there seemed to make up her mind, for she immediately turned back to Celia with a polite—and patently false—smile wreathing her features. "Oh, I think you need not wonder overmuch about that," she said soothingly. "All in good time, Celia. For the present, you need only adjust to your new home and learn your way about. We shall undertake your instruction in deportment, as I mentioned. You are a member of the family, recently rescued from a distressing situation and restored to your rightful place. That is all."

But that was obviously far from all. Had the duchess begun with that assertion of family feeling, rather than ended with it, Celia might have been persuaded to take it at face value. As it was, however, she felt a shiver of fear.

What undergame was the duchess playing? And why would she not say outright what she wanted? She surely had some hidden motive—and she must have reason to believe that Celia would not like it, whatever it was.

Chapter 4

Celia's days soon settled into a routine. Since her cousins consistently rebuffed her, she stopped making friendly overtures to the other young ladies of the household. She sat silently through breakfast with whatever members of the family were present, then withdrew to the duchess's rooms. There she would endure several hours of daily instruction in the rules of polite conduct, in the history and glory of her ancestors, and in the attitudes and beliefs deemed proper for an aristocratic maiden.

Most of Her Grace's pronouncements struck Celia as petty, and some seemed downright wicked. But the first thing she learned was that a young lady, if she *must* have opinions, must keep them to herself. Since this was difficult for Celia, the mere maintenance of a calm demeanor was, in itself, a lesson in self-discipline. She hoped this would do her some good. Apart from learning self-control—and, of course, pleasing her benefactress—it all seemed a pointless exercise.

Her impatience finally showed itself when Her Grace recommended, for what seemed the hundredth time, that Celia pattern her behavior on that of her cousins. "Do you know what your daughters call me behind my back?" blurted Celia, her voice shaking a little. "They call me Cinderella."

A slight frown disturbed Her Grace's masklike serenity. "Nonsense. You are imagining it. I have instructed my daughters to welcome you."

Celia gave a despairing little laugh. "Your Gr—Aunt Gladys, you cannot command what others *feel!* I overheard them quite by accident, but I tell you truly, they resent me. They do not understand why you have brought me here and shown me so much kindness. And frankly, ma'am, I cannot blame them. I do not understand it myself."

She clenched her hands together tightly, trying to rein in her frustration. "Pray do not misunderstand me. I am grateful for your invitation, I am grateful for your support, I am grateful for—oh, everything! I am all too aware of how much I owe you. I do not like to contradict you, but—but I cannot understand why you wish me to model my behavior on that of your daughters. They are women of rank and fortune. The manners that are appropriate for them are, in a lesser being, an intolerable affectation! Can you not see how it strikes them? They despise me."

"They will not do so when you have learned to conduct yourself with dignity," said the duchess severely. "As I have told you time and again, your manners are far too informal. Your kindness to the staff borders on *familiarity*. Nothing could be worse! I am disappointed, but not surprised, that my daughters keep you at a distance. Your status is beneath their own, and your ill-chosen behavior reinforces that unfortunate fact. But your lineage is not, after all, so far removed from theirs. If you would *act* the lady, you could easily pass for one. It is precisely that end that I am trying to achieve, Celia. Strive to be a little more conformable."

Celia felt her cheeks flush angrily. "I *do* try. But I must tell you, ma'am, I heartily agree with my cousins! The behavior you deem *appropriate* for me is, in a penniless orphan, simply putting on airs!"

"You are expressing yourself again, Celia."

Celia closed her eyes for a moment, struggling, and

then opened them again. "I beg your pardon, madam," she whispered, choking on the words, and was rewarded with a tiny smile from the duchess.

"I understand how difficult this training is for you," said Her Grace mildly. "All the Delacourt women are strong-minded. I do not take offense at your frankness, Celia. I merely point it out, so that you might be on your guard. In public, any such outburst would put you beyond the pale."

"Yes," said Celia tonelessly. "I shall confine my remarks to the weather."

Amusement flickered briefly in Her Grace's ice blue eyes. "You would like very much to point out to me that we are not in public," she remarked. "Quite right. You may express yourself to me, Celia, so long as we are alone, and so long as you do it without *heat.* You have a temper, my dear, and that has been the downfall of more than one young lady."

More than one young lady in this very house, I'd wager, thought Celia resentfully. *And I am not your* dear. But she said nothing. She was learning fast.

The duchess was a difficult woman to fathom. She was hardly a warmhearted individual, and did not seem to have an altruistic bone in her body, so her staggering generosity to Celia was baffling. To give her a home—and *such* a home!—and to take a personal interest in training her to occupy the position thrust upon her, was definitely an act of kindness. On top of that, she had forced Celia to accept the ministrations of the hairdresser, dressmaker, and dancing master employed for her own daughters. These gifts should have caused Celia to glow with gratitude. Even affection. But, somehow, they did not.

Celia continually reminded herself how kind, how extraordinarily kind and generous, the duchess was being. It was strange, and rather sad, that she had to remind herself—but the thought refused to come unbidden. Kindness and generosity simply did not sit naturally upon Her Grace's shoulders. There was a missing piece to this puzzle, and Celia could not make sense of the picture.

Her Grace had just said something clearly meant to be kind, for example, and yet her affect was as detached and indifferent as ever. She was eyeing Celia in a decidedly calculating manner. Celia schooled her own features to mirror Her Grace's inscrutability and waited.

"Have you been taught to revere frankness, Celia?" asked the duchess suddenly. "Do you admire it?"

Celia blinked. "Yes, ma'am."

"I wondered if that might be so. Your habit of speaking your mind is very firmly entrenched." Her Grace paused, still studying Celia with her lips pursed in consideration. "I trust, then, that you will not object to a little plain-speaking on my part," she said at last.

Celia tried to look neither relieved nor eager, although she felt both. "No, ma'am," she said woodenly. When Her Grace still did not speak, she ventured to add: "I would welcome it."

Her Grace inclined her head. "Very well." She frowned at her hands suddenly, as if finding it easier to speak truth when not looking directly at Celia. "I am displeased that my daughters have so far forgotten themselves as to express themselves unbecomingly within your hearing—or, indeed, at all. You need not tell me which of them you overheard. Neither Augusta nor Elizabeth would demean herself by openly displaying such a degree of spite. However, I have often been disappointed in the tone of Winifred and Caroline's conversation. I do not doubt that it was one, or both, of them who indulged in a feeble witticism at your expense."

Her Grace was, as usual, correct. But, also as usual, there was no need to tell her so. Celia remained silent.

The duchess looked up again, her expression unreadable. "Nevertheless, their characterization of you as 'Cinderella' is more apt than they know."

Celia stiffened, and Her Grace smiled humorlessly. "I do not mean to imply that you are dirty, or pitiable, and I trust no one here has asked you to perform the tasks of a servant. But I am hopeful—I put it no higher than that—I am *hopeful* that you will achieve a similar fate."

"Oh," said Celia, relaxing slightly. "Is this the end for which you are grooming me? That I might marry a prince and live happily ever after?" This time, her chuckle sprang from genuine amusement. "Thank you, ma'am, for wishing me so pleasant a future! I hope you do not have your heart set on it, however. I am an unlikely choice for a prince. And—" She stopped, fearing that her tongue was running away with her again, but the duchess looked inquiringly at her. Thus encouraged, Celia plunged ahead. "Forgive me, ma'am, but—but I must have mistaken your meaning. If a prince is available, surely he would be better matched with one of your own daughters. The stepmother in the story certainly thought so."

The duchess moved impatiently. "You and I do not dwell within a work of fiction, Celia. The partner I have in mind for you is not literally a prince, and he is rather too closely related to my own daughters."

For a brief instant, Celia wondered whom the duchess meant. Then she guessed. One could not help guessing. But her guess was so startling, she felt her mind first shy away from the idea, then dance round it in morbid fascination. Surely Her Grace did not mean—it was, it *must* be, impossible—absurd—oh, no, she *couldn't* mean—

"I am speaking of my son John," said the duchess, banishing all doubt.

Celia felt almost as if the breath had been knocked out of her body. "You say that so calmly!"

One of the duchess's finely etched brows lifted.

"Why, how should I say it? There is no cause for alarm or excitement. I have a son, the only son who will survive me. He shall be Duke of Arnsford one day. I mean to provide him with a duchess who will not disgrace the family. One who has been groomed, as you put it, by me."

Celia experienced an odd, dreamlike sensation that they had somehow slipped from reality into the realm of fantasy. She swallowed hard, and managed to speak. "But, Your Gr— Aunt Gladys, there must be any number of well-bred women who are far more qualified than—"

"Do not speak to me of well-bred women!" said Her Grace sharply, raising one hand to cut off Celia's speech. "There are, as you say, a number of women who would cut off their right hands to be the next Duchess of Arnsford. Many of these ambitious females would, in fact, be admirable choices. However, my son is already acquainted with the majority of them, and none of them has, to date, struck his fancy."

The tale of Cinderella swirled again in Celia's dazed brain. "Perhaps you should give a ball," she murmured, suppressing a mad urge to giggle.

The duchess, who always sat ramrod-straight, somehow straightened further in her chair. Her eyes snapped fire. "Do you mean to disoblige me in this, Celia?" she demanded. "Are you *opposed* to the idea?"

Celia could not help shrinking a little. Fear hammered at her. She had seldom felt more powerless. Of course she could not disoblige the duchess. For one thing, what would become of her? For another, oh, how ungrateful she would seem! It would be shabby treatment indeed. Shameful, in fact.

A dizzying picture flashed across her mind of all the gifts she had accepted since she had come to Delacourt. The clothes that had been ordered for her were doubtless worth more than the whole of her inheritance. She had no hope of repaying the duchess. She was in no position to argue. Speechless, she shook her head.

"I should hope not, indeed," said Her Grace crisply. "I have given you many things, Celia, and I shall give you many more, but marriage to my son is the greatest gift I can bestow upon any young woman. I am extremely vexed to see it received with so little gratitude."

Celia plunged into a morass of stammering, incoherent disclaimers, but the duchess cut her off impatiently. "I see that you are Richard Delacourt's descendant after all. You have been stuffed full of nonsense, I daresay—romantic claptrap and vulgar ideas fit only for the stage! You must abandon such notions, Celia. They are beneath you. You are no longer among the unwashed hordes who choose a partner the way *beasts* choose partners, with no regard for family, duty, or posterity. Persons of our rank choose carefully, and choose well." Her Grace's eyes blazed wrathfully, and her knuckles whitened where she gripped the arms of her chair. "I do not understand this modern tolerance for romantic love as a foundation for marriage. It is preposterous to base a decision that affects every aspect of one's life, and determines not only the quality of life but the very *identity* of every generation to follow, on a mere emotion—or, worse yet, on nothing more than animal attraction! What basis is that for earthly happiness? What basis is it for happiness in the hereafter? It is beyond foolish. It is vulgar."

Celia had never seen the duchess so moved. Her face had gone quite pale, with two spots of color high on her cheekbones, and her breathing had started to come in short, panting gasps. As she finished her last sentence, she actually fell back against the cushions of her chair. It was the first time Celia had seen the duchess's back touch the back of any chair she sat on. Alarmed, Celia moved forward to assist her.

"Madam—Aunt Gladys—are you unwell?"

The duchess glared impatiently at her, but seemed unable to speak. Celia reached quickly for the bell, but the door communicating between the morning room and the duchess's apartments had already opened. Hubbard glided swiftly forward, a glass full of some medicinal draught in her hand. Celia stood helplessly by as Hubbard, murmuring soothing sounds, forced a little of the liquid past Her Grace's lips. Her Grace seemed unwilling to receive these ministrations, and as soon as she was able she sat upright again and shook her henchwoman off.

"There is nothing in the least wrong with me," said Her Grace pettishly. "Thank you, Hubbard, but pray take yourself off. I don't want you."

Hubbard immediately curtseyed and withdrew. Celia watched her go in some bewilderment, then glanced dubiously back at the duchess. Her Grace certainly seemed herself again. She had recovered her strength almost immediately. The entire episode had passed so quickly, it was almost as if Celia had imagined it.

There were still two spots of color on the duchess's cheeks, but if Celia had had to guess, she would have guessed that they stemmed from embarrassment. Her Grace looked extremely uncomfortable. "I beg your pardon," she said at last. "I must be careful not to upset myself." She glanced sharply up at Celia, who still hovered anxiously near her chair. "Sit down, child. These spells are nothing new. I have been subject to them since girlhood."

Celia obediently sat, although she wasn't entirely sure she believed Her Grace. Something in the duchess's words rang false.

"John will come home for Christmas," announced Her Grace, returning to the subject at hand as though nothing were amiss. "You will have an opportunity to become acquainted with one another. It is a pity that you will still be in mourning, but that cannot be helped. You will support my efforts by being on your best behavior. It will please me very much if you exert yourself a little to entertain him. We do not often see John at Delacourt, and I rather fancy it is because he finds the society of his family—irksome. You will provide some diversion."

"Yes, ma'am."

Her Grace's nostrils flared, as if scenting rebellion beneath Celia's meek demeanor. "You will do your duty, Celia."

"Yes, ma'am." Celia hesitated, then decided to ask. "Is he coming here because—that is—does he *know* about me, Aunt?"

The duchess's fingers tapped rhythmically on the arm of her chair. "No," she said finally. "He is coming home for Christmas. That is all. And that is why, Celia, you must put yourself in my hands and do as you are told. I mean to do my utmost to bring about this match, but John is of age, and it will not hurt matters if you—assist me a little."

By the time Celia left the duchess, her mind was whirling with conjecture and alarm. She desired nothing more than to hide somewhere for a time and think, but as she closed the door behind her she saw Delacourt's elderly butler loitering in the passage. Munsil was a fatherly soul who had taken her under his wing almost immediately after her arrival. His manner was very correct, and he bowed the instant he saw her, but Celia could tell that he had been waiting for her to emerge. His eyes were twinkling in a most unbutlerish way.

Celia was uncomfortably reminded of the scolding

she had just received for her familiarity with the servants. Rebellion stirred in her heart. She didn't care what Her Grace thought. Why, Munsil was worth ten of that useless duke!

They were still within earshot of the duchess, so she dropped her voice to a conspiratorial whisper.

"What is it, Munsil?"

Munsil's twinkle became pronounced. He addressed her in the measured tones of the starchiest of butlers, but with a self-conscious primness that added humor to his delivery.

"I regret to inform you, miss, that your cat—er, that is, his lordship's cat—has run afoul of Monsieur Andre. Again."

Celia's troubles immediately receded. She stifled a laugh with one hand. "Oh, dear. How bad is it?"

"Thus far, the encounter has not proved fatal. To either of the combatants."

"Well, I'm glad of that, at any rate! What happened?"

"A slight dispute arose regarding a certain guinea fowl. Each was of the opinion that the bird fell under his jurisdiction. And neither could be convinced that the other had any claim to it whatsoever. A battle of wills naturally ensued."

"Munsil, you terrify me! Do not leave me in suspense, I beg you. Who won?"

Munsil paused, as if considering. "I would call it a draw, miss."

"A draw! Did they split the bird?"

"No, miss. Not intentionally, at any rate."

Celia choked back a giggle. "It split of its own accord, I suppose."

"Eventually, miss, yes, it did. It being the nature of poultry to tear apart when subjected to vigorous tugging."

"Why, then, I would say that Manegold won the day."

"Well," said Munsil cautiously, "he succeeded in destroying the bird, which was certainly an object with him. But it failed to provide the satisfaction he expected. Monsieur Andre managed to douse the carcass with red pepper at the very moment when Manegold believed himself to have triumphed. The result was unhappy for the cat."

"I hope it did not make him ill," said Celia anxiously.

"Oh, I do not mean to imply that Manegold *ate* the bird. He was merely—surprised. He fell into a sort of fit, and while he was occupied with sneezing and yowling, Monsieur Andre was able to gain the upper hand."

"My word! Then I suppose Monsieur Andre won in the end."

"Well," said Munsil, with the same cautious delivery, "he succeeded in thwarting the cat, which was certainly an object with him. But—"

Celia choked. "But it failed to provide satisfaction!"

"Precisely, miss."

"Where are they now?"

"Monsieur Andre's wounds are being salved by the kitchen maids, and Manegold is enjoying a period of solitary reflection in the buttery."

Celia was startled. "The buttery! Oh, you must be mistaken. Only think how dangerous!"

Munsil coughed. "The animal, miss, was first confined within a small crate. I believe he was persuaded to enter the crate against his better judgment, but Monsieur Andre's assistant had the happy thought of placing an unpeppered portion of the guinea fowl in the back of it, thus overcoming Manegold's initial objections."

"Dear me. We shall have to rescue him posthaste. It might occur to Monsieur Andre to replace the ruined guinea fowl with roasted feline."

Munsil led her to the buttery, where they discovered

the prisoner. The crate might easily have held a lesser beast, but Manegold was the largest cat Celia had ever seen. Since he was boasting his winter coat, and was currently fluffed with both anger and cold, he completely filled the makeshift cage. He no sooner saw his friend Celia than he hailed her in a loud and insistent voice. He was obviously explaining his predicament and requesting an immediate release, but Celia thought it prudent to postpone that for the time being. She carried the crate away, with Manegold still hotly protesting within it, to her own chamber. Once there, and with the door firmly shut behind her, she placed the crate before the fire and opened its hinged end. Manegold stalked coldly out, turned his back upon Celia, and began washing his face.

"Yes, but I had nothing to do with it, you know," Celia told him. "There's no use your taking it out on me. Besides, I need your advice. Who is to counsel me if you will not?"

Manegold ignored her.

"Very well. Two can play at that game," said Celia severely. She crossed to the bed, knelt beside it, and pulled a large sheaf of papers and a box of jumbled charcoals and pencils from their hiding place behind the wooden step unit. These she took to the window seat. She then wrapped herself in a thick shawl against the December chill, hopped up on the seat, tucked her feet beneath her, propped her well-wrapped shoulder against the cold window, and searched through the papers for a clean sheet. She found one and took out a pencil. A dreamy expression softened her features as she tapped the pencil against her lower lip for a moment. Then she began to sketch.

This proved irresistible to Manegold. When he heard her pencils rattle in the box, he swiveled his head to watch. A few swift, sure strokes of Celia's pencil and his image began to take shape: the enormous ruff of thick, golden fur, the absurdly sweet pink triangle that was his nose, his round eyes like molten amber, their expression wise and wild as a hoot owl's. Soon Manegold left the fireside and sprang onto the window seat, graceful despite his bulk, to stare, fascinated, at her pencil darting over the page. When he reached out a paw and gently patted the side of it, she smiled.

"You great, soft, hulking thing," she murmured. "Are you ready to be friends again?"

Manegold looked expectantly at the pencil. His tail twitched. "No, I am not playing with you," she informed him. "I'm thinking."

She set the pencil down and reached for the cat, who stretched his neck obligingly toward her, eyes half-closed, and permitted her to scratch his chin. "What's your master like, Manegold?" she whispered. "They tell me you're his cat. What's he like?"

Manegold closed his eyes and leaned into her hand. "Yes, all right, then! But you haven't answered me," complained Celia. She sighed. "It's not that I mind the idea of living in luxury the rest of my days. And, heaven knows, I had no *other* plans for my future! But—" She grabbed the big cat and hauled him into her lap. "There's something rather horrid about arranged marriages, in my opinion." She frowned. "I can't help having opinions, Manegold, try as I might! And I do think this says something about the duchess, don't you? Imagine! Bringing me here to whip me into shape for her boy John. It's perfectly medieval. And she doesn't seem to think he'll fall in with her plans, either, or why would she ask me to behave any particular way? She's afraid he won't like me."

Manegold collapsed limply against her thigh, gazing up at her with frank adoration. Celia could not help laughing a little. "Flatterer," she scolded him.

He butted her hand with his head and she began

absentmindedly stroking the thick fur behind his ears.
"I think I should bide my time, don't you?" she asked
the cat. "It would be silly to enact a scene, or stamp
my foot and cry 'I won't!' like a baby. Nothing may
come of this preposterous idea. In which case I would
have behaved disgracefully for no reason at all. And
whatever you may think of Her Grace—" She looked
warningly at Manegold, but he seemed disinclined to
argue. Satisfied, Celia continued. "Whatever you may
think of Her Grace, I owe her a great deal."

She leaned down and pressed her cheek against the
top of Manegold's head. His throaty purr rumbled
against her fingertips. "I'll tell you what I think," she
whispered. "I think Her Grace is the most powerful
woman I ever met. She frightens me, Manegold. But
I think—I really think—that no amount of power sat-
isfies her. She would control everything and everyone
around her if she could. I believe she has chosen me
for her wretched son only because she believes she
can control me. I certainly have nothing else to recommend me."

Manegold bumped his cold nose into her chin, his
eyes closed in feline bliss. She smiled. "Don't argue
with me," she admonished him, pulling back to gaze
with mock sternness at the furry face. Manegold
blinked owlishly at her, then closed his eyes and continued to purr.

"I'm rather fond of my theory," mused Celia, still
stroking the cat. "If Her Grace has the power to insist
that her son marry a girl of her choosing, why not
choose someone born and bred to the role? Hmm?"
Manegold did not venture an opinion. "I'll tell you
why. Because such a girl would have powerful friends.
She would have a family. She would have ideas of her
own as to how to go on in the world, or how to run
a great house like this, or how her children ought to
be educated." Celia shivered. "Here am I, a sort of

quasi cousin, so, at the very least, my surname is acceptable. But I have never moved in aristocratic circles. I am utterly alone, and utterly dependent upon Her Grace. I am a blank slate upon which she can write. Or so she believes."

Celia took Manegold's ruff in both hands and gently shook his face. He opened his eyes just a slit and purred loudly at her. "I knew you would agree with me," murmured Celia. "How much of what she is telling me is utter rot, would you say? What of that nonsense about never speaking one's mind? And her notion that it is our solemn duty to preserve the social order, because rank is bestowed by divine providence? I think it wicked and prideful. What do you think?"

Manegold sneezed.

Celia chuckled. "Quite right. *Your* rank has been bestowed by divine providence. But I am speaking of the humans in the household." She sighed, and shifted the heavy cat to hug him a little closer. "You're a great comfort to me, Manegold."

She sat for a while, her face pensive, as Manegold drifted off to sleep on her lap. The window's cold began to penetrate her shawl. Her papers lay scattered across the window seat. She ought to move and address these circumstances, but still she sat, turning her morning's interview with Her Grace over and over in her mind. It seemed to her that the most likely outcome of the duchess's matchmaking would be failure. In which case, of course, there would be no harm done. If her efforts were crowned with success, surely it would be because both Celia and the unknown Lord Lynden desired the match—wouldn't it? So then again, there would be no harm done.

And yet her nerves were jangling with alarm. Why did she feel so apprehensive? What was she dreading? Every girl dreamed of marriage. And here she was being offered a chance at marrying far, far above herself. This was a triumph, surely? She ought to be marveling at her luck, not shaking in her shoes.

Perhaps she would fall in love with Lord Lynden. Now there was a cheerful thought. And why not? It wasn't as if she loved another. He might turn out to be a perfectly agreeable young man.

But her optimism faded as she mentally reviewed the members of his family. Whether he resembled his humorless and controlling mother or his rude and imbecilic father, she knew she could not stomach him as a husband either way. His sisters seemed to take after their mother for the most part. Elizabeth, the eldest, was as chilly as she was handsome. Augusta was nearly as handsome but more openly shrewish; she had a petulant and whiny way with her that set Celia's teeth on edge. Caroline and Winifred, the youngest, were two peas in a pod—sniggering little prigs who thought far too highly of themselves, and for no reason that Celia could fathom. Caroline had her father's tendency to corpulence and his goggling eyes. Winifred was arrogant and pert. Neither was attractive by any stretch of the imagination. What would their brother be like?

Celia looked down at the sleeping cat, warm and limp on her lap. She knew two things about the mysterious John Delacourt that gave her a glimmer of hope. One was that he had chosen Manegold for a pet, and apparently held the cat in so much affection that even Monsieur Andre, the kitchen despot, who detested cats in general and Manegold in particular, dared not harm the animal.

The other was the duchess's statement that he found his family "irksome."

Lord Lynden might turn out to be human after all.

Chapter 5

Shortly after noon on the twenty-second of December, Jack Delacourt strode up the shallow marble steps approaching the facade of his ancestral home. He hoped he wasn't about to make a cake of himself. If he had misread the signs and there really *was* no girl, he was going to look a fool.

Well, he was going to look a fool regardless. But if some fledgling harpy was lurking about the place, ready to sink her talons into the Marquess of Lynden, it would be awfully good sport to foil her—and have a bit of fun in the bargain. He supposed that one day he would outgrow the delight he took in annoying his mother, but that day had not yet arrived.

During the journey, it had occurred to him that his mother might have prevailed upon Lady Elaine what's-her-name's parents to bring her to Delacourt for Christmas. Lady Elaine was a prim and colorless schoolgirl who had unaccountably taken his mother's fancy a year or two ago. The duchess had been trying halfheartedly to foist her onto Jack ever since. He almost hoped it would be she; the practical joke he had devised would work perfectly on Lady Elaine.

As he reached the top step his eyes lit with genuine pleasure to see Munsil himself, not some nameless footman, waiting for him.

"Munsil, by Jove!" Jack exclaimed, seizing the butler's hand and vigorously wringing it. "Merry Christmas! Well, I suppose it's a few days early for that, but it feels like Christmas, eh? Devilish cold out here in Oxfordshire. I daresay it shall snow tonight. I say, I *am* glad to see you looking so well, dear chap. At your age, too! Don't know how you do it. This place wears me down in a fortnight."

The butler gently disengaged his hand from Jack's and bowed, his cheeks tinged faintly pink with mingled pleasure and embarrassment. "And a merry Christmas to you, my lord, I'm sure. May I say how very glad we are to see you?"

"Say anything you like. It's been the deuce of a long time, hasn't it? Six months or more. If you're looking for Hadley, he's not coming," Jack added, seeing Munsil's eyes traveling past him to the mud-splattered chaise at the end of the front terrace.

Munsil's eyes returned to Jack's face, their expression almost startled. "Not coming, sir? I trust he has not met with an accident."

"Oh, no, nothing like that! I've given him leave to visit his own people for Christmas, that's all." It wasn't all, however. There were additional reasons why his devoted valet had been left behind. Jack bit back a laugh at the thought, and waved a careless hand. "I say, didn't you have a nephew or something who had ambitions to become a valet? If you'd like to send him up to my rooms, I've no objection. He can wait on me as well as any other."

Had Munsil not been a paragon among butlers, his jaw would have dropped at this. "My nephew? Well, as to that, sir, I don't like to put Will forward—"

"Why, you didn't, man! I suggested him myself."

"Yes, but—forgive me, my lord, but he's young yet, and has no real experience. I wouldn't care to send you a member of my own family unless I were perfectly certain he'd give satisfaction—"

"Pooh! Nonsense. Send him along. It'll be good experience for him, what? I promise not to thrash him if he scorches my shirts."

Munsil bowed deeply, apparently overcome by Jack's generosity. "Thank you, sir. It will be an honor. I'll see to it that he does his best for you, of course."

By this time several footmen had arrived upon the scene, and Munsil began swiftly directing them as to the transportation of his lordship's baggage from the coach to his chambers. Jack turned toward the wide marble staircase, idly beginning to strip off his gloves, but paused at the sight of a stranger.

It was a girl, all right, and not the witless Lady Elaine. Jack froze, every sense on the alert as he assessed her. He had caught her in the act of coming through the door to the north passage, where she had hesitated, one hand on the doorknob, as if ready to whisk herself back out of sight. When she saw that her presence had been noticed, she apparently decided, with every sign of reluctance, that she must stay. Her hand dropped from the doorknob and she stood like a wild creature at bay, staring tensely at him with wide, apprehensive eyes.

She was nothing like what he expected. She resembled none of the girls who had previously found favor in his mother's eyes. She looked small and soft and vulnerable, traits the duchess generally despised. A halo of silky brown ringlets framed her face, which was really quite lovely in a blurred, soft-focus way, as if some artist had drawn the prettiest face imaginable and then gently smudged the edges of the portrait. The effect was appealing—sweet, rather than beautiful. Her eyes were huge and velvety brown. Her skin was fair and fine-textured, but not fashionably pale. Her complexion was more like ivory than porcelain. As he watched, the apprehension faded from her eyes and a tentative little smile wavered across her face. She looked—why, she looked rather adorable.

And she was in mourning. What the deuce—?

Almost too late, Jack remembered his role. He straightened, digging beneath his thick greatcoat for the quizzing glass he had secreted there, and pulled it out, raising it to his eye. He then fixed his gaze, with his eye hideously magnified, upon the unfortunate young female and adopted what he hoped was a repulsive leer. "Oh, I *say*! What have we here? Aphrodite in black! How simply awful! Too, too depressing!"

The girl's smile faded. Jack turned to find Munsil staring at him as if he had just sprouted horns. "Munsil, old thing," drawled Jack, "would you be so good—?" He indicated the muffler and greatcoat that covered him from neck to heel, and Munsil, all emotion wiped from his expression, stepped forward to divest him of these outer garments and hand them to a waiting lackey. As his outfit was revealed, Jack was careful not to meet the eyes of anyone who knew him well. Fortunately, apart from Munsil, the only two footmen present who had seen him before were occupied with the baggage.

He turned back to the girl, striking a careless pose. "Now *this* is more the thing, don't you think? The festive season is upon us, you know. Festive! Fa-la-la-la-la!"

The girl's eyes, already enormous, widened further as she took in the glory of his pink pantaloons and the waistcoat garishly striped in lime and puce. The purchase of that waistcoat had nearly brought Hadley to tears. As a kindness to his valet, Jack had not allowed him to see the pantaloons, and had immediately packed him off to spend Christmas with his relatives. Pink pantaloons were not generally worn, and Jack had searched in vain for a tailor with a sense of humor strong enough to willingly make him a pair. He had had to pay through the nose to obtain the ghastly things, and promise the tailor that he would never divulge the name of their reluctant creator. Still, now that he saw the electric effect they were having on everyone within sight, he was sure they were worth every penny.

The girl was looking speculatively at him, her mouth slightly pursed in the expression of one who has decided that, despite her doubts, she will reserve judgment.

"By the by," drawled Jack, peering at her in a fair imitation of his father's shortsighted stare, "who the devil are you?"

He was sure the strong language would offend her, but it had no discernible effect. "Celia Delacourt," she replied promptly. "And who the devil are you?"

Jack was so surprised, he burst out laughing. "Jack Delacourt, at your service!"

Munsil stepped hastily forward. "Miss Delacourt, allow me to present your cousin, the Marquess of Lynden."

She inclined her head and curtseyed. Jack resisted the urge to bow. "Cousin, did you say? Cousin?" He raised the quizzing glass again. "Balderdash. Never saw her before in m'life."

Munsil looked appalled, but as he opened his mouth to speak the girl intervened.

"I am, more properly, the daughter of your father's cousin, my lord."

"Eh?" said Jack blankly.

"My grandfather was your father's uncle."

"Eh?"

She bit her lip and tried again. "My grandfather was Lord Richard Delacourt. Younger son of the fifteenth duke, you know." When he still stared uncomprehendingly at her, she repeated patiently, "Your father's uncle."

"Never met him, either," said Jack. He then startled Munsil by digging an elbow suddenly into the butler's ribs. "Not my father! His uncle! Haw! Haw! I've met my father. Eh?" He threw back his head and emitted the laugh he had been practicing for the past three days. It was painfully loud, and struck all the notes of a horse's whinny. It had caused John Emerson to laugh so hard that the boy had fallen off his chair, right in the middle of Boodle's. Jack was frightfully proud of it.

Before the group assembled in the entrance hall could recover from the stupefying effect of Jack's new laugh, Augusta appeared on the landing above. He galloped up the stairs to wring her unresponsive hand. "Gussie!" he shouted. "Practically my favorite sister! How have you been, old thing?"

Augusta scowled, and tried in vain to remove her hand from Jack's grip. "Oh, John, for pity's sake! You make my head go round and round," she complained. "Let me alone, can't you? And don't call me Gussie!"

He immediately seized her and bussed her cheek. She let out a smothered squawk and swatted ineffectually at him. Jack jumped away, let out another peal of loud, whinnying laughter, and galloped off down the hall toward his bedchamber.

Once there, he collapsed into whoops.

His hilarity was interrupted by a hesitant scratching on the door, followed by the entrance of Will Munsil. Jack grinned at the lad. He looked to be no more than sixteen or so, a shy boy, ready to burst with excitement and pride at being called to wait upon his lordship. He bowed nervously and began a rather breathless and stammering speech acknowledging the honor Jack's notice had bestowed upon him, how he meant to do his utmost to give satisfaction, et cetera, but Jack cut him off with a wave of his hand.

"Never mind all that," said Jack. "You may unpack my bags, if you think you're up to the task."

"Yes, my lord! Certainly, my lord!" Will rushed to

begin, and Jack watched covertly as Will, rather nervously, lifted out the contents. The lad never paused once. He seemed to handle each garment with equal reverence, and not to notice any peculiarities of color or cut. This was just what Jack wanted: a temporary manservant who would neither suggest what Jack ought to wear nor argue with the choices he made. But at some point, Jack decided regretfully, he would have to disabuse the boy's mind of the idea that he would ever be a valet. He obviously had no eye at all.

Back in the hall, Lady Augusta continued down the stairs, still scowling. Celia took a deep breath. "Your brother is certainly—unusual, cousin," she said hesitantly. "Is he always so—so boisterous?"

"Oh, there is never doing anything with John," said Augusta crossly. "He's always been utterly mad. It's my belief he gets worse every year. Nothing he does astonishes me anymore. I say, have you seen my novel lying about? I've misplaced it."

"No, I'm sorry," said Celia. "Perhaps—"

"I shall alert the staff," said Munsil, bowing. Augusta departed, still apparently in search of the novel she had been reading, and Munsil returned to his supervision of the busy footmen struggling with his lordship's baggage.

Celia went quietly to the small drawing room adjacent to the library and sat on one of the satin-covered divans. She had begun to tremble. She could scarcely take in the enormity of the thing.

Lord Lynden was mad. Utterly mad, and getting worse every year. How casually Lady Augusta had imparted the information! And that frightful woman who controlled the entire household and all its inhabitants, that dreadful, despotic duchess, meant for Celia to *marry* him.

Why, it was monstrous! But it explained everything. Celia felt the missing piece of the puzzle had just fallen into place, and she understood Her Grace's inexplicable kindness to a poor relation. No wonder she had chosen Celia to succeed her, rather than some highborn lady, bred to the role! Who better than a powerless orphan to coerce into marrying the family lunatic?

God bless Grandpapa for leaving this ghastly family! How had he found the courage? And, more important, how would Celia find the courage? For leave she must. That much was clear. She hadn't the strength, she hadn't the power, to fight the duchess on her own turf. And that poor, afflicted young man would be no help whatsoever. He had seemed so pleasant and jolly at first, when she had accidentally overheard him speaking to Munsil, that she had almost hoped, for a moment—but it was useless. No girl in her right mind could find happiness with the creature she had just met.

It hardly mattered what Lord Lynden's opinion of her might be. However little he might want to marry her, Celia was sure his mother would find a way to force him. Her only hope was escape.

She was startled from her reverie by a gust of wind rattling the windowpanes. The weather was turning dark and nasty. Celia rose and went to look out. The very thought of being out in that cold made her shiver. It was all very well to talk of leaving Delacourt, but until she had a place to go, she was well and truly trapped here.

And then anger came to her rescue, stiffening her spine. Celia knew she was a nobody, but she was also a Delacourt. She *would* stay and fight the duchess on her own turf. At least she need no longer feel guilty for accepting Her Grace's largesse! The duchess had an ulterior motive. It would serve her right if Celia smiled, and accepted gift after gift, and then refused to do her sinister bidding. What was the worst that could happen? Banishment from Delacourt? Her grandfather had survived it, and so would she. Dr. and Mrs. Hinshaw would take her in, as a last resort.

Perhaps.

At any rate, she would not panic. She was a Delacourt, and not a coward.

Celia dressed for dinner in a martial frame of mind. The family gathered every evening in the drawing room, punctually at half past seven, to await Munsil's summons. Tonight, Celia was deliberately late. She was well aware that a footman would be sent to her chamber to find her, so she readied herself early, buttoned herself into a warm pelisse, and then hid in the dark library. Let them search! she thought mutinously.

When she heard the library clock chime again, signaling that it was now a quarter to eight, she crept out and went quietly up to the drawing room. She still did not go in. She lingered in the passage, hugging herself against the chill and watching the stairs, until she saw Munsil rounding the corner of the hall below. Then, and only then, did she paste an unconcerned expression on her face and enter the drawing room.

The duchess had spent many hours drilling Celia in how to hide her thoughts and emotions. It was time to put her training to the test, and see how the duchess liked it! Celia did not think the duchess would like it at all.

A fire roared in the grate and the room was warm. Lady Winifred and Lady Caroline sat side by side on the sofa, their heads bent over a copy of *La Belle Assemblee,* arguing in hissing whispers over its contents. Lady Augusta slouched discontentedly in a chair, scowling vacantly into space. Lady Elizabeth, poised and elegant as usual, sat with her mother before the fire. The only servant in the room was Hubbard, standing motionless behind Her Grace's chair. The duke, whose labored breathing could be heard across the room, was stuffed into a suit of dinner clothes that his bulk had long since outgrown. He was huddled in the corner of the room, sneaking some dark liquid from a decanter as surreptitiously as if it belonged to someone else.

It was Lord Lynden, however, who irresistibly drew the eye. He stood before the fire, conversing with his mother and eldest sister, wearing an ensemble more appropriate for performing at Astley's Amphitheatre than dining at Delacourt. He was clad, correctly enough, in knee breeches—but the knee breeches were of lilac satin. And his coat was so covered with gold and silver lace, braid, and ornaments of various types, it was impossible to judge whether it matched the breeches or not. If this evidence of his dementia had not been so pitiful, Celia might have been hard-pressed not to laugh out loud.

The duchess was obviously in a rare temper. She normally showed so little emotion, it was rather frightening to see anger glittering in her eyes. The anger seemed at first to be directed at her son, but her head swiveled when Celia entered, and her gimlet gaze fixed on the new arrival.

"You are late," snapped the duchess.

"Yes," agreed Celia. She crossed calmly to the chair opposite Lady Augusta and seated herself gracefully upon its edge.

Yesterday, Celia would have been scarlet with distress. Yesterday, she would have apologized profusely. Yesterday, in fact, Celia would not have been late at all. But this was today, and everything had altered.

The duchess visibly swelled with wrath. "In future, Celia, you will be punctual."

Celia smiled brightly. "Oh, yes! I daresay I shall."

A brief, electric silence fell. All eyes fixed upon Celia, with varying degrees of fascination. The duchess looked both baffled and enraged. "Why are you wear-

ing a pelisse?" she demanded. "Where have you
been?"

"In the library, madam. It was cold."

"Do not force me to send you to your chamber like
a child, Celia. You cannot wear a pelisse at table."

Celia's smile never wavered. "Thank you, ma'am,
but, on the contrary, I can easily wear a pelisse at
table. There is no need for your kind concern. I rarely
become overheated."

Lord Lynden abruptly began coughing. Celia
thought at first that he was covering a laugh, but of
course that was impossible—wasn't it? Before she
could decide, Munsil appeared in the doorway and
announced dinner.

Everyone rose, like a herd of obedient sheep. The
duchess was still pale with anger, but Munsil's entrance had struck all expression from her features. She
calmly delivered a few words to direct the disposition
of the party. All fell meekly into place at her bidding.
Hubbard silently arranged Her Grace's shawl, then
slipped out of the room.

Lord Lynden was ordered to take Celia down on
his arm. This was alarming, but Celia hadn't the heart
to use the unfortunate young man as an instrument of
her rebellion. She was certain that the poor, mad thing
had had no part in his mother's schemes. The duchess
had even told her as much. So she took his arm and
suffered herself to be led to dinner.

Dinner was ghastly. The duke, who was generally
impossible to distract from his meals, was inspired by
the presence of a fellow male at the table to lift his
eyes from his plate and bark out a remark from time
to time. He asked his son a question or two—
apparently about sport; Celia did not understand the
questions, and the marquess was given no opportunity
to reply. The duchess deftly intervened each time her
husband spoke, turning the conversation into paths

that she deemed appropriate for the dinner table. She was ably assisted by her eldest daughter; between them, Her Grace and Lady Elizabeth almost managed to maintain an illusion of normal dinner conversation.

Almost, but not quite. Winifred and Caroline poked each other whenever their mother was not looking, and snickered each time their father was squelched. Augusta never spoke unless directly addressed, and then replied in a monotone; she was sulking over something. Celia was likewise silent, as was her habit when in the company of her newfound relatives.

It was a terrible thing, she thought as she glanced round the table, that she felt no affection for a single one of them. Terrible, and terribly sad.

The duke generally disappeared after dinner. Tonight, the heir's presence changed the routine somewhat. The duchess gracefully withdrew, all the females trailing in her wake, so that the gentlemen might enjoy their port in solitude. Her Grace led the petticoat parade slowly back to the drawing room.

So long as servants hovered, serving the meal and then lighting the ladies' way, so long did the duchess's forbearance toward Celia last. The instant the door closed behind the departing footmen, Her Grace ordered Celia, in a voice of steel, to join her by the fire. Her daughters disposed themselves at a tactful distance—Winifred and Caroline with obvious reluctance; they were fairly quivering with curiosity.

Celia waited until the duchess had seated herself, then sat nervously across from her. The ubiquitous Hubbard had reappeared and stationed herself nearby. Celia hoped that the duchess's dislike of plain-speaking, especially before servants, might shield her somewhat from the brunt of her anger. One look at Her Grace's face, however, told her that her hope was vain. The duchess never bothered to hide anything from Hubbard, and disapproved of frankness only in women other than herself. Her eyes glittered in her masklike face, and she wasted no time in polite fencing.

"I am extremely vexed with you, Celia," she snapped. "What is the meaning of your extraordinary conduct this evening? And, for heaven's sake, take off that pelisse!"

Hubbard glided forward. Celia rose, her cheeks burning, and allowed the duchess's henchwoman to remove the offending pelisse. Beneath it she was correctly attired in a dinner dress of black velvet—a gift, of course, from the duchess. She sat stiffly back down, but was unable to maintain the pretense of being unaffected by Her Grace's displeasure. She had always dreaded making people angry, and now found she had to swallow hard before she could speak.

"It is not my desire to vex you, madam."

"I am glad to hear it! You could scarcely have chosen a worse time to arrive unpunctually, and unsuitably dressed. I had already been sorely tried by—" She abruptly stopped speaking, and Celia saw her lips compress into a thin line. "By something else. Well, never mind. I shall address that later. But as for yourself, I own I was astonished to see such behavior in you. I honored you with my confidence because I deemed you worthy of it, and because I require your assistance to achieve my object. An object that, you know well, is entirely in your own best interests! And yet tonight, of all nights, you embarrass me—and embarrass yourself!—with wayward and peculiar behavior such as I have never seen in you before. Had I not known better, I might have fancied that I perceived *defiance*. Defiance! But such a thing must be impossible. I am sure you know your duty better than that—do you not?"

Celia's voice was quiet but firm. "I hope I do, ma'am. Indeed, I hope I know my duty."

The firelight burned against the planes of the duchess's face, throwing into bold relief the cheekbones, the high-bridged, aristocratic nose, and the finely arched brows. Half in light, half in shadow, she looked beautiful, regal, and deadly. Her sharp eyes missed nothing, Celia was certain. No mealymouthed skirting of the question would satisfy her. Sure enough, the duchess's white, ringed fingers clutched the arms of her chair, and she leaned forward in a way that struck Celia as nothing short of menacing.

"I have *told* you your duty, Celia," she said, the eerie flatness of her tone somehow worse than a raised voice could have been. "You will obey me in this, or I promise you, you will regret it. You will rue the day you ever dreamed of crossing me. Do you understand?"

Celia shrank back against her chair, staring at the duchess in frightened amazement. "Yes," she whispered automatically. "Yes, ma'am."

But she did not. She did not understand at all. She did not understand what the duchess would do, nor why she would want to do it. Why was it so important to her to control and bully Celia? Why was it so important to her to arrange this marriage with her son? She seemed as mad as the marquess, and far more dangerous.

Bewildered, Celia watched as the duchess regained mastery over her features, resumed her sphinxlike expression, and straightened in her chair. "It is well," said Her Grace shortly. One finger moved in an almost imperceptible signal, and the devoted Hubbard stepped out of the shadows and slipped something into the duchess's hand. Celia could not tell what it was.

The duchess dismissed her and she curtseyed shakily, then moved off to join the other ladies. But she was not cowed. No, indeed, Celia told herself firmly. If anything, she was more determined than ever to escape the silken noose she felt tightening round her neck.

Chapter 6

When the gentlemen entered the room, Lady Augusta was strumming moodily at the pianoforte, Lady Caroline and Lady Winifred were engaged in a game of checkers, Lady Elizabeth was pensively studying her sisters' discarded copy of *La Belle Assemblee,* and the duchess, still seated by the fire, was resting her eyes. Celia longed for her sketchbook to pass the time, but, lacking this diversion, sat curled on the sofa, leaning her cheek against her hand and listening to the meandering melodies issuing, one after another, from the pianoforte. Her mind was so busy considering and rejecting various means of escape from her predicament that she had entirely forgotten the gentlemen. The duke rarely joined the ladies after dinner—or, indeed, at any other time—but the presence of his son altered this habit. Celia was caught completely off guard by the opening of the door. She looked up, startled, and then hastily sat up and placed her feet on the floor, twitching her velvet skirts into place.

If the duke had come to the drawing room hoping to enjoy the refreshment of a man-to-man conversation with his heir, he was destined for disappointment. The duchess opened her eyes at their entrance and straightened in her chair. "Ah, John, there you are," she said, stretching out one hand so that her son must, in common courtesy, walk forward and take it. "You have met your cousin Celia, of course, but I fancy you are unacquainted with her. Celia, dear child, come and sit with us for a moment."

She spoke as cordially as if she had never been annoyed with either of them a day in her life. Bemused, Celia rose obediently from the sofa and came hesitantly forward.

Lord Lynden seemed to be as wary of her as she was of him. They stood, one on either side of the duchess, and eyed each other askance. Her Grace's voice droned gently on. "Celia is the granddaughter of Lord Richard Delacourt, John. I am sure you have heard your father speak of his uncle Richard."

The marquess flicked an imaginary speck of dust from his sleeve. "Oh, aye! The infamous Uncle Richie. Ran off with one of the tenants, didn't he?"

It was a shock to hear this cavalier disparagement of her dear grandmama, but Celia remembered the marquess's affliction and managed to keep her tongue between her teeth. Her Grace looked nearly as angry as Celia felt, and spoke sharply. "Pray recall to whom you are speaking, John! Your great-uncle Richard wed a vicar's daughter. The match was far from brilliant, but there was certainly no scandal attached to their marriage."

He opened his eyes in mild surprise. "Really? Then why the deuce did the family banish him?" Lord Lynden then threw back his head and emitted an earsplitting laugh. All conversation and music ceased. The entire assembly stared at him in startled amazement.

Her Grace looked murderous. "There is nothing humorous in the situation, and no need to air the family's differences here and now. Pray sit down, John, and mind your manners!"

The duchess waved Celia and her son into chairs. They both sat, but neither looked comfortable. Her Grace looked keenly from one to the other. "My son has a lively sense of humor," she informed Celia—by way of apology, Celia supposed. "When you have come to know one another, I am persuaded you will become great friends. Hubbard will take me upstairs now. I am fatigued. Do you sit here a while and talk. You will find Celia a more interesting conversationalist than your sisters, John.''

It was the sort of thing any hostess might say, but it sounded more like a command than a polite platitude. Celia felt that she had been ordered to be interesting, and supposed that the marquess had been ordered to find her so. Would the poor young man realize it, however?

Celia watched in some trepidation as Hubbard assisted Her Grace with her shawl and reticule and escorted her from the room. It was rather terrible to be left alone with a lunatic. She had no notion how to go on. The presence of other people in the room, however occupied in other pursuits, was a comfort.

The madman himself seemed disinclined to offer any help. After the departure of his mother he leaned back in his wing chair and crossed his legs, regarding her with a sort of cynical amusement. He said nothing at all. He seemed to be waiting for her to put herself forward. There was no indication that he had heard the veiled instructions in his mother's parting remark. Really, it was most awkward.

Well, she was under no obligation to be interesting, whatever the duchess might wish. In fact, she had no desire whatsoever to interest the marquess. She tried to recall the various strictures Her Grace had drummed into her head regarding polite conversation. The foremost of them was, Never say anything in public that could not as easily have been said by someone else. Under the circumstances, that sounded like good advice. She found an innocuous remark, cleared her throat delicately, and began.

''I trust you had a pleasant journey from London, my lord.''

''I didn't. It was devilish.''

A brief silence fell while Celia struggled to think of a response to this. "I suppose travel at this time of year is always a bit of a trial," she ventured.

"Why do you suppose that?"

"Well, it—it's very cold, of course. And I daresay one encounters mud and snow and—and such. They do say the roads in England are shocking."

"Nonsense. The roads in England are kept as well as any other roads."

"Really? I have never traveled abroad."

"Neither have I."

"Then how—" Celia broke off, with an effort, and pasted a smile on her lips. *Mad as a hatter,* she reminded herself. It was a pity, because he was a good-looking fellow; tall and well proportioned, with a distinct resemblance to his mother and Lady Elizabeth. The strong, lean, well-bred features she thought so handsome in them seemed even more handsome in a male face. He had their unusual coloring, too: dark hair and blue eyes. Her favorite, she thought wistfully. Had he been blessed with a normal brain, she might have found herself strongly attracted to him.

She paused for a moment, hoping Lord Lynden would introduce a topic of conversation, but he merely sat and regarded her fixedly. She began again.

"I believe it has begun to snow."

"It will soon stop, however."

"Will it? This is my first visit to Oxfordshire, so I am not familiar with—"

"It has nothing to do with Oxfordshire, you ninny."

Celia could scarcely believe her ears. "Wh-what?" she stammered.

"Spring arrives everywhere. It won't snow forever."

"I—I thought you meant—well, you said it would stop *soon,* and I thought you meant rather sooner than that."

"How soon did you think I meant?"

"I don't know—tonight, I supposed, or perhaps within the hour, or perhaps in a few days."

"Why did you suppose that?"

"I—I'm sorry. I misunderstood you."

"Well, don't let it happen again."

Celia stared, completely nonplussed. He did not look angry. He did not even look particularly crazed. He looked, in fact, perfectly amiable. But the things he was saying were so contrary, they were actually belligerent! What should she do? How could she soothe this poor, witless young man? He surely had no idea how impossible he was being.

Another silence fell while Celia hoped in vain for a topic of conversation to arise naturally. Lord Lynden merely looked at her and waited for her lead. She tried again. "Delacourt is a lovely place."

His lip curled in something like a sneer. "Of course it is."

Indignation rose, and she again choked it back. But this was terrible. She was strongly tempted to leave him to his disordered thoughts and go join Lady Elizabeth. Would he even notice her departure? But just as she opened her mouth to make some excuse, the marquess unexpectedly spoke.

"Tell me, Miss Delacourt—what brings you here?"

His tone was definitely hostile. She looked apprehensively at him and saw that his gaze had become as keen as his mother's. She comforted herself with the knowledge that Her Grace had informed her that her son did not expect to find her here, and had no idea of his mother's plans to promote a match between them. Whatever the root of his animosity, it could not be that he suspected anything of that nature. But madmen saw imaginary enemies everywhere.

She smiled gently at him and spoke soothingly. "I am here at the invitation of your mother."

"That does not surprise me," he said bitterly, although the source of his sarcasm remained a mystery. "I daresay she is immensely gratified that you like Delacourt so well."

"I hope she is. But everyone must admire Delacourt."

"Has she, by any chance, encouraged you to make a *lengthy* stay?"

Celia blinked. "Why—why, yes, she has—she has told me that I may consider Delacourt my permanent home."

At that, Lord Lynden's antagonism vanished in a look of pure surprise. "Has she, by Jove! I never knew Mother to rush her fences."

For the first time, his voice sounded completely normal. But his words had made no sense. Puzzled, Celia considered whether she ought to ask for an explanation. Might it worsen his symptoms, to be forced to examine them? The last thing she wanted to do was to excite or distress the poor deranged creature.

His eyes flicked over her black velvet gown, and a different sort of frown creased his handsome forehead. "Would you mind terribly if I asked you why you are in mourning?"

Celia tensed. It was a trial to speak of her loss under any circumstances, and to expose her private grief to an addlepated and hostile young man was an extremely distasteful prospect. But his face had lost that guarded, strange expression and was suddenly so compassionate, she had to look away. She stared down at her hands and swallowed past the lump that had formed in her throat. "I am in mourning for my family," she said tonelessly.

She closed her eyes, praying miserably that he would ask no more questions. There was a terrible moment while she waited, dreading his inevitable exclamation of sympathy or curiosity. But her prayers were answered. When he finally spoke, all he said was, "I am sorry."

"Thank you," she said, feeling she could breathe again. He immediately launched into a lively story of some mishap he had encountered in his journey from London, forcing her to look up and regain control over herself.

She was deeply grateful for this tactful gesture—although more puzzled than ever. His instantaneous transformation from a bellicose madman to an affable, immensely attractive young gentleman was the weirdest manifestation of his illness she had yet seen.

He underwent several more transformations in the next three-quarters of an hour. If she hadn't known better, she might have suspected that his madness was feigned. It almost seemed that he caught himself conversing normally from time to time, became vexed with himself, and then went out of his way to say or do something outrageous. It was most strange. By the end of an hour, Celia was exhausted. She sincerely pitied the unfortunate marquess, but his company was trying. The kinder one tried to be to him, the ruder and sillier he became. She took her cue from the duchess and, pleading fatigue, made an early escape from the drawing room.

Jack watched her go, feeling almost ashamed of himself. It was shocking, the way he had treated her. Still, he reminded himself firmly, he would rather play the fool for a week or two than find himself bullocked into marriage. He had no wish to marry a girl who conspired with his mother. Not even a sweet-faced, rather lost-looking girl.

But the sight of her tired little face, pale above the somber black of her gown, tugged at his conscience. She left the room so quietly, too—clearly not even expecting acknowledgment of her departure from his self-absorbed sisters. How long had she been living here? he wondered. And why did she accept her status as a cipher in this house, if she thought herself destined to rule it one day? Odd, that.

He noticed that his sister Elizabeth was regarding him, her eyebrows wryly lifted. He grinned, and left the fire to sweep her a magnificent leg. "Admiring my lilac unmentionables, sister?"

"Your entire outfit is unmentionable, in my opinion," she replied tartly. "I have been wanting all evening to ask you what you are about."

"Mother doesn't care for my new tailor."

"No sensible person could. Really, John! I suppose you think you are amusing, but you are not."

He straightened, laughing. "How would you know? You haven't any more sense of humor than this footstool."

She flushed. "Just because I don't care for undignified silliness—"

Jack, instantly contrite, reached over and gave her shoulder a friendly shake. "Sorry. Sorry! That was a wretched thing to say, and I ought not to tease you. Forgive me! It's been a long day." He dropped into the chair across from her. "Besides, I did not don this finery for your amusement."

Elizabeth's angry flush faded. "Well, there are worse things you could accuse me of than having no sense of humor," she allowed. "It's true that I have never shared your admiration of laughter for its own sake. Nor your fondness for hilarity. And indeed, you must know I do not entirely approve of it. Your sense of the ridiculous has often led you to go too far." She looked pointedly at Jack's attire.

"Has it? Then I hope it has done so again."

Elizabeth frowned. "Pray do not talk in riddles."

"Very well. How have you been? It seems to me there is less of you today than when I saw you last."

Elizabeth's face went still and shuttered. "I have been well enough."

He regarded her gravely. She looked, in fact, as if she were unhappy, and as if she had been unhappy for some time. She had always been slender, but now she was almost too thin, and her fair skin was nearly translucent in its paleness. No lines marked her face, and she was still a good-looking woman, but whatever traces of girlishness she had once had were gone forever. She was twenty-six, and looked it.

But Elizabeth was not the only family member whose appearance troubled him. "Tell me, how has Mother been?"

Elizabeth seemed almost amused by the question. "Need you ask? Mother is always the same."

Jack leaned back skeptically and crossed one leg over the other. "Well, then something's up with Monsieur Andre. Is he not feeding you enough? If he's trying to help Father reduce, he's missing his mark."

"Has Mother lost weight? I hadn't noticed."

"I daresay when you see her every day, the changes are not apparent, but I was struck by it. And why does Hubbard shadow her everywhere she goes?"

"Pooh! She has done so for years."

Jack looked unconvinced. "Has she? Well, I never knew Mother to take to her bed before ten o'clock. Although," he admitted, "she may have had other reasons for doing so tonight. Wanted to get herself out of the way, I suppose."

Before Elizabeth could ask him his meaning, their father came rolling up to pounce on Jack. Elizabeth moved off to join Augusta, and Jack spent the next hour listening with a good grace to the duke's wheezy, and increasingly boozy, sporting anecdotes. It bored him, but it seemed the least he could do to ease his parent's burdensome existence.

His father's misery, reflected Jack grimly, provided a useful object lesson in why a man should *not* allow his parents to choose a bride for him. The Duke of Arnsford was probably the least well equipped of any man in England to be cooped up willy-nilly with a set of elegant and powerful females. His intellect was even weaker than his eyes, and in every respect that mattered—personal appearance, manner, education, strength of will, and authority—he was dramatically inferior to his wife. As a result, he had lived under the cat's foot from the day of his wedding forward.

Jack was the third person to plead fatigue and make an early escape from the drawing room. He took a candle, although the route was so familiar to him he could make his way blindfolded if need be. Still, it was a good thing he had a little light; a flash of pale fur against the dark wood of the wainscoting in the passage alerted him to Manegold's presence before the cat succeeded in tripping him.

"Manegold, old friend!" said Jack fondly, as the animal wound himself adoringly around his ankles. "How've you been, chappie, eh? How've you been, then?" He reached down, balancing the candle carefully in his other hand, and thumped the enormous kitty's ribs as if it were a dog. Manegold chirped joyously at this rough treatment and collapsed on the carpet, showing Jack his belly invitingly. Jack laughed. "No, I'm not going to stop in this deuced cold corridor. Come on, mate. Let's go and see if young Will managed to stay awake."

The cat trotted at his heels as Jack proceeded to his rooms. They found Will manfully waiting up for his new master, although his eyelids seemed rather heavy. He assisted Lord Lynden out of his outlandish garb and into his night gear while Manegold bathed before the fire. As soon as Will had finished his duties and stumbled off to bed, Jack picked up the enormous cat, who immediately went limp in Jack's hands.

"Oof! Here's one member of the family who hasn't lost any weight," remarked Jack. He settled into a deep-bottomed chair before the fire and settled the cat comfortably in his lap. Manegold began to purr.

"I've missed you, old chum," said Jack. "I wish I could keep you in London with me, but it'd be a cruelty to take you there." He scratched Manegold's ears. The cat surrendered to bliss and began kneading Jack's thigh with his huge paws. Jack automatically stuffed a fold of his dressing gown beneath the cat's front feet, cushioning his skin from the rhythmic appearance of Manegold's claw tips. "Easy, mate! You don't know your own strength."

Manegold tilted up his face, eyes almost closed, and fixed an unfocused gaze on Jack, his purr rumbling loudly. Jack chuckled. "It's good to see you, too," he said. "Are you ready to settle in for the night, then? Eh?"

A faint whistle sounded out in the hall. Jack looked up, surprised, and Manegold's purr stopped as abruptly as if a switch had been thrown in the animal's brain. He was suddenly the picture of eagerness. He leaped lightly down off Jack's lap and trotted to the closed door, where he sat, tail twitching, and stared earnestly at the door handle.

"What is it?" asked Jack.

Manegold patted the door with one paw, then looked back over his shoulder at Jack.

"You want me to let you out?"

The whistle sounded again, faint and sweet. *"Row,"* said Manegold plaintively.

Mystified, Jack crossed to the door and opened it. The cat was through it in a flash, disappearing into the darkness down the hallway. Jack stepped out to follow his pet with his eyes, and saw a bar of light far down the passage where someone's door was partially open. He could not think whose door that was for a moment; no member of the family was placed so far down the passage. He had just realized whose door it must be when Manegold appeared in the light, tail high in greeting, head tilted back on his neck to gaze ecstatically at the face of the person opening her door to him.

A small, barefooted figure in a white nightgown slipped partially into view. The murmuring of high-pitched, inarticulate blandishments reached Jack's ear. Manegold stamped his feet in a blissful dance of love, pressing his furry body against Celia's slim legs, tail quivering with joy. Her low laughter sounded then, musical and warm with affection. The sound of it made Jack catch his breath. He saw the tableau only for a moment—his cat, apparently in love with another, which gave him an odd feeling of loss—and his cousin Celia, unaware that she was being watched, her unconscious sweetness giving him an odd feeling of discovery. Then they were both gone, slipping into Celia's room, and the bar of light disappeared as the door closed behind them.

Jack let his breath go. "Well, I'll be damned," he told the empty hallway. He didn't know whether to be amused or annoyed. Manegold's defection was bad enough, but to lose one's pet to the charms of a mercenary was worse.

"I always thought you a good judge of character, my furry friend," he murmured to the absent cat. "But I'm afraid you're mistaken this time. Only the most determined of fortune hunters would have put up with the treatment I dished out tonight."

Still, he reflected as he closed the door, he could see the attraction. There was something about Celia that made one forget why she was there and whose game she was playing. Several times during the course of the evening he'd been lulled, himself, into liking her. It was difficult to bear in mind, somehow, that she was scheming with his mother to trap him into marriage. Her eyes were so direct, her expression so sweet, her whole person so soft and unassuming . . . why, a man just couldn't believe that a girl like that would marry for any reason but love.

The picture of her in her nightrail, so fleetingly glimpsed, returned to tantalize him. Her bare feet had looked so small and white and—defenseless.

Defenseless! What the devil did he mean by that? He gave himself a mental shake, disgusted by his own gullibility. Yes, little cousin Celia was dangerous. He could hardly blame his infatuated cat. He was rather fascinated with her himself.

Chapter 7

Jack had just blown out the candle when a soft tap sounded on his door. "Yes? What is it?" he called.

The door did not open, but a voice he recognized as Hubbard's replied, sounding muffled and apologetic. "Beg pardon, milord, but have you gone to bed?"

He had, of course, but immediately threw back the comforter and picked up his dressing gown. "I'll be with you in a moment," he told her, hastily making himself decent.

His first thought was that something was wrong with Mother, but of course that was nonsensical. Nothing was ever wrong with Mother, and if it was, a physician, not her son, would be called to her bedside. Noticing her weight loss had made him fanciful. He supposed, in reality, her loss of weight was probably deliberate. Most of Mother's actions were. She had doubtless decided she was growing plump and had rectified the situation with her usual ruthless efficiency.

When he opened the door, he found Hubbard standing there, lamp in hand, her strange features making her look like a gargoyle lit from below.

"What is it? Is Mother all right?"

A surprised expression flitted across her homely face. Jack had the oddest sensation that Hubbard, of all people, longed to confide in him. She did not, however, but merely said, "She'd like to speak with you, sir, if you have the time."

He grinned ruefully. "You're very polite! That's not Mother's wording, is it?" Hubbard looked a little embarrassed at this, so he took pity on her. "Never mind," he assured her. "I've all the time in the world."

"Thank you, sir," said Hubbard in her usual gruff monotone. She lit the way for him back to his mother's sitting room, announced him, then vanished into the adjacent dressing room.

The duchess was seated before the fire in her dressing gown and cap, a shawl draped round her shoulders and a most fierce expression on her face. It made her look older, somehow, and frail. When her eyes fell upon her son, she bent upon him the glare that had always reduced him to abject groveling when he was a child. It no longer struck terror into his heart, but it did make him feel a bit chastened.

Well, he hadn't supposed she'd called him in for a comfortable little gossip. He strolled forward with an inward sigh and dropped a quick kiss on her unresponsive cheek before the scold began.

"Hallo, Mother," he said cheerfully. "Looking forward to Christmas?"

Her forbidding expression did not alter. "I have not called you in here at this hour to discuss Christmas," she informed him icily.

"No? Well, frankly, I didn't suppose you had," he admitted. "I thought you had gone to bed hours ago."

Her eyes flashed balefully. "I am fatigued, but not so fatigued that I could sleep peacefully while you prepare to humiliate us all. Really, John, I am so displeased with you, on so many levels, I hardly know where to begin! What was that disgraceful outfit you were wearing called? Or had it a name?"

He blinked. By George, he had forgotten all about that. But then, he was the only one who hadn't had to look at himself all night. "Do you mean my dinner ensemble? I could see you didn't like it, but as for humiliating the family—no, no, that's going too far!"

She shuddered and pulled her shawl a little closer round her shoulders. "I can scarcely credit the monstrosities that pass for fashion nowadays," she complained. "I suppose you will tell me it is de rigueur in London to come to dinner dressed all by guess, but I will tell you, John, that it is not the fashion at Delacourt! While I am mistress under this roof, you will dress with sobriety and decorum or, by heaven, you will eat from a tray in your room."

Jack looked thoughtful. Here was something he hadn't bargained for. He wondered if it might thrust a spoke in Celia's wheel if he vanished at mealtimes. After all, that would be the only portion of the day when he could not avoid her. Delacourt was so enormous, it would be child's play to make himself scarce the rest of the time.

His mother's gaze had sharpened. Perhaps that was occurring to her, too. Her tone was slightly milder when next she spoke. "Sit down, John. I am craning my neck to look up at you, you've grown such a height."

He sat, and tried to look meek. It had never been possible to dupe Mother, however, and it still was not. "Take that foolish look off your face," she said crossly. "It puts me out of all patience. Dressing like an idiot is bad enough, but you also seem to have adopted the manners of a buffoon. Has behaving like a dolt become the rage as well?"

He waved his hands vaguely. "Well, you know, Mother, mannerisms do go in and out of style—"

She snorted with derision at this, and he was startled into silence. He had rarely seen her show emotion of any kind, and was surprised at the unexpected strength of the effect his little joke was having. His normally unperturbable mother was evidently much moved.

"Nonsense!" she huffed. "Utter nonsense! I have long deplored that circle of friends with which you surround yourself, and now we see its natural effect. You have chosen, heaven knows why, to associate with those who are beneath you, with commoners and vulgarians—"

Jack straightened in his chair, frowning, but his mother continued wrathfully, "If your conduct this evening is a sample of what your *friends* think amusing, I tell you point-blank that you need new friends! Unfortunately, however, your manners have deteriorated to the point where you will find it difficult to cultivate any friends worth having. Your boon companions are a motley set of mismatched care-for-nobodies. They may find it amusing when you utter ill-considered remarks and laugh like a hyena, but I promise you, no person of worth will admire such behavior! I suggest you make an effort, John, to remember who you are! I was never more vexed with you in my life than I was this evening."

"For that, ma'am, I am sorry," said Jack quietly. "But even if you were correct as to the source of my behavior, you could not seriously expect me to abandon my friends at your command. Nor will I. We are unlikely to agree on this issue of what defines a worthy individual, so in the interests of harmony I respectfully suggest that we let the matter drop."

A muscle jumped in the duchess's jaw, but she managed to keep her teeth firmly clenched as she struggled to suppress her frustration. Jack waited in polite, but unyielding, silence. Finally his mother said, tight-lipped, "Very well. It is not my purpose to quarrel with you."

He inclined his head in acknowledgment of her sacrifice. Really, one had to admire her self-control, he thought wryly. She would obviously love to rake him over the coals. But Her Grace never, ever, slipped from the standards she set for herself. She studied him a moment longer. He waited.

"I shall not browbeat you, John," she said at last. "You believe that your life in London is no concern of mine. Very well. You are a man grown. Beneath this roof, however, I feel sure you will respect my preferences and accede to my requests. I am asking you, as a favor to me, to dress conventionally and behave mannerly while at Delacourt."

Jack felt a stab of dismay. Dash it all, how could he accede to her requests and still manage to frighten off his would-be bride? "I shall endeavor not to embarrass you, Mother," he said carefully.

"Thank you. It will also oblige me if you make an effort to become acquainted with your cousin Celia."

The frontal attack startled him. She had never done such a thing before. In the days when she tried to match him with Lady Elaine, she had kept a careful distance, in fact—all too aware that any hint of interference or pressure would cause him to bolt. It struck him as uncommonly odd that she would change her tactics.

He frowned. "Why?" he asked, matching her bluntness.

The duchess regarded him calmly. "Because it is my hope that you will make her an offer of marriage. At your earliest convenience."

"Good God!" This unexpected frankness propelled him out of the chair with astonishment. He took a hasty turn about the room, raking his hand through his hair. "Good God!" he repeated, stunned.

The duchess appeared unmoved. "Pooh! There is no need for these theatrics. You are making a great piece of work about nothing. Sit down, John."

He fell, rather than sat, into the chair across from her and stared at her in wild-eyed amazement. "I never thought I'd see the day when you, of all people, abandoned subtlety."

Her mouth quirked. "And I never thought I'd see the day when you, of all people, expressed a preference for it! What has become of your much-vaunted love of plain dealing? I find it highly ironic that I have offended your sensibilities merely by directly stating a truth."

"No, no—you are right. I still prefer the word with no bark on it. I just never expected to receive it from *you*. Forgive me if I seem a trifle—taken aback."

"Certainly. May we now discuss the matter like rational creatures?"

Jack blinked dazedly at his mother. She looked perfectly composed. There was no trace of the anger with which she had greeted him just a few minutes ago. He supposed that since she wanted something from him, she had decided that anger would not achieve her ends. He raked his hands through his hair again, then sighed. "By all means," he said politely. "Shall we start with the obvious?"

Now she looked a trifle wary. "What do you consider obvious?"

"Well, for one thing, I have never before seen, or heard of, Celia Delacourt. Who in blue blazes is she, and why the devil should I marry her?"

The duchess stiffened. "There is no need to employ strong language, John. I have already told you, she is the granddaughter of your father's Uncle Richard. His *favorite* uncle, you know."

"That's no recommendation," said Jack grimly. "My father and I have hardly a single taste in common."

"Nevertheless, I gather Lord Richard was generally considered a charming individual. He was rather after your own style, I believe. He had a reputation as a jokester."

"Excellent. Cousin Celia is the granddaughter of a jokester. Well, that is all I need to know. I'll go wake her up and make her an offer."

The duchess glared reprovingly. "You are being sarcastic, John," she informed him.

"Yes," he agreed. "But pray continue. What is the

cause of Miss Delacourt's former obscurity? I have never heard that branch of the family mentioned—at least not by you. In fact, I have no idea what became of Uncle Richie and his progeny. If I have the story straight, he thumbed his nose at the family's choice of a bride for him, married to please himself, and, as a result, was disinherited."

By the lengthening of the duchess's upper lip, Jack gathered that she found the subject distasteful. "That is true," she said repressively. "He married most unwisely."

"Ah." Jack stretched his long legs out before him. "Then I can guess the rest. His granddaughter has been sent to rectify the situation. She will atone for her ancestor's sins by marrying very well indeed, thus ending the breach. How commendable! I only wonder why you have volunteered in her cause. It isn't like you, Mother, to busy yourself in the concerns of others—particularly those whom you deem to have come by their just deserts."

"Celia was not sent. I invited her. And she cannot be held responsible for events that occurred long before she was born."

Jack shook his head in amazement. "But this is odder and odder! You invited her? She told me so, but I assumed it was a euphemism. Most uncharacteristic of you, Mother! There is something havey-cavey about this entire scenario. Give me a round tale, if you please! I know you are afraid that I, like Celia's unfortunate grandfather, will eventually—as you put it— marry unwisely. But how did you hit upon cousin Celia as the proper person to save me from this fate? Good God! We don't even know her. And what advantage is there in my marrying her? Does she have political connections? Unsuspected wealth? She must have *something* to recommend her, or you never would have singled her out."

The duchess's face became more than usually mask-like. She regarded her son for many moments in silence, with an expression so wooden that he was tempted to poke her, as one does a waxwork, to see if she was breathing. It was impossible to guess what thoughts were revolving in her brain. At last she heaved a tiny sigh and gazed into the fire.

"I cannot tell you all my reasons," she said slowly. "You are correct that the succession has been very much on my mind of late. Your way of life has caused me—concern. I do not deny it. Your taste for low company distresses me. You have deliberately placed yourself among what I can only term a *dangerous* set of persons, the very sorts of people who might be depended upon to introduce you to their sisters and cousins—well, I shall say nothing further on that head, since you have made it plain I cannot interest you in confining your friendship to *gentlemen.*" Her voice dripped with contempt. "Suffice it to say, I have long considered what the family's response ought to be, should you propose marriage to a girl so far beneath yourself that—" She glanced fleetingly at Jack's face, and something in her son's expression warned her that she should stop. "Very well. To date, such a calamity has not occurred. It is, perhaps, foolish to worry over-much about an event that may never occur."

"You are right, however, that no consideration of what my family may find acceptable will deter me from offering marriage to a girl of my own choosing." Jack's voice was quiet, but there was a note of implac-ability in it. "Pray do not delude yourself into the belief that my opinions were carelessly formed, or that I can be dissuaded from them by argument. I have thought long and hard about this."

The duchess's hands clenched on the arms of her chair, belying the calmness of her demeanor. "I, too, have thought long and hard about it. Allow me to point out to you that I have rather more experience than one acquires in a mere three-and-twenty years! You would do well to heed the advice of your elders. The choice of a marriage partner is the most important decision you will ever make."

"On that, madam, we are agreed. And that is why I must reserve the right to make that decision, and not permit anyone else to make it for me."

The duchess's expression grew fierce. "You speak as if you will be the only person affected by your choice."

His brows lifted. "I am certainly the person who will be *most* affected by it."

"No, you are not," she snapped. "You are not a merchant, or a farmer! The livelihood and well-being of hundreds of people is in your hands. What will happen to them, if you are cozened into marrying a girl whose professed adoration of you is entirely false? Such things have happened to other rich men, as you know well. Even if you succeed in finding a girl whose love is genuine, you will discover that her family's love for you is a little less disinterested! It is the way of the world, John. If you marry beneath yourself, your bride's relatives will attach themselves to you like so many leeches. You cannot afford to be distracted from your duties by a wife who does not know how to go on, or by in-laws who embarrass you, or who hang upon your sleeve, forever with their hands out, begging you for money, for introductions to influential persons, for invitations to gatherings where they will be completely out of place—and where you will be loath to acknowledge your relationship to them! You cannot afford to have your tenants and your peers resent your bride, or hold you in contempt for choosing her. You will not like to have your children looked upon as mongrels, a little less fit, themselves, to marry well—by heaven, the thought is insupportable! Do not burden your sisters, do not burden your unborn children, with relatives of whom they must be ashamed. You will be the Duke of Arnsford, John! You, of all men, should choose a bride with your eyes wide open."

It was an admirable speech, and obviously deeply felt. Jack looked thoughtful. "It is something to consider," he admitted. "For posterity's sake, we must hope that I fall in love with a girl of my own rank. But frankly, ma'am, I would place no strong dependence on the likelihood of that. And I will not marry a girl I do not love."

Two spots of color appeared on his mother's cheekbones. "How dare you be flippant, sirrah? I am speaking to you most earnestly."

"I beg your pardon, ma'am, but I, too, am speaking earnestly. And you have yet to explain to me how you picked cousin Celia, of all unlikely prospects, to become the next Duchess of Arnsford. What became of Lady Elaine?"

"You disliked Lady Elaine."

Jack's tender heart felt a pang. He hoped inoffensive little Elaine had not realized how dull he found her. "Well," he temporized, "I did not dislike her, precisely—"

"It was clear you would never take her to wife."

He sighed. "True. But that still does not tell me why you are pushing Celia under my nose."

The duchess moved impatiently. "I will not fence with you, John. You are aware that I would have preferred you to marry a woman of birth and fortune. But I am correct, am I not, that you do not share that ambition?"

"You are correct. I've no ambitions in that area at all."

A faint sigh shook the duchess. "Then Celia will have to do," she murmured, almost to herself. "Her birth is respectable, at least, and she seems healthy and sensible. She is not unattractive. You could certainly do worse."

A short bark of laughter escaped Jack. "Left to my own devices, you mean, I am *likely* to do worse! And yet, ma'am, I prefer to be left to my own devices. I will take my chances, I think, and pick my own bride."

Anger flashed in the duchess's eyes. "It is of the *first importance* that you marry respectably. You could marry brilliantly, and you would, but I suppose there is no hope of that."

"No hope at all! But what's your hurry? I am not yet in my dotage. Surely there's no immediate need for me to step into parson's mousetrap."

"I would like to see this matter wrapped up before—" She broke off, then went smoothly on. "Before you 'fall in love,' as you call it, with someone wholly unsuitable."

Jack had the distinct impression that she had been about to say something else and had abruptly changed course in midsentence. His eyes narrowed in suspicion. "I am in no immediate danger of falling in love, Mother. I have met no one."

"But once you do, it will be too late to act," she said, her lips curving in a dry little smile. "Come, John! What is the harm in getting to know Celia? You may like her very well."

"Oh, I've no objection to befriending her. But I've every objection to finding myself compromised! If she is under the impression I am dancing attendance on her, about to offer her marriage—"

"Pooh. To whom will she complain?"

"Why, to her par—" Jack stopped, suddenly remembering what Celia had told him. A frown descended upon his face. "She has no parents, has she?"

"No," said the duchess placidly. "They died, I believe, in early September."

"Good God," whispered Jack, appalled. "Both of them at once?"

"Yes, and her siblings as well. Celia is completely alone in the world. I received a letter from someone— the local squire or landholder, I suppose—describing her plight and begging me to help her. After her family died, she had continued to reside in the vicarage where she was born, but apparently the man who wrote to me had just engaged a new vicar. Naturally, he required that Celia vacate the premises posthaste. That is why I invited her here. She has nowhere else to go, so we are likely to find her on our hands forever unless we can find a suitable husband for her."

The calmness of his mother's tone spoke volumes to Jack. He found himself moved against his will, and rose to take another turn about the room. The last thing he had expected was to find himself roused to anger and pity on Celia's behalf, but that is what he was feeling. When he finally trusted himself to speak, he said, trying to match his mother's calmness, "What you are telling me is, Celia has no one to defend her if we abuse her."

His mother's brows flew up in momentary surprise. "Abuse her? What a strange concern. It is unlikely that we will do so, I think."

"It is abusive, madam, to lead the girl to believe that I will marry her, when I will not."

The duchess's brows snapped together. "Nonsense. Celia is extremely grateful for the chance to reside at Delacourt. Regardless of what happens, she will not fly into odd humors or fancy herself ill-used."

"She cannot, can she?" said Jack bitterly. "She is completely dependent upon us. She has no choice but to be grateful for whatever crumbs drop from our table."

The duchess looked exasperated. "I do not understand your attitude. You seem upset by a circumstance

that works wholly in our favor. It is this very dependence that has enabled me to assume control of Celia's education. How else, pray, was she to become
accustomed to our ways here at Delacourt? How else
was she to learn how to manage a ducal palace, or
how to behave in polite society? It is no mean feat, I
assure you, to present a creditable appearance to the
world when one is a duchess. Certain expectations of
appearance and deportment must be met. Celia was
reared in a vicarage, in surroundings so modest that
they verged on squalor! No servants to command, no
stable, no Season in London, *none* of the elegancies
of life—why, without my advice and assistance, it
would have been impossible for her to step into her
role here at Delacourt."

An arrested look crossed Jack's features. "Aha.
This is the real reason why Celia appealed to you,
isn't it? You have brought her here to mold her into
your own image. Well! That is certainly an *advantage*
no female of birth and fortune, as you phrased it,
would enjoy. I fancy Lady Elaine's parents had strong
ideas of their own on how to train their daughter.
Most parents do! But your ideas, naturally, are superior to everyone else's; that goes without saying. No
wonder you switched your allegiance to an orphaned
and unsophisticated girl. Such a defenseless chit would
have to accept your tutelage without question. And if
you treat her abominably, or fill her full of nonsense,
no one can say you nay. No one will step in and inter-
fere. I congratulate you, ma'am. Cousin Celia is quite
a find."

He dropped back into the chair and scrubbed his
face tiredly with his hands. "Your mania for control
has led you astray this time, Mother. If you prepare
Celia for her new life by making her like yourself, you
will only place the prize further out of reach. The
more like you she is, the less inclined I will be to offer
her marriage."

The telltale signs of anger were cracking the surface of the duchess's rigid calm. Her knuckles were white where she gripped the chair, and her voice, although she did not raise it, had taken on a tight, furious note. "You are insolent. How did I manage to rear a son with so little sense of duty? You defy me, you are unmannerly and insulting—your way of life, your entire demeanor, is slipshod and slovenly—you are nothing, *nothing,* like the son I hoped you would be."

"Yes, I know, and I am sorry for it," said Jack, with quiet candor. "A pity Harry did not live. But he did not, and here I am, Mother. I am all you have. You must make the best of me."

The duchess's breathing quickened. "Make the best of you? I can make nothing of you! You take a perverse delight in thwarting me. I have gone to great trouble and expense to find—or make!—a suitable bride for you. You seem to think there is something wrong with that! I do not understand you. Persons of rank have chosen marriage partners for their children for centuries. You must marry one day. Why, *why* do you scorn my advice and assistance?"

A slight frown crossed Jack's features. His mother's anguish was so extreme, it appeared physical. "I do not mean to insult you. But you must be as aware as I am that you and I rarely agree on any matter of importance. It seems unlikely that we will agree on this one."

The duchess's back remained ramrod-straight, but her head fell back to rest against the top of her chair back. With her head thus supported, she continued to glare at her stubborn son. "The importance—of romantic love—in marriage—has been vastly overstated," she panted. "You would do well—to consider—what I have said—"

Jack rose, perturbed. He had never seen his mother so overset. "I will do so," he promised quickly. "Do not perturb yourself. Really, there is no need for this distress. May I bring you something?"

"No. No, nothing." She seemed to be struggling to control herself again, and her strange, panting breathing became more even. "Please go, John. We shall—address this—tomorrow."

He bowed, tight-lipped and worried, and removed his disturbing presence. The instant the door closed behind him, the duchess took a huge gulp of air. A low moan escaped her and she writhed, speechless, in her chair. Hubbard immediately appeared at her side, medicine glass in hand, and slipped one arm behind the duchess's arched back.

Despising her own weakness, the duchess drank. "I hate this—vile stuff," she gasped.

"Yes, Your Grace," said Hubbard soothingly. Her hand rubbed gently, rhythmically against her employer's back, distracting the duchess from her pain. The duchess closed her eyes, knitted her brows in fierce concentration, and struggled to banish the terrible burning sensation.

It was growing more difficult every day to keep the pain at bay. She was growing weaker, there was no denying it. Her strength was ebbing. Soon she would no longer be able to hide her torment from those around her. The realization sent a stab of such intense anger through her, she was able to open her eyes and straighten in her chair once more.

"Thank you, Hubbard," she said, managing to sound almost normal.

Hubbard respectfully withdrew her arm. "You're quite welcome, Your Grace."

Normally Hubbard would bow herself out at this point, but this time she did not go. She remained, standing at a respectful distance, watching the duchess with compassion in her eyes. Her Grace hated to be observed like this, but she did not have the strength to argue with Hubbard or order her away. In a moment, she promised herself, still fighting back the grinding waves of pain. In a moment, I will tell Hubbard to go. She clamped her teeth tightly and stared at a point on the wall directly ahead of her, willing the pain to recede.

Whether through the strength of her iron will or the assistance of the laudanum, the pain eventually retreated far enough to enable her to look at Hubbard again.

"Well? Why are you still here?" she asked, in a voice that should have sounded more formidable than it did. She had meant to snap at Hubbard, but only a whisper came out.

"I was thinking, Your Grace, that if you're feeling a bit poorly, I might sleep on a pallet in your dressing room," said Hubbard quietly.

The two women looked at each other. They had known each other a long, long time. Gertrude Hubbard had waited on the duchess when she was still Lady Gladys, fresh out of the schoolroom and enjoying her first London Season. How long ago it seemed, thought the former Lady Gladys.

For the first time, it occurred to her that Hubbard had devoted her entire life to serving her. In truth, Hubbard was her most intimate friend. What a strange thought. And she knew nothing about her.

For a moment, she felt an urge to ask Hubbard, Why did you do it? No husband, no children, no family. No life. Has it been worth it? Did you have any choice?

But, of course, one did not have personal conversations with servants.

Her gaze was clouding over, and she blinked, focusing with difficulty on the soberly clad woman who stood so humbly before her. Her Grace's mouth twisted in a strange little smile. Hubbard looked as diffident as if she were still the meek and lowly servant, and Her Grace the strong and all-powerful employer. But the balance of power had shifted. Both of them knew it. It was kind of Hubbard to keep up the pretense, but Her Grace was almost completely helpless now.

The duchess realized, blearily, what Hubbard's offer really meant. She would never again sleep without a nurse nearby. Day and night, someone would watch over her. This was a moment she had dreaded. Now it was here. And she was too exhausted to feel more than a fleeting pang of regret as she bid farewell to solitude.

She was taking one more step, she thought. One step closer to the end. But for as long as she could, by heaven, she would step gracefully.

"Thank you, Hubbard," said the duchess mildly. "You are very good."

Chapter 8

Jack stood in his dressing room in his shirtsleeves, studying his wardrobe. His mouth pursed thoughtfully. Will Munsil hovered at a respectful distance, awaiting instructions. A cold winter sun lit the room with blinding brilliance, illuminating the obvious: most of Jack's wardrobe was handsome and tasteful. Confound it. He ought to have made more provision for this. He could not wear the pink pantaloons every day. Besides, his mother had requested that he dress soberly. It would be entirely too disrespectful to flout her request by inflicting pink pantaloons upon her.

Very well. No loud colors. But something mismatched, perhaps. Something silly. He quickly chose a morning outfit of buff and brown with a bottle-green waistcoat, but when he saw them laid out together he realized that the combination was unexpectedly attractive. He frowned.

"Is something amiss, sir?" asked Will anxiously.

Jack thought about changing the waistcoat, but his stomach rumbled in protest. No, he was too hungry for all this folderol. He had no intention of hanging about in his dressing room all morning.

He eyed his temporary valet speculatively. "Will, do you know how to tie a cravat?"

"No, sir."

"Ha! Excellent! High time you learned. Try your hand at this one." Jack pointed to a formidable swath of starched linen and seated himself confidently before the looking glass.

The hapless lad gulped nervously. As Jack had hoped, poor Will handled the cravat exactly as if it had been a dangerous snake. He held it at arm's length, approached his master gingerly, and, blushing for his ineptitude, attempted to wrap it round Jack's outstretched throat. His timidity resulted in a loose and lopsided mess. When he was done, Jack's head appeared to be sitting atop a wasps' nest.

"Perhaps I should try it again, sir," suggested Will, scarlet-faced.

"No, no! You have done an admirable job. If only we were in London! We'd set a new fashion."

Will looked doubtful. "Do you think so, sir? P'raps if I just redid that last bit, where it's higher on one side than the other—"

Jack rose, waving him away. "Do not change it one iota. I like it as it is. I only hope you can duplicate your efforts in future."

Will beamed, dazzled by this vote of confidence, and happily helped his lordship into his waistcoat and coat. Jack went down to breakfast devoutly hoping that the unfortunate boy had an interest in horses or something. He really had to be distracted from this valet ambition of his, and the sooner the better. "No aptitude," muttered Jack to himself. "No aptitude at all."

The breakfast room was occupied, but only by Elizabeth and Celia. When Jack entered the room, Elizabeth's teacup paused halfway to her lips.

"Good morning! Good morning!" Jack boomed, rubbing his hands together in feigned enthusiasm and making a beeline for the side table. "Beautiful day, what?"

"Good morning," said Elizabeth repressively. "For pity's sake, lower your voice! And what is the matter with your throat?"

Jack picked up a plate and, since he could not turn his head, rolled one eye at her. "Eh? What's that?"

"Your throat. Have you a sore throat?"

"Lord, no! Never better in m'life." He lifted the cover off one of the serving dishes and sniffed appreciatively. "Buttered eggs! Hurrah!" He attempted his whinnying laugh, but his voice had not yet warmed up. It broke halfway through and petered out, rendering his new laugh even less convincing than usual.

Elizabeth looked alarmed. "It appears to me that you have wrapped flannel round your throat, and then tied your cravat over it to hide it," she said accusingly. "Are you quite certain you are well?"

Jack busied himself in heaping buttered eggs upon his plate with the maximum amount of clatter. "Perfectly fine. Very well indeed, thank you, very well indeed. Hah! Where's the toast?"

Elizabeth frowned. "You will have to ring for some. You know, John, if you are unwell, it's quite selfish of you to come downstairs and inflict your sore throat on the rest of us."

Jack dropped his heavily laden plate onto the breakfast table beside his scowling sister. He offered Celia a rather vacuous smile. "My sister has a horror of illness," he explained.

"Many people do," said Celia diplomatically. She sat composedly at her place, some distance from theirs, and calmly addressed her breakfast. She was garbed this morning in a high-necked round gown of black bombazine. Mourning did not flatter her, decided Jack. Black was a ghastly color for an ivory-skinned, brown-haired girl. And still she managed to look rather sweet. He felt a stab of anger as he pictured this pale, sad-eyed child at the mercy of his ruthless mother. Mother ought to scrap with someone her own size, he thought. This defenseless girl is not a worthy opponent.

But then he remembered: Celia was not necessarily Mother's victim. She might be a willing, even eager, accomplice. He ought not to be so hasty, letting his guard down merely because she had a tragic history and a sweet face. Really, it was unsettling to discover what a softhearted chap he was! Mercenary females were not immune to life's vicissitudes. A harpy might lose her family and still be a harpy. It was difficult to keep that thought in mind while actually looking at Celia, so he tore his eyes away from her and dug determinedly into his breakfast.

Elizabeth had lapsed into offended silence. Jack slurped his coffee and made as much of a racket with his silverware and china as he could, hoping that Celia would prove to be one of those females who abhorred bad table manners. The audience he was aiming for seemed to take no notice. Elizabeth, on the other hand, was growing visibly cross.

"Do not tell me again that there is nothing wrong with you, for I will not believe it," she announced at last. "Why must you be so provoking? Go upstairs at once and take to your bed like a sensible person."

"I don't wish to go to bed," said Jack, with his mouth full. "Nor am I a sensible person, as you have frequently told me."

Elizabeth rose angrily from the table and flung her napkin onto her half-empty plate. "Very well. If you stay, I go. I've no wish to spend Christmas nursing a sore throat."

Jack, swallowing hastily, reached out a hand to stop her, but she was gone. He looked remorsefully after her. "Now look what I've done. I ruined Elizabeth's breakfast."

Celia looked skeptical. "You meant to, didn't you?"

Jack opened his eyes at this. "No, no! Not in the least. I told her I wasn't ill, but she wouldn't believe me. Should I go after her, d'you think?"

"I daresay if she is still hungry, she will order a tray to be sent up to her."

"I hope so." Jack looked guiltily at the plate she had left behind. "She needs her breakfast. Too slender by half, my sister. Awfully touchy, too. Dash it, she knows better than to pay any heed to my antics! I wonder what the matter is? I hope she's not pining over Kilverton after all."

"Who?"

"Richard Kilverton. Chap she almost married." Jack looked up. Celia's eyes were round with surprise. He grinned and reached for the pepper. "Didn't you know?"

She shook her head. "No, I'd no idea. What happened?"

"Oh, it caused the deuce of a scandal," said Jack cheerfully, thickly peppering his eggs. "Kilverton is Lord Selcroft's heir. A thoroughly decent chap, too. I liked him. Pity! But there it is. They were actually engaged last Season. Notice in the papers, wedding date set, betrothal parties and all that. But then Elizabeth flew into one of her rages. Broke it off in a fit of pique, I believe. Six months ago, or thereabouts."

"Gracious! What a ghastly thing to happen."

"Pho! If you're picturing Elizabeth as a tragic heroine, you're wide of the mark." Jack chewed thoughtfully. "I hope."

"But it sounds as if it were nothing more than a misunderstanding. Everything might yet come right, if Elizabeth apologized to the gentleman."

Jack shook his head, chewing, then swallowed. "He's married someone else."

Celia's spoon clattered onto her plate as she dropped it. "No! *Already?* How can that be?"

His eyes twinkled at her dumbfounded expression. "When a fellow like Kilverton is determined to marry, he marries. Plenty of females ready to take him the instant he dropped his handkerchief. Elizabeth ought to have known that. Well, that's just it: she did know it! Flew into a rage anyway. I would have sworn, at the time, that her heart wasn't seriously engaged. But the way she's declined ever since, I don't know." He shook his head gloomily. "I must say, I'm a bit worried about her."

"I did wonder, you know, how it was that she was single. She is such a handsome creature."

"Yes," agreed Jack, spooning cream into the bottom of his cup. "That's Elizabeth, all right. Handsome. She's elegant, she's rich, she's wellborn, she's accomplished—in fact, she's dashed near perfect. That's been her undoing."

"Really?" Celia, fascinated, seemed to forget where she was. She rested an elbow on the table and leaned her chin on her hand, pondering Jack's remarks. "I see what you mean," she said thoughtfully. "It must be difficult to find a suitor high enough on the ladder for someone like Lady Elizabeth."

"Precisely." Jack reached for the coffeepot. "For a while, they thought of trying for royalty—but Mother disapproves of the male members of our own royal family and Elizabeth dislikes foreigners, so nothing came of that! In the end, it was decided the only Englishman good enough for our Elizabeth was the Duke of Blenhurst. They held up their noses at everyone else and bided their time, waiting for poor old Blenhurst to come to his senses and offer for Elizabeth."

"And he never did?"

Jack shook his head. "He sniffed around for a bit. Raised their expectations, I'm afraid. Elizabeth wasted two or three Seasons on the chap. But when all was said and done, he couldn't bring himself up to scratch."

Celia's nose wrinkled in momentary puzzlement. Jack quickly swallowed his mouthful of coffee and corrected his last statement. "Couldn't force himself to do it. Offer for her, I mean."

"Oh."

"I daresay he might have done the deed eventually, you know, if he hadn't met Lord Joyce's youngest—what was her name? Esther. But once he met her, Elizabeth's tale was told."

Celia's eyes softened with sorrow. "Poor Elizabeth."

Jack pulled a wry face and tucked back into his eggs. "You needn't pity Elizabeth. She cared for Blenhurst no more than she cared for Kilverton. It was all ambition. I've known her all my life, you know. Elizabeth cares deeply for no one but herself."

"Yes. She hasn't any friends," said Celia slowly.

Jack looked up, surprised. Celia was staring at the tablecloth, her expression troubled.

"What do you mean?"

Her brown eyes focused and lifted to his, their velvet depths still filled with concern for the absent Elizabeth. "It isn't right," she said softly. "Everyone should have friends, don't you think? If she's in trouble, she has nowhere to turn. No one to talk to. No one to comfort her. At least—" A faint blush was creeping up Celia's neck, and she lowered her eyes to her plate. "She may have friends elsewhere. Or perhaps she is closer to Lady Augusta than she seems. After all, I haven't been here very long—"

"No, you're right," said Jack thoughtfully. "Very perceptive. I've always thought of her as just like Mother, you know. Never needing anyone. Completely self-contained. But I don't suppose anyone is, really."

"No. Everyone needs someone."

Her face had turned so sorrowful, Jack couldn't bear it. He leaned back in his chair and stuck his thumbs in his waistcoat. "Pretty fine talking, for a girl who steals companions from others," he said, with mock severity.

As he had hoped, her melancholy vanished in surprise. "I'm afraid I don't quite understand you."

Jack rolled his eyes. "Don't feign innocence, cousin. You stole my favorite foot warmer last night."

Celia folded her hands in her lap. Her eyes darted to the closed doors on either side of the breakfast room. She looked almost afraid of him. When she spoke, she enunciated her words slowly and adopted a soothing tone. "I think you may have imagined something, cousin. Something that didn't really happen." She leaned forward, urgency and compassion written all over her face. "Think back, and I feel sure your recollection will clear. I stole nothing from you last night. Do you remember now?"

Jack stared at her in the liveliest astonishment. She seemed to be reacting very strangely to his jocular reference to the cat.

"I remember perfectly, thank you. You stole a foot warmer from me. A certain fat, furry foot warmer whose habit it has always been to sleep at the end of my bed."

Celia blushed crimson. "Oh! Oh, dear. You mean—you mean Manegold? I—I quite forgot he was your cat."

"Humph! He seems to have forgotten it, too."

She glanced apprehensively at him. "You aren't really offended, are you? I do beg your pardon. It's just—" She bit her lip, and stared back down at her plate. "While you were gone, you know, no one seemed to pay him any heed. No one in the family, I mean. Munsil did, a bit, and I've seen the housekeeper give him tidbits and talk to him from time to time, but—well, he's such a friendly cat, isn't he? It seemed to me that he wanted a little attention."

A slow smile crept across Jack's face. Manegold was

not, in fact, a friendly cat. To a chosen few, he was almost oppressively affectionate; to everyone else, he was completely indifferent. "So you took pity on his loneliness, and comforted him."

Celia lifted her eyes anxiously to his. When she saw that he was neither scolding her nor laughing at her, a shy smile lit her features. "Yes, that's right. At least, I hope I did."

It was all too clear that the shoe was at least partially on the other foot. Manegold had comforted Celia's loneliness. *Good for you, Manegold,* Jack thought approvingly.

What was there about this girl that moved him so? She aroused his chivalry, he supposed. She seemed so alone, and her eyes were so sad. He wished he could reach across the table and hug her. Instead, he tossed his napkin down and rose from the table.

"Come on," he said. "Since you've robbed me of my best friend, you owe me a replacement, don't you think? You must keep me company while I try to infuse a little Christmas spirit into this cold heap of limestone."

Her quiet little face suddenly lit with the first expression of genuine pleasure he had seen in her. She even clapped her hands. "Oh, do you mean it?" she cried. "I thought no one cared for Christmas here."

He grinned. "I do," he said simply, and held the door for her. "I say, are you sure you're a Delacourt? I never met a Delacourt quite like you."

She paused on the threshold and looked up at him. Her smile was actually saucy. "I might say the same about you." Then a shadow seemed to cross her features, and she shrank back a little, eyeing his neckcloth.

"What is it? I'm really not ill," he assured her.

What the deuce—? Was that *pity* he saw in her eyes? Whatever it was, her fear seemed to recede. She laid a gentle hand on his sleeve. "Ill or well, I think I shall be safe enough with you," she murmured.

He was still puzzling over that remark when they met, by agreement, in one of the back porticos some twenty minutes later. Jack had decided to abandon acting the fool, at least for the time being. It was tiring, and he couldn't remember to keep it up. Hang it all, he liked Celia. Whatever she was, at least she didn't seem the formidable type. He couldn't imagine her bullying, coercing, or intimidating a man into making her an offer of marriage. He still wasn't sure what she was doing, ensconced in Delacourt and basking in his mother's favor, but he meant to get to the bottom of the mystery before making up his mind what to do about it.

He had discarded Will's cravat and tied his own— a much simpler affair, but it was invisible anyway beneath the muffler he had wrapped round his throat. He had also donned an overcoat, sturdy boots, and a hat and gloves suitable for a December outing in the woods. He was strapping a handsaw to an ancient sledge when Celia joined him. He looked up to greet her, then froze in surprise.

She was wearing colors. He had been right; mourning did not flatter her. Now she was buttoned into a thick, hooded pelisse in a rusty, orangey shade that seemed to warm up her complexion and bring out the highlights in her hair. A few tendrils were escaping from her hood and curling softly round her face in proof of this fact. Her hands were buried in a muff made of some sort of blond fur that further lightened her appearance.

She blushed when she realized he was staring at her, and looked a little anxious. "It's my warmest pelisse. I'm afraid I have nothing suitable in black—" she began, but he cut her off with a wave.

"You look very pretty," he said firmly. "And it's

Christmastime. In honor of the season, I believe there is nothing wrong with wearing colors for an hour or two."

The shy smile flitted across her face again. "And no one else will see me, I daresay. Thank you, cousin John."

"My friends call me Jack."

Her smile brightened. "Jack," she repeated. "And you may call me Celia."

"I mean to," he assured her, grinning. "I'm a shockingly informal person, you know."

"I like it," she said happily, and almost danced out the door and toward the sparkling fields of snow. He followed, his smile widening into a rather besotted grin. *What a dear little thing she is,* he thought. It was impossible to keep one's guard up in the face of so much sweetness.

The cold snow crunched underfoot, but the sun was deceptively warm to two persons bundled up as they were. Jack was glad when they reached the edge of the wood, where a decidedly chilly temperature greeted them.

"Oh, this is delightful!" exclaimed Celia, sniffing the spicy, pine-scented air. She spread her arms wide in exultation. "Fancy owning your very own woods!"

Jack, who had owned his very own woods since infancy, blandly agreed. "The only ivy I know of at Delacourt is ornamental, and attached to the gatekeeper's house, so perhaps we'd better confine ourselves to evergreen boughs," he told her, looking about for a likely stand of trees.

"What about holly?" she asked eagerly. "Have you any holly? Or hawthorn? You must have hawthorn."

"Hawthorn is far too commonplace," said Jack firmly. "Let's hold out for holly."

"Very well," she said gaily, then paused, frowning in concentration. "What day is today?"

"It's Wednesday. The twenty-third."

Her face fell. "Must we wait until tomorrow then, before hanging the green? Perhaps we shouldn't gather anything until tomorrow."

He had to bite back a laugh. She looked as disappointed as a child. "Rubbish," he said firmly. "We'll hang it whenever we please. Besides, I daresay it will rain this afternoon and ruin the snow. And if it doesn't rain, the sun will do the job. Tomorrow will be a muddy mess. Come on!"

They tramped through the wood for over an hour, ostensibly hunting for holly but mostly ending up with evergreen boughs, and chatting as comfortably as if they were old friends. Celia reminded him of a houseplant starved for sunshine, suddenly set outdoors on a bright morning. One could almost see tiny leaves unfurling and reaching for the sky. She became effusive in her eager chatter, taking in deep gulps of the fresh, cold air and exclaiming over the beauty of the day, the wood, the snow, the landscape. She behaved, in fact, like a caged thing unexpectedly set free.

Celia's enjoyment was contagious. The sledge, however, grew heavier and heavier as they piled greenery atop it, and he was dragging it for the most part over bare ground beneath the trees, rather than snow. He eventually was forced to stop and remove his muffler. Celia ran lightly on ahead. He heard her quick footfalls halt at the top of the rise and her lilting voice cry out, for the dozenth time, "Oh, Jack! Jack! Come and see!"

He grinned. He knew what had excited her admiration this time. He left the sledge at the bottom of the hill and trudged up to join her. She stood, entranced, where the wood suddenly cleared at the top of the rise. A vista had opened up at her feet. From this spot, one could see for miles. The palace, which was still behind them and to their left, was not visible.

Below them lay acres of open space dotted with stands of trees, a meandering stream rippling over rocks, a magnificent lake—complete with a sculptured stone bridge that led to a small island in its center, and then arched beyond it to the opposite shore—and, in the distance, the sleepy village. It was considered by all the guidebooks to be one of the loveliest views in England. The air was very clear today, and the pristine snow added to the beauty of the scene.

Jack had loved this overlook as a boy. Later in life, he had realized that there was little about it that was natural. That knowledge had somehow taken the edge off his appetite for the spot. A famous landscape artist had carefully created this magnificent view, wrestling with God until His stubborn earth surrendered and displayed the artist's genius rather than the Creator's. Last night's snowfall helped to mask the heavy hand of the landscape artist, wiping out the geometric pathways that, to Jack, marred its perfection even as they enabled one to get about and enjoy it. The snow also concealed the fact that the open spaces were, for the most part, beautifully manicured lawn rather than natural meadow.

Celia appeared spellbound. "I have never seen anything prettier," she said softly, gazing reverently over the valley.

Jack smiled. "Nor have I," he said, but he was looking at Celia. She stood beside him, her eyes wide with awe, her cheeks rosy with cold and exercise, and her glossy brown curls blowing softly round her face. It was a pleasure to see her deep delight. Some of Jack's love for the place returned as he witnessed Celia's heartfelt enthusiasm.

"Let's sit and look at it for a bit," he suggested, dusting the snow off the handy log the landscape artist had placed there for this purpose.

Celia's eyes lit with pleased surprise. "Oh, how perfect!" she exclaimed, without a hint of irony. She seated herself on the smooth, level surface revealed by Jack's dusting and peered rather anxiously up at him. "I hope you are not growing tired?"

"Not in the least," he assured her. He sat beside her, but turned so he could watch her face. It was more entertaining to watch her ever-changing face than to gaze at the view.

She seemed relieved. "I shouldn't like to be blamed for—that is, I don't wish to tire you excessively. I daresay it isn't good for you."

He laughed out loud. "What a poor creature you must think me! I know you have lived in the country all your life, and I know that country folk have a low opinion of anyone who chooses to live in London, but I assure you I am not a *complete* puddingheart."

"Oh, no! On the contrary, I think it's very brave of you to live in London. Frightfully brave." She bit her lip and looked shyly down at her hands, nervously pleating a fold of her pelisse. "Do you—do you *choose* to live in London, then? I don't mean to pry, but—well—it seems rather extraordinary, to me. Surely you don't—you can't—live entirely alone?"

He grinned and stretched his legs out before him, crossing them casually at the ankles. "Not entirely," he admitted. "I have my man Hadley, you know, to look after me. He's very good indeed. Rules me with an iron fist, of course. But, on the whole, I consider that a fortunate thing, so I generally submit without a fight."

"Ah," she said quickly, with a swift, compassionate glance up at Jack. "I think I understand. But—you *like* this man, this Hadley?"

Jack laughed. "Oh, I wouldn't change him for the world! I pay him a shocking wage, in fact, for fear he'd go off and find an easier job! There are any number of chaps who'd be glad to take him off my hands and give him a soft life. But he's a loyal sort."

"Really? That's good. He is not here with you now, however, is he?"

"No. Looking after me is pretty hard work, you know, and poor Hadley had been at it for many months without a holiday. So I sent him home for a bit of a rest before the New Year."

Jack's tone was jocular, but Celia only nodded absently. "I suppose that's best," she said, "but it does seem a pity that you can't have a little more help while you are home for the holidays. Forgive me, but it seems to me that you need it." Her gaze had traveled to his neckcloth. She appeared thoughtful.

He remembered, then, that the removal of his muffler had revealed his cravat. The last time she had seen his neck, it had been swathed in Will Munsil's badly botched Mailcoach. Or whatever that was. No wonder she thought he needed his valet. He touched the retied cravat self-consciously and cleared his throat. "Oh. That. My—er—eccentricities. I daresay you may have been wondering—" he began, feeling a bit sheepish, but to his surprise, she immediately held up her palm in a gesture of silence.

Her expressive eyes turned up to his, hot with indignation. "You needn't tell me, for I have guessed the truth," she assured him passionately. "It's your family, isn't it? They make you—nervous."

He blinked. "Well, I wouldn't put it quite that way. I suppose they do bring out the worst in me. Unfortunately."

"I knew it!" she exclaimed. Her small fists balled in her lap. "You are a completely different person when they are nowhere about. Oh, it is wicked! Positively *wicked*!"

He winced. "I'm sorry, Celia. It hasn't been fair to you, has it? But you must understand—"

"I do understand," she interrupted. "I understand *perfectly*. I ought to have seen at once how it was, because I knew you lived in London. And now you tell me you live alone, with only *one man* to look after you! Well! How could that be, unless you felt better there? And why would you feel better there, rather than living quietly in the country? It can only be because your family is not there to torment and worry you."

He eyed her doubtfully, suddenly no longer sure he understood her anger. It did not seem to be directed at him, after all—and her words made little sense. But something had put her in a rare taking. Every muscle in her body appeared tense, and she was suddenly blinking back tears. She looked fiercely back at the view, although it was clear her eyes no longer saw it, and gave a defiant sniff.

"I have felt it, myself, ever since I arrived," she told him. "It has been a blessing, more than anyone can know, for me to be away from home at this time. To be *anywhere* else. And, even so, this house—the people in it—your family—I tell you truly, sometimes they are almost too much to bear! And if they oppress my spirits, how much more must they affect a—a *sensitive* person? For you must know, my spirits are not easily oppressed. I have always been excessively strong-minded."

"Have you?" said Jack, at a loss but feeling something was expected of him.

She nodded. "Strong-mindedness is my greatest failing," she confessed. "It is a terrible fault in a female. Although, to speak truth, I have been glad of my strong-mindedness lately."

In the natural way of one who is consumed with grief, her thoughts had irresistibly veered from the topic at hand to the topic that gnawed endlessly at the edges of her mind. Her features twisted in the unmistakable expression of someone who is struggling to hold back tears.

Jack thought he had never seen anyone look less strong-minded than Celia Delacourt. "Fragile" described her more accurately. But he did not say so. Instead, he silently located his handkerchief and handed it to her. Her gloved fingers clutched it spasmodically, seeming hardly to know what it was. She still stared blindly out at the snow-softened valley.

"Tell me what happened," he said quietly.

Chapter 9

"Tell me what happened," he said quietly, and Celia felt her carefully built defenses crumbling. Panicked by her impending loss of control, she struggled a moment more to resist his kindness. Kindness is worse than anything, she thought despairingly. I wish he would say something silly or mean. I wish he would turn this into a joke. But he did not. He sat and looked at her, gravely and compassionately, and with a perfect semblance of sanity. And Celia discovered, wretchedly, that even a calamity too deep for tears expressed itself somehow, anyhow, in tears.

Misery crashed down on her like a blow. Had she been standing, she would have staggered and fallen. As it was, she simply clutched herself and gasped, sobbing uncontrollably. His arms must have gone round her then. She was dimly aware of warmth, and rough wool against her cheek.

It didn't matter that she was being comforted by a virtual stranger. It didn't matter that she was making a disgraceful spectacle of herself. She simply could not help it. She clutched Jack like a lifeline in the darkness, and wept, and wept, and wept. Once she started crying, she couldn't seem to stop. Her breath came in great, hitching gasps. She shook like a frightened puppy. She buried her face in Jack's coat, ashamed to the core of her being but completely unable to stop.

He held her, and rocked her, and murmured to her

for a very long time. It was only when she noticed that his soothing murmurs were interspersed with curses that she was able to push away from him and bury her face in her hands. "Why—why—why are you sw-swearing?" she gulped, her teeth chattering as she regained a little control.

"Sorry," he said, his voice sounding strained. "I made a rather colossal error, didn't I? I hoped it might make you feel better to talk about it. I was obviously wrong."

She could not look at him. She held her head, which now ached fiercely, and rested her elbows on her knees. She concentrated on breathing. In. Out.

Dear saints in heaven, she had just wept all down the front of a madman. She wondered wearily if every madman was as kind as this one. If Jack was an example of what she might find in Bedlam, she would gladly exchange life in a ducal palace for a home among the lunatics.

What a crazy thought. Perhaps she was going mad, too.

"Do you feel better?" he asked, still in that quiet, compassionate voice that had been her undoing.

"No," said Celia shortly.

"I've heard it said that tears can ease the heart."

"So have I." She took another deep, shaky breath and expelled it slowly. "Just an old wives' tale, I sup-sup-suppose. Doesn't help a bit. Tears are com-completely useless."

"Ah. Well. At least you have stopped."

"One must stop, eventually," said Celia dully. Her ribs hurt from sobbing. She was exhausted. She wished with all her heart she could lie down somewhere and go to sleep.

How she longed for sleep. Sleep, deep and dreamless sleep, sounded lovely. No more thoughts. No more memories. No nightmares. Even Manegold's comforting presence, although infinitely helpful, had yet to bring her a night of unbroken sleep. She couldn't remember the last time she had slept the night through. Not since her summer visit to Wiltshire, surely. That must have been the last time. The last time for everything.

She straightened her spine, aching, and returned her gaze to the valley. It seemed strange to see it still there, nestled peacefully beneath its blanket of snow. Some irrational corner of her mind had half expected the storm raging within her to have ripped through the landscape as well. But the world was utterly indifferent to the personal sorrow of its inhabitants. And that was well and good, she thought tiredly, or happiness would not be possible. For anyone.

Her mind was traveling in strange little circles, her thoughts floating in some weary, peaceful place where she was aware of sorrow but could no longer feel it. She was too tired now to feel it. Maybe that was the much-vaunted benefit of tears. They did not heal anything, but at least they wore a person out.

Jack's hand reached over and clasped hers. His hand felt large and strong and comforting. Without thinking, she curled her fingers round it and clung. And then, holding Jack's hand and gazing sightlessly at the beautiful valley below, Celia felt words forming. It was as if strength flowed from Jack's warm hand and coursed through her, giving her the power to speak at last.

"I went to visit my old governess," she began. She spoke haltingly—but dreamily, as if she were telling a story. "In Wiltshire. You see, once Benjy was born, and with Margery and I nearing marriageable age, it was decided that we could no longer afford a governess. And Mrs. Floyd was of a mind to—retire, I suppose. So she left us, and went to live with her brother in Wiltshire. But she had always been a particular friend of mine. We corresponded regularly. And she frequently begged me to come to Wiltshire and visit her. And finally—this past summer—I was able to go."

She took a deep breath, closed her eyes, and sighed. "I had not been there a week when . . ." Could she say it? she wondered numbly. Yes, she could. "A message came. My younger brother had been taken ill."

Jack's hand moved, clasping hers a little tighter. She opened her eyes slowly and looked once more at the valley, as if she could see the words there, written on the snow, and all she need do was read them aloud. The only emotion that touched her was a dim gratitude for this respite from grief.

"That was all the warning I had. That message. I came home immediately," she said. "Mrs. Floyd came with me. But by the time I arrived . . ."

Memory—and, with it, pain, sharp and swift—suddenly stabbed through her precious fog of detachment. She took another deep breath to hold the tears at bay. Surely, surely, she had no tears left at the moment. But when she spoke again, a quaver had crept into her voice, and the thread of her story was more difficult to follow. Her mind wanted to jump from point to point, as anguished as her feet would be were she walking on hot coals. Images formed, nightmarish but compelling, impossible to ignore. Words tumbled out. She felt she must speak or suffocate beneath the weight of her memories.

"I knew something was wrong. Something terrible was wrong. No one came out to meet the carriage. Everything was so still. The apothecary's cob was hitched in the yard. I—I went into the house. I ran. There were—there were bodies in the parlor. I did not stop to look. They were laid out under sheets. In the parlor. I could not look. I could not. I ran upstairs." Her teeth were chattering now, but the words poured out. "Mama was still alive. But she could not speak. I think she recognized me. I—I think she could hear me. At first. But she could not answer. Margery—"

More images. Unbearable.

"Margery was unconscious. Barely breathing." Celia swallowed hard and closed her eyes against the pain. She forced the words past her chattering teeth. "They were the only ones left alive. Mama, and Margery. Margery died later that afternoon . . . Mama died the next day."

"Good God," whispered Jack. His voice was full of horror. Celia tensed against the waves of sympathy emanating from her companion; if she gave in to his sympathy, she would collapse. She pulled her hand from his and clenched her fists tightly together in her lap. She opened her eyes again, but would not, could not, look at Jack. Compassion would cause her to crumble yet again, and she felt driven to finish her story. If she did not, she would have to revisit it in future. If she could get the terrible words out, just this once, she might never have to say them again.

"They th-think it was the f-fish." A strange little smile shivered briefly across her features. How absurd it was, in a way. Life and death hingeing on such a simple matter. Such an everyday occurrence: dinner. She took another gulp of clear and frosty air and continued the tale, more steadily now. "But no one knows, really. Mrs. Miller—she's a woman in the village who would come to us three or four days a week, you know, helping Mama with this and that. Mrs. Miller had arrived one morning and discovered the house in an uproar. Benjy had been taken ill in the night. He couldn't see properly. Could barely lift his head. He was having trouble speaking. . . . So they sent for the apothecary. It was he who thought it must be the fish. He believed—he—he told them they might lose Benjy. That was when they sent for me." Celia stared at her feet. "The message I received didn't mention that by that time Papa and Jane had also started to feel unwell."

Remembering, remembering how they couldn't breathe, how her dear ones could not breathe, she found she had to concentrate on her own breathing again. In. Out. The iron bands that had tightened round her ribs loosened a bit, and she went doggedly on. "Benjy faded very quickly. By the time he died, everyone was ill. Jane went next. Then George. Then Fanny. Then Papa. They told me—they told me Papa died just an hour before I arrived." She took another deep breath. Almost done. Almost done now. "I already told you, I think, that Margery and Mama were still alive. They were still alive when I came home. But not for long."

There. She had said it. She had told the story. She hadn't told it clearly, perhaps, but she had told it. There was much more she had not told . . . of their dear, joyous lives, and of their deaths, and of the unending nightmare her own life had been in the aftermath. But she had told the worst of it.

And she had told it to Jack, of all people. That was strange.

She turned her head, then, to look at him. Her neck almost creaked as it turned, it felt so stiff. It would be horrible beyond belief to discover that the tension of the moment had pushed him back into his own illness. But he sat, still and watchful, his long body turned to face her. He looked pale, and his blue eyes had darkened with emotion, but he appeared perfectly grave and sane.

"If you're not going to use that handkerchief," he said hoarsely, "I would like to have it back."

She glanced down in surprise at her hands. She was clutching his handkerchief and had wadded the fine linen folds into a crumpled mess. "Oh, dear," she said, handing it to him. "I'm afraid I've shredded it a bit."

"Doesn't matter." He took it and blew his nose

fiercely. "Thank you. I shall be a man again in a moment."

She gave a rusty chuckle. "You've been a man all along. And an excessively kind one."

"Well, there's no doubt I'm a tenderhearted chap," he agreed, stuffing the ruined handkerchief into his coat pocket. "But that story would crack a heart of stone. And to think, after going through all that, you fell into my mother's clutches. Why, it's enough to make a frog weep."

Jack was trying to gentle her into a better humor, she realized, and felt her heart warm toward him. Mad or sane, he had to be the kindest man she had ever met.

The glow of her gratitude enabled her to actually smile at him. She tried to match the lightness of his tone. "Your mother's clutches haven't been so very bad. Why, look where I am! I might have ended up in a workhouse, you know, or hired out as a governess or something. And since I've never been bookish, I don't know which fate would have been worse! I don't imagine I would have been hired by one of the *better* households. My only talent is for sketching."

"Really? I don't believe I have any talents at all. The only marked propensity I have is for making friends, and that tends to be more of a nuisance than anything else."

"I think that's a lovely gift," said Celia softly. She could certainly vouch for the fact that he had it. She could not recall feeling so drawn to anyone in her life as she felt to cousin Jack.

"My family wouldn't agree with you."

He was smiling, but Celia wondered if poor Jack was, indeed, an easy touch for unscrupulous persons. There must be any number of villains who would take advantage of a fellow whose heart was as soft as his head.

Celia remembered Augusta's crossness at seeing her brother again after an absence of many months, and her ill-natured observation that his affliction grew worse every year, and a wave of protectiveness surged through her. Jack might very well *improve,* rather than worsen over time, had he the benefit of decent care and regular exercise! Why, it was really astonishing to see the improvement in him this morning, simply by removing him from the oppressive atmosphere of Delacourt—and his wretched family—and letting him tramp about in the fresh air. She hoped his man Hadley was a sensible and easygoing person, and that he was not being quacked too much by high-priced London physicians. She wished there were something she could *do* for him.

He rose and stretched out his hand to her. "I think we should move along before we freeze solid, don't you?"

"By all means." She allowed him to pull her to her feet, then paused, looking at the view one last time.

The tolling of church bells floated briefly across the valley. The sound tugged at her heartstrings, as sweet and ethereal as the promise of heaven. As familiar and comforting as home.

"Listen," she whispered, closing her eyes. "How beautiful they sound. I haven't heard church bells since I arrived at Delacourt."

"You can't hear them in the palace," he said softly.

"No." It seemed a metaphor for her entire experience of the place. Celia opened her eyes and sighed. "This really is a lovely spot," she said wistfully. "I hate to leave it, even if it is a bit cold."

"I shall bring you back here one shining day in April. I promise you, everything will look completely different in a few months."

Something in his voice made her look up at him. He was looking not at the view, but at her. Why, he meant something else entirely. He meant that things would look different *to her.* Surprised and touched, she gave him a shaky smile. "I suppose it will, one day."

"I have frequently observed," he said seriously, "that a harsh winter is almost always followed by a particularly glorious spring."

Celia felt tears sting the back of her eyelids. "I do hope you are right," she whispered. "One is so glad to reach the end of—of a harsh winter."

He nodded, then took her hand again. "But in the meantime," he told her bracingly, "we have Christmas to warm our hearts. Excellent placement, isn't it? In the midst of winter's darkest days, just when one needs it most! I say we go hang some greenery and get on with it."

Celia managed a little laugh. "Very well, sir! I trust your sledge is where you left it."

"Oh, no one would dare abscond with our hard-gleaned trimmings," he assured her, helping her down the steep path.

Her heart lightened with relief at his return to friendly raillery. "If the sledge has gone missing, we will simply follow the tracks until we find the thieves."

"And woe betide them! Evergreen poaching carries the stiffest penalties in these parts. Anyone caught decking their halls with ill-gotten holly is—is—"

"Yes?" prompted Celia.

"Is made to change places with the Yule log."

"No! How horrid. You shock me, cousin."

"Well, it's a good thing I am here to protect you. You've been crashing about the woods all morning without a license. You wouldn't care to be slowly consumed by fire while the rest of us make merry."

"No, indeed." They had reached the sledge, which was, of course, exactly where he had left it. Celia fell into step beside Jack as he threw the rope over his shoulder and began hauling the sledge back toward the edge of the wood. "What a mercy it is that you did the actual cutting of the branches today," she commented. "I'd no idea I was in danger of running afoul of the law."

"I wondered why you hadn't thanked me."

Celia, idly enjoying this nonsensical conversation, was brought up short by the realization that Jack might be serious. Her smile faded and she looked up at him anxiously. Perhaps one ought not to joke with a lunatic. She knew little of these things. What if she caused him to go off into a fit of some kind? But, really, he seemed so normal—

Jack glanced down at her. "What's the matter?" he asked, seeming a bit surprised by her scrutiny.

She blushed and looked away. "Nothing!" she said hastily.

"You're looking at me as if you thought I might suddenly sprout wings and fly away."

Her blush deepened. "No, I'm not."

"Yes, you are. And it's not the first time." He stopped, right in the middle of the path. "Out with it! What's bothering you? Is it the way I acted yesterday?"

Scarlet-faced, Celia bit her lip. "P-partly. But, really, cousin, you mustn't worry about it! *Pray* do not. Come along!" She grabbed the edge of his sleeve and tugged encouragingly. "Let's get the sledge back to the house, shall we? Such a lot of holly and evergreen we've gathered! We'll have a lovely time, hanging the green—"

He looked amazed. "You're talking to me exactly as if I were three years old."

"Oh, dear! I—I don't mean to." Since Jack had not budged, Celia dropped his sleeve and pressed her hands together beseechingly. "Pray do not be angry," she said breathlessly.

"I'm not angry. I'm baffled." He tapped his face to indicate his expression. "This is bafflement," he explained. "If it disturbs you, you can eradicate it by simply revealing to me what the *deuce* is going on in that pretty head of yours."

Celia was mortified. She wished she had had time to consult with someone—Lady Augusta, or Munsil, or *someone*—to prepare for this conversation. She had often heard it said that madmen were unaware of their own oddness and believed themselves to be perfectly normal. Here she was, all alone in the wood with one, and she did not even know whether Jack himself was aware of his condition. Perhaps that was the best place to begin.

She scanned his features with some trepidation. He did look baffled. And also a bit amused. And handsome—but that was irrelevant, of course.

"I am wondering," she began hesitantly, "if you are aware—if you think you have been—quite well, these past few years. Or during your youth, for that matter." She saw his baffled look widen into astonishment, and hurried on. "I mean—were you sickly, as a child? Have you been plagued with physicians and whatnot? More than you liked, I mean? More than—normal?"

He stared at her. "Forgive me if I seem a bit surprised. I had thought of many things I expected might be bothering you, but you have chosen something that was not on my list." He rubbed his chin thoughtfully. "Physicians! Because I was the only surviving son, do you mean? Are you thinking I was cosseted and fussed over? Do I seem overly indulged? A bit—spoiled, perhaps?"

"Well—not exactly. Not quite. I was thinking—I was thinking—I don't know what I was thinking," she finished lamely, blushing for her evasion.

"Ah," he said, his expression inscrutable. "The answer is that I have been blessed with an amazing degree of good health, was never sickly as a child or a youth, and haven't the foggiest notion why you should ask such an extraordinary question."

His tone was pleasant enough, but Celia's embarrassment increased. "I beg your pardon!" she said hastily. "It's none of my business, of course."

"I was, in my youth, fussed over a good deal," he offered. "But the uproar was always over my *behavior*. Not my health. I was forever being scolded for this transgression or that, by one parent or the other. I always found it difficult to toe the line, you know, and do the 'done thing.'" He grinned. "You may have noticed that I still have trouble with that."

"Yes. I see." His behavior had caused a constant uproar, had it? Of course. Poor lad. At some point his parents must have realized that Jack's consistent failure to "toe the line" arose from something more serious than youthful rebellion.

But—did it?

A rather breathtaking idea occurred to Celia. She studied Jack's honest, amiable countenance, wondering. Was it possible—was it *possible*—that Jack was not mad at all?

It was difficult to believe that a madman could converse so naturally and pleasantly, hour after hour. It was even more difficult to believe that a madman would show her so much kindness, and listen so attentively, and joke with her. Weren't madmen supposed to be feebleminded? He seemed, if anything, more clever than most people.

From what she knew of his parents and sisters, it suddenly seemed not only possible but *probable* that what struck the Delacourts as outright lunacy might be just . . .

Just what? she wondered, confused again. It wasn't only Lady Augusta's word she had for it, after all. Her heart sank as she recalled Jack's demeanor and behavior yesterday. And even this morning at breakfast, she had to admit, he had not seemed quite right in the head. She was hardly qualified to make a diagnosis, but anyone could see that there was *something* wrong with him.

And then there was his mother, who was taking great pains to arrange his marriage—a duke's heir!—to a penniless orphan. Strong evidence, indeed, that something was amiss, either with Jack or with the duchess!

Perhaps his madness was of the sort that ebbed and flowed, changing from day to day. Perhaps she had just spent a few hours with him during a phase of clarity, but his befuddlement could return as swiftly as it disappeared. She had heard of such afflictions. Perhaps—

Jack interrupted her train of thought. "Are you going to tell me, or aren't you?"

"What?" stammered Celia.

He looked exasperated. "Very well," he said, picking up the rope again and beginning to drag the sledge down the path.

Celia trotted after him, contrite. "I'm sorry, Jack. I don't mean to be secretive. Was I—was I staring at you?"

He shot her a wry glance. "First you looked as if you were afraid of me. Then you talked to me as if I were still in short coats and blushed when I asked you why. Then, when I tried to discover what you were thinking, you asked me about my *health*. And then you studied me for several minutes, as if I were a beetle on a card! I can't force you to confide in me, cousin, but I do wish you would."

It seemed impossible to ask him outright: Jack, do you know you're mad? And yet Celia wished she could, in fact, ask him about it. Whatever his condition, he seemed such a *forthright* person at heart. If any madman could talk about his own disorder, he could.

As she wrestled with this problem, Jack stopped so suddenly that she slid into him. He caught her, steadying her on the slick path, and gazed intently into her eyes. "I know what it is. And I know why you won't tell me."

"You do?" said Celia faintly. Jack was still gripping her arms. His hands felt large and powerful. She had to tilt her head back to look at his face. A sudden, overwhelming impression of his size and strength rushed along her nerves. The sensation was not unpleasant, but it made her feel—strange.

"I think we should be honest with each other, cousin," said Jack slowly. "You and I have good reason to keep each other at a distance, haven't we? But I think . . . I think I've changed my mind about you. You're no more a fortune hunter than I am."

Celia almost gasped aloud. "A *fortune hunter?* Is that what you thought me?" She pulled herself out of his grip, shaken. He must know about the duchess's plans after all. How humiliating. Unless—she glanced again at him, uncertain. Maybe he simply thought her a fortune hunter because she was accepting charity. "You mean—you thought me a fortune hunter because I came to live at Delacourt?" she asked cautiously.

"No. Because—" To her surprise, Jack's face was reddening. He looked completely nonplussed. "That is—I thought you were part of—or at least I thought you knew about—" He turned and walked a few steps away, clearing his throat. "Confound it! If she doesn't know, it's not my place to tell her," he muttered.

Celia had heard him quite clearly, but it behooved her to pretend she hadn't. Indignation helped to hold her silent. Had the duchess *lied* to her? She had definitely been told that Jack knew nothing of this ridiculous marriage scheme. But he obviously did know of it, and thought her a fortune hunter! Which, by the by, lent credence to the idea that he was unaware of his own illness. He must fancy himself quite a prize, Celia thought, far above being matched with the likes of her! Well, if he were sane, so he would be. She felt torn between exasperation and pity.

He turned to face her again. "At any rate, whatever I thought of you, I don't think it now," he said firmly. "You may have my hand on that, if you wish." He walked back to hold out his hand to her, and she hesitantly took it.

"Thank you, cousin," she said stiffly.

He reached out his other hand and enveloped her hand in both of his, smiling down at her. She could feel the warmth of his grasp even through the thickness of their gloves.

"I like you," he said simply. "I hope we will be friends."

All uncomfortable emotions fled, and Celia flushed with pleasure. What a dear man he was. It was impossible not to respond to such frank goodwill.

"I like you, too," she said warmly, and meant it.

Chapter 10

A brief silence fell. Elizabeth looked more than appalled, she looked stricken. "Mother, how *could* you?" she uttered, and covered her face with her hands.

The duchess's brows twitched together in an exasperated frown. She had been forced to witness too many emotional scenes lately, she thought irritably. First from Celia, then John, and now Elizabeth. She was tired and unwell, and disliked displays of strong emotion to begin with. Elizabeth was her favorite child, but she could not refrain from snapping at her. "For heaven's sake, Elizabeth! I have not acted out of spite. I have acted in your best interests."

Elizabeth, pale with agitation, rose from her chair as if compelled and crossed swiftly to the window, where she stared sightlessly at the snow-dusted lawns. Her hands, held stiffly at her sides, clenched, unclenched, and clenched again.

Since her daughter seemed incapable of speech, and was obviously making a praiseworthy effort to control herself, Her Grace addressed her in a milder tone. "I did not speak of this to you earlier, because there was no point in doing so until I knew what the outcome of my efforts would be."

"You might have consulted me, however!" cried Elizabeth. "You might have ascertained my wishes in the matter. *Before* you acted!"

"To what purpose?" asked Her Grace, her voice sharp with exasperation. "You would have been on tenterhooks these three weeks and more. I sought to protect you from disappointment. It seemed to me unlikely that Blenhurst would accept my invitation. And if he did, I certainly thought to receive word prior to today." She flicked the creased paper lying open on the escritoire before her. "It was most unfortunate that his letter was delayed. However, that cannot be helped."

Elizabeth drew a shaky breath. "When do you expect him?"

"Possibly this afternoon. No later than tomorrow."

"Then he might arrive at any moment!"

"I suppose he might. Pray calm yourself, Elizabeth! You will not be sent to open the door."

Elizabeth's only reply was an inaudible exclamation. She paced the room, her hands still jerking spasmodically. The morning room, although high-ceilinged, was not a large apartment. Five swift strides brought her to the fireplace. Five strides back and she was at the window embrasure again. The movement seemed to help her regain some measure of calm, however. She returned to face her mother, her eyes glittering like flint-hard sapphires.

"You had better tell me all. I will not, I *cannot* face him unless I know in advance where I stand in this. I set my cap for him years ago—at your direction, ma'am!—and was humiliated for my pains. And the lessons I learned last Season with Kilverton are still quite fresh in my mind. Painfully so! I've no desire to play the fool a third time. *Why* is Blenhurst coming here? His wife has been dead less than a year—only eight or nine months, surely. What is his purpose in spending Christmas at Delacourt, of all unlikely places? He is no connection of ours."

The duchess met her daughter's eyes levelly. "Precisely. I am sure he found my invitation surprising, and I am sure he recognized that there is only one reason why I would invite him. His Grace of Blenhurst is not a stupid man. His acceptance of my invitation, therefore, must indicate that he is considering making you an offer of marriage."

Elizabeth seemed once more bereft of speech. Her mother calmly watched the various emotions chasing themselves across her eldest daughter's face. Among them, she recognized hope—and the fear of hope. Whatever the rest of Elizabeth's feelings, they could be sorted out later. It was enough, thought the duchess, that Elizabeth hoped. Hoped so much that she was afraid to hope.

"Sit down, my dear. Let us contrive a little."

But instead of sitting, Elizabeth clasped her hands tightly on the high back of the chair before her. "I do not wish to contrive," she said, her voice shaking. "I have done nothing but scheme and contrive and plot for the past eight years, and it has achieved nothing. I am done with contrivance, Mother. I do not wish to speak disrespectfully to you, but I must tell you that I am *mortified* that you wrote to Blenhurst and invited him to spend Christmas at Delacourt. As you say, he will easily guess why you have done so, and what purpose you have in mind. If this should become *known*—" Elizabeth's voice broke, and she pressed her knuckles against her mouth.

"Nonsense," said the duchess bracingly. "Blenhurst is not a common gossip."

"I will be even more of a laughingstock than I am now."

Her Grace stiffened. "*You,* a laughingstock? You are nothing of the kind! I will not countenance such careless speech from you, Elizabeth. You must be well aware that you are an object of envy, with your birth, your breeding, your personal gifts—"

Elizabeth gave a short, bitter laugh. "Envy! I have long been the target of cruel gossip, Mother. Perhaps, as you say, it originally stemmed from envy. Lately, however, people have begun to *pity* me. I find it intolerable. And now you, of all people, are providing grist for the gossip mill with this *shameless* invitation—"

"Do you dare to criticize me?" Her Grace's eyes narrowed dangerously.

Elizabeth's face took on a sulky expression that made her look strikingly like Augusta. "I beg your pardon, ma'am."

The duchess's mouth tightened. "You may rest assured, Elizabeth, that I am as eager to avoid disgrace as you are. Who will gossip about this, pray? If he comes and goes without making you an offer, who will carry the tale to town? This is a family gathering, not a party of strangers."

Elizabeth's eyes widened in fresh horror. "Does Blenhurst know it will be a family gathering?"

Her Grace's eyes slid away from her daughter's. "I did not mention the particulars," she said evasively.

"Good God, ma'am! He will naturally assume that it is, in fact, a party to which he has been invited! He may be very angry when he arrives to discover that there are no other guests!" Furious tears sparkled in Elizabeth's eyes. "How could you make him so conspicuous? He will feel honor bound to offer for me."

The duchess smiled grimly. "Let us hope so," she said shortly. "It would give me great pleasure to see you settled before—to see you settled, that is, so advantageously. His Grace of Blenhurst is a wealthy man, and sensible. His character is steady and his disposition mild."

"Oh, yes, yes, yes, yes, yes!" snapped Elizabeth, dashing the tears impatiently from her eyes. "And it has long been your ambition to thrust me into the arms of the only eligible duke in England!"

"It has long been your ambition as well, has it not?" said Her Grace acidly. "Comfort yourself with the recollection that *if* you secure an offer from Blenhurst, the gossips will be silenced at last. Your ill-advised jilting of Lord Kilverton will be miraculously transformed from a shocking misstep to a clever gambit."

She had thought this might actually give Elizabeth pause, might cheer her and fortify her for the coming days. Once Elizabeth's ambition was rekindled, Her Grace had little doubt that she would throw herself into this project with determination—and, this time, succeed. But Elizabeth's shoulders were tense with misery, not eagerness. "It *was* a misstep, as all the world knows. Kilverton set a trap, and I stepped into it."

"Yes," said her mother dryly. "You lost your temper—the very thing I had specifically warned you not to do. Had you heeded my advice, we would not be having this conversation today. But let us not cry over spilled milk. Perhaps in future, Elizabeth, you will follow my instructions more carefully."

Elizabeth shot her mother an angry glance. "Has it not occurred to you, madam, that there is a certain *pattern* to these setbacks we have suffered? On the very occasion when you warned me not to lose my temper with Kilverton, you also warned me that you had observed him at Almack's, dancing with the lady who is presently his wife! It was this observation that prompted your advice, was it not? Blenhurst, also, was very near the sticking point—or so we believed!— when he met Esther Joyce. Once he had done so, his retirement from the list of my admirers was disconcertingly abrupt." Her face was suddenly haggard. "You have taught me that a man of breeding does not require, does not even *desire,* romantic love in marriage. Yet twice I have been discarded by men of breeding who apparently not only desired love, but refused to marry without it."

The duchess snorted. "You are reading far too much into these events, Elizabeth."

"Am I? Am I indeed? I have had a great deal of time in which to reflect, of late, and my reflections have not been—comfortable." Elizabeth took a deep breath. "I think it possible that you and I have been wrong."

The duchess stared at her daughter in disbelief. A sharp stab of pain wracked her, the inevitable result of surprise. The unexpected always ruined her concentration, breaching her defenses. She automatically pressed her hand to her abdomen—then, with an effort of will, removed it and placed it back on the arm of her chair. When she spoke, her voice sounded thin but controlled.

"I never thought to hear such rubbish from you, Elizabeth. I have endured Celia's mewlings because I know her to be ignorant, and John's because he makes a habit of opposing my will. But you! You have had the benefit of my teaching and my example all your life, and we have always thought as one. I have long been proud of your elegance, both of person and of mind. You have always behaved just as you ought. Your conduct has been above reproach since the instant you made your curtsey to the Polite World. It is nonsensical—it is *heretical*—for you to doubt yourself. It is an insult not only to you but to me."

Elizabeth flushed. "Very well, ma'am. I shall not trouble you further with my thoughts on the subject. But if Blenhurst does *not* offer for me, I beg you to relinquish your ambitions. I have done so. Or, rather, I have tried to do so! But I cannot reconcile myself to spinsterhood while you continually burden me with false hope."

Elizabeth's eyes looked suspiciously bright. Good heavens! Was she weeping? Before the duchess could recover from her astonishment, Elizabeth dropped a stiff little curtsey and vanished out the door.

Her Grace felt her world tipping into chaos. Now that there was no one to see, she clutched her belly, panting, until the miasma of pain receded and her clouded vision cleared. Elizabeth, defying her! Elizabeth, doubting her! It was inconceivable. Why, it almost caused her to doubt herself.

She gazed anew at Blenhurst's carefully worded acceptance of her Christmas invitation. So polite, so neutral. So brief. It had originally struck her as businesslike and unambiguous, a clear message of his intent. Now she felt less confident. Had she read more into his message than he intended? She banged her fist on the escritoire in a futile expression of frustration.

Hubbard, who was never out of hearing now, immediately appeared in the doorway. The duchess waved her away impatiently. "Thank you, Hubbard, but I require nothing. Or—wait. Stay a moment. I would be obliged to you if you would arrange for Mr. Willard to pay me a visit. At his earliest convenience."

Uncertainty flickered in Hubbard's eyes. "The solicitor, Your Grace?"

"Yes, yes, our solicitor! Pray take care of it for me. Munsil or one of the footmen will know the best way to send a message to him."

"Yes, Your Grace." Hubbard curtseyed and, with one last searching look at her mistress, departed on her errand.

The duchess leaned her head against the back of her chair for a moment, exhausted. "Sharper than a serpent's tooth, to have a thankless child," she quoted bitterly. It seemed she had three thankless children on her hands, if one counted Celia.

Well. They would all thank her one day.

And now she would have Blenhurst to entertain. She had already sent a message to the housekeeper and one to the stables. She had broken the news to Elizabeth. What else was there to do? Ah, yes. She forced herself to straighten in her chair, and blearily

took up the menu Monsieur Andre had sent for her
approval. It was entirely in French, and she was finding it difficult to concentrate. She made a few quick
strokes, replacing one suggested sauce with another,
vetoing tomorrow's dessert course as too common—
Blenhurst would almost certainly be present for that
meal—and requesting a crème brûlée instead. She
lacked the energy to quarrel with the rest of it. Let
Monsieur Andre decide. For heaven's sake, she paid
him an exorbitant wage to do so.

The day-to-day management of Delacourt was becoming ever more difficult for her. High time she
made use of Celia, she supposed. A pity that Elizabeth
could not fill her mother's shoes. Elizabeth was born
and bred to the role; she would make an admirable
duchess.

Her Grace's lips tightened. Elizabeth would, if all
went well, make *Blenhurst* an admirable duchess. Delacourt would be handed to Celia, a callow girl who
knew no more of running a great house than—well.
No sense repining. This is why she brought Celia here,
after all. Celia would learn, and she would teach her,
thus ensuring the smoothest possible transition. Her
management had made Delacourt perfect. Nothing
must change.

Celia's training must begin without delay, and Elizabeth *must* marry Blenhurst. It was already apparent
to Her Grace that she would not have the strength to
travel to London for the Season, let alone engineer
Augusta's come-out. The child had been kept dangling
in the wings, waiting for Elizabeth's marriage before
being allowed to make her own curtsey. Elizabeth's
marriage had failed to materialize, and Augusta was
twenty now. Twenty! Her first Season simply could
not be put off any longer. Once safely wed, Elizabeth
could take on that responsibility, and the duchess
could devote what remained of her energy to Celia's
training.

But she would have to stay alive, she realized tiredly, until summer. Augusta was already in a perpetual temper, believing her chances had been blighted by Elizabeth's prolonged spinsterhood. She would be frantic if her mother's death forced her into mourning and put off her Season another year. Whatever it cost her, then, she must hang on as long as she could. For Augusta's sake. It was her duty.

This grim train of thought was interrupted by Munsil's discreet cough. "Forgive the interruption, Your Grace, but the Duke of Blenhurst has arrived."

Jack and Celia were crossing the last expanse of rapidly melting snow, heading for the rear of the palace, when two stout footmen came through the side door and headed purposefully toward them.

Jack indicated them with a nod. "The general is sending reinforcements. We'll win this battle yet."

"We didn't even tell anyone we were going to gather greenery," marveled Celia. "What an efficient staff you have."

"Frightening, isn't it? Let's test them. I say we stop right here, climb up on the sledge, and wait for them to drag us the rest of the way."

Celia giggled. The bed of the sledge was invisible beneath the stack of boughs, piled so high that she could not see over the top. "Too dangerous," she averred.

"Well, I'm stopping here, at any rate," said Jack, doing so. He pressed one hand to the small of his back and stretched. "Faugh! That's warm work, even in December."

Celia was instantly contrite. "I should have thought of that. I'm so sorry. Why did you not ask me to push it from behind?"

His eyes twinkled down at her. "You persist in believing me a hothouse plant, don't you?"

"Oh—not that, exactly—"

"Too soft to pull a rubbishing sledge."

"That isn't what I—"

"Weakened by my idle life of luxury and privilege."

She placed her fists on her hips and glared at him. "That is *not* what I meant."

He grinned, and lightly flicked her nose with one finger. "Had you pushed from behind, I would not have had the pleasure of your conversation. You were far more useful by my side."

She was so surprised by this casual, almost brotherly contact, she did not immediately reply. Then the footmen were upon them to take the sledge from Jack. The younger of the two men seemed to be laboring under suppressed excitement. As Jack and Celia fell into step behind the sledge he blurted, in a congratulatory tone, "I think you should know, my lord, that His Grace of Blenhurst has arrived."

"Blenhurst! *Blenhurst?* You're joking."

"No, my lord."

"Ha! Then someone is hoaxing you, my good man."

The young man ignored the older footman's admonishing frown. "No, my lord," he said eagerly. "For I saw him myself."

Jack looked startled. "By Jove! Is he staying for dinner, d'you know?"

The young man swelled with importance. "I daresay he'll be stopping for some several days, my lord. He had a quantity of baggage with him, and Her Grace has put him in the Blue Room."

"You don't say!" Jack seemed to cogitate for a moment. "Thank you, William. Most interesting."

Celia, burning with curiosity, felt an almost imperceptible tug on her elbow. She glanced up and met Jack's eyes. In response to his clear signal, they dropped a little farther behind the sledge. "What does it mean?" she asked softly.

"It can only mean one thing. Mother's got her hooks into the poor fellow again."

"How can that be? I thought you told me he was married."

Jack nodded thoughtfully. "Seems to me there was more to the story. I'm afraid I don't keep track of people as closely as I ought. Forgive me; I have a constitutional dislike of gossip."

Celia nodded with quick sympathy. If Jack had been kept in London, with his oddities on public display, he had probably been the target of gossip himself. "Perfectly understandable," she told him staunchly.

"Yes, but my failure to read the columns, and my avoidance of conversations about the personal lives of others, often leaves me in the dark regarding matters that are common knowledge." He scratched his chin, perplexed. "Did Blenhurst's duchess run off with another man? Seems to me that was one of the on-dits last summer. No, begad, it must have been someone else. Blenhurst made a love match."

By now they had reached the back entrance and the stone-floored room where they had found the sledge and saw. The footmen stood impassively by, awaiting instructions.

"Hm," said Jack. "Under the circumstances, I think you should pack the boughs in snow and we'll deck the halls tomorrow rather than today."

"Very good, my lord."

As they entered the main portion of the house they encountered Munsil, who confirmed that His Grace of Blenhurst had in fact arrived and that refreshments would be served shortly in the tea room. Jack was hungry and Celia was curious, so they both sped to their chambers to change their outdoor clothing for more suitable attire. Celia could not help smiling as she reflected on the astonishing change in her circumstances: she thought nothing now of sitting down to tea with an unknown duke. And thanks to the Duchess of Arnsford's generosity, she actually owned frocks that were suitable for drinking tea with dukes. It made one's head swim, to unexpectedly reach such heights.

The orange pelisse went back to its place in the far depths of her wardrobe, and Celia donned sober black once more. For the first time since she had gone into mourning, she was conscious of a twinge of regret. It was a shame, she thought, that black did not become her.

She regarded her reflection in the looking glass over her dressing table and sighed. Such beautiful, well-made clothes! She had never owned such garments in her life. And every last one of them made her look sallow and haggish. She frowned, then rummaged briefly through a drawer until she found a modest lace collar. She tried it with the dress, and the narrow edge of white seemed to brighten her face a bit. Feeling faintly cheered, she went down to the tea room.

Jack had not yet arrived. The room's sole occupants were Lady Elizabeth and a gentleman whom Celia had never seen. Both looked up as Celia paused on the threshold. Their expressions of relief were almost comical; Celia had evidently interrupted a rather strained tête-à-tête. The gentleman rose.

"Ah, here is my newfound cousin," announced Elizabeth, her voice overbright. "You have not met Miss Delacourt, I think. Your Grace, may I present my cousin Celia? Celia, the Duke of Blenhurst."

"Your Grace," murmured Celia, curtseying very low.

The duke bowed. "Miss Delacourt."

She looked at him with interest. He was older than Celia had expected, a slightly built, modest-looking man who appeared to be nearing forty, with thinning brown hair and a mild, pleasant face. Although there was nothing particularly distinctive about his appearance, he had a certain dignity that sat naturally upon his shoulders and lent him a distinguished air. He looked thoughtful and educated. She liked him at once.

Almost the instant Celia sat down, the awkwardness in the room returned. They drank tea. Elizabeth poured. Celia cleared her throat and commented gamely on the weather. The duke politely agreed that yes, it was pleasant to see a little snow at last. An uneasy silence fell. His Grace opined that the snow would be gone by Christmas, however, unless it snowed again. Celia and Elizabeth concurred. More silence.

Celia pointed out that one always associated snow with Christmas, even though one frequently celebrated Christmas with no snow at all. His Grace seconded this observation and wondered whether there really had been a great deal more snow at Christmastime when he was a boy than there was nowadays or whether everyone simply remembered childhood Christmases that way? Celia was sure she didn't know, but she also remembered Christmas as a snowy time, and wasn't that odd? Yes, yes, yes, most odd, very interesting.

Silence.

Of course, nothing compared with the winter of 1814. Oh! Heavens, no. No, that was a shocking winter, completely out of the ordinary. Not a typical English winter at all. Dreadful, dreadful. Of course, the Frost Fair was amusing. But, on the whole, a shocking winter. Shouldn't care to have a winter like that every year, no, indeed.

Silence again.

His Grace turned at last to Celia. "How is it that we have never met, Miss Delacourt?" he asked, with a pleasant smile. "I feel sure I would have remembered you."

Celia was in no danger of reading anything other than common courtesy into this gallant statement, so she was a little startled when Elizabeth rushed into speech before she could reply.

"Oh! Celia has lived all her life quite buried in the country," said Elizabeth, with a hostile little laugh. "We never even knew of her existence until a month or so ago."

Blenhurst looked mildly surprised. "And yet, you say, you are cousins? How can this be?"

"We are—" began Celia, but Elizabeth cut her off.

"The connection is remote," she said. "We call each other 'cousin' as a formality. May I pour you a little more tea, Your Grace?"

"Thank you," said Blenhurst absently. His eyes still rested on Celia, who had relapsed into silence. "You have never been to London, then, Miss Delacourt?"

"No, Your Grace," said Celia woodenly. She was keenly aware of the angry glitter in Elizabeth's eyes, and knew it was His Grace's polite interest in her that had earned her that crushing snub. She would not make the mistake of attempting to converse with him. Expressionless, she sipped her tea and stared at the carpet, waiting for Elizabeth to take the lead. She did not have long to wait. Elizabeth seized the reins at once.

"How are your sisters, Your Grace?" asked Elizabeth gaily. "I vow, it is an age since I last saw them!"

Blenhurst turned back to Lady Elizabeth, and she artfully led him into talking of people whom Celia had never met. It was unfortunate, thought Celia, that it took misplaced jealousy to spark Elizabeth into showing a little animation. Now that she had been roused, however, she was able to maintain it, and the conversation flowed much more naturally—without Celia's participation. She sat, mouselike, and meekly nibbled a biscuit.

The duke was far too well-bred, however, to exclude Celia from the conversation indefinitely. Munsil and one of his underlings brought more tea, and while Elizabeth was occupied in directing the servants His Grace turned back to Celia, saying quietly, "I hope you will not think me impertinent if I offer the condolences of a fellow sufferer, Miss Delacourt. Is your loss of recent date?"

The understanding in his eyes, and the fact that he was also wearing mourning, eased the tension that always gripped her at such questions and enabled her to answer him with a fair degree of composure. "September, Your Grace." She felt that something more than this bald answer was required and managed to add, "I lost my family. But the duchess very kindly took me in." This last was added hastily, in case he thought her pitiable. He looked shocked anyway, of course, and bowed his head in an expression of concern.

"I am sorry."

"Thank you. Was your loss . . . recent, Your Grace?"

Pain crossed his features. "Not as recent as yours. I lost my wife last spring. And my newborn daughter with her."

She felt a strong pang of sympathy. They were kindred spirits, she and this melancholy duke. For he was melancholy, she saw. There was bone-deep loneliness in every line of his face.

"I'm so sorry," she whispered, and, forgetting the differences in their rank and gender, she gently laid her hand on his sleeve.

Chapter 11

A footman intercepted Jack on his way down to tea with a message from his mother. He stopped by her rooms on his way to the stairs and, with only a quick knock to precede him, entered.

"You wished to speak with me, ma'am? I warn you, I'm headed for tea and devilish hungry." He accompanied this disrespectful greeting with a grin that robbed his words of offense.

The duchess looked up from the neat stack of household bills on the desk before her, a faint smile lightening her features. "I shan't keep you long, John."

"Did you wish to inspect my costume?" He spread his arms wide. "Perfectly dull and respectable, you see."

But even the smallest touch of humor was lost on Her Grace. "I had no doubt you would accede to my wishes, once I had made them known to you," she replied calmly. "No, I merely wished to confirm whether you spent the morning with Celia. Did you?"

He stiffened, frowning a little. "Yes. Why?"

"So I was told, but I am glad to hear it directly from you. She sent word that she could not meet me this morning, as is our habit. If she spent the time with you, I shall not reproach her. I trust you had a pleasant time. Thank you."

She returned her attention to the bills. It was clear he had been dismissed, but Jack did not go. His frown deepened. "Reproach her? Is she under some obligation to spend her mornings with you? I hope you do not keep her dancing attendance on you, ma'am. She is no servant."

His mother looked up at him again, her finely arched brows lifted in frosty surprise. "Certainly not. Quite the contrary. Celia spends her mornings with me in preparation for the role she has been asked to play. You must be aware, John, that her upbringing has not equipped her in any way to be a duchess. If she shall be one, one day, it is by no means too early to teach her how to go on. She has a great deal to learn." She tapped the edge of a paper with her pencil, returning his frown with one of her own. "You seem surprised. Did I not tell you of this last night?"

Jack was more than surprised. He was dismayed. And what was truly surprising to him was the depth of his dismay. His mind replayed that brief scene in the forest—the moment when he had tried to speak openly to Celia about his mother's scheme to marry them, when the words had died on his lips because he was so sure she did not know. Had Celia misled him? Was she really hand-in-glove with his mother? And if she was, why did that upset him?

For it did upset him, and that was the most surprising thing of all. He had met her only twenty-four hours ago. It was absurd to think he knew her well, and yet he felt he did. And somehow it mattered, mattered very much indeed, if he now discovered he had been mistaken in her character.

His eyes narrowed. "You told me that you meant to undertake her education. I did not realize that you had already begun. Let me be sure I understand you, Mother. Is Celia aware that you are preparing her to be the next Duchess of Arnsford? Have you, in fact, told her that you hope to install her here as your daughter-in-law?"

The duchess's eyebrows climbed higher. "I saw no

point in hiding it from her," she said impatiently.
"Certainly I told her. Had I not, she would have
thought my interest in her inexplicable."

So Celia knew. Jack felt himself turning pale. "And
has she been a *good* student? Has she been eager
to learn? Biddable?" He raked one hand distractedly
through his hair. "But you need not answer. Celia's a
clever girl. I'm sure she has learned quickly and well."

The picture of Celia sitting attentively at his mother's knee, soaking up her instruction, striving to be
exactly like her and secretly plotting how best to at-
tract him, was sickening. The fact that she had succeeded in attracting him was more sickening yet.

"Forgive me," he said abruptly. "I believe I am expected in the tea room." He bowed quickly to his
mother, who was regarding him in speechless astonishment, and quit the room.

He found he had to linger in the passage, taking
deep breaths to steady himself, before entering the tea
room. He was angry, and not entirely sure why. It was
disconcerting to feel that one had been preyed upon,
but after all, wasn't that what he had expected? What
was the matter with him? This was the way of the
world. Penniless girls like Celia set traps for wealthy
men every day. They had to, to keep the wolf from
the door. He shouldn't blame her. If he was angry
with anyone, it ought to be his mother, not Celia.

Hell's bells! He was angry at both of them. And if
anything, he was more angry at Celia than the duchess. After all, one expected such cloak-and-dagger
rubbish from Her Grace. But Celia—! He couldn't
explain why he felt betrayed. What did it matter *why*
he felt what he felt? He was too angry to care.

He stopped arguing with himself and pushed open
the door. Tea, he thought sarcastically, was *exactly*
what he needed.

The room was filled with the last light of a brilliantly

sunny day, and he was briefly dazzled after the dimness of the passage. He nearly collided with Munsil and a lackey pushing an empty tea cart on their way out. He stepped aside, his eyes gradually taking in the scene.

Tea had been set for a larger number of persons than had, as yet, arrived. Elizabeth sat stiffly over the tea service, its enormity and gleaming silveriness separating her from the room's other two occupants, who sat side by side at the opposite end of the tea table.

Elizabeth's solitary state gave her an air, simultaneously, of power and helplessness. She was in control, but only of the teapot. Her eyes blazed with fury and suffering. All of her attention was focused, miserably, on Celia and the Duke of Blenhurst.

Celia and Blenhurst seemed utterly oblivious.

Jack was conscious of a strong desire to land Blenhurst a facer. The rogue was gazing intently into Celia's upturned face. And—God save the mark!—Celia had her hand on the fellow's arm! What the deuce—?

A killing rage swept through Jack, immediately followed by a black and bitter mood. Ha! cried an ugly little voice in the back of his mind. So that's the way of it, is it? And why not? An unattached duke is an even bigger prize than an unattached marquess.

Then his eyes met Elizabeth's, and his fury swung back to target Blenhurst. The cur was not only stealing Celia, he was making Jack's sister unhappy. Hanging was too good for the villain. He felt his hands clenching into purposeful fists.

All this occurred in the space of a few heartbeats. Then Blenhurst noticed Jack's entrance and rose, a smile of pleasure lighting his face. Jack glared at him for a moment, then nodded brusquely. "Blenhurst," he said shortly, as the duke bowed.

He was not well pleased when the duke approached him, but it was impossible not to shake the fellow's hand. "Lynden, how have you been?" inquired the duke heartily. Some of Jack's belligerence must have registered at this point, for he fell back a pace and his smile became strained. "It's been a long time. Too long, I suppose."

Not long enough, thought Jack. "It has been a while," he said stiffly.

The duke flushed. "Yes. Indeed. I hope to make amends for my—neglect."

Jack's gaze sharpened. Why, the rascal thought he was angry because he had never offered for Elizabeth! When he looked at Jack he saw a protective brother shielding a brokenhearted sister. The absurdity of this tickled Jack's reprehensible sense of humor. An unholy grin tugged at his reluctant features. Elizabeth had no heart to break, but Blenhurst couldn't know that. Probably fancied that Elizabeth had been weeping into her pillow every night for years, mourning his defection. Well, let him think it.

He clapped a hand on Blenhurst's shoulder, his good humor partially restored. "Excellent," said Jack grimly. "Where's the tea?"

Only then did he allow his eyes to stray to Celia. She looked perfectly placid, not guilty or self-conscious at all. He could not decide whether that observation ought to make him feel even more cynical or whether it ought to relieve his mind. He sat rather crossly beside her.

Elizabeth handed him a porcelain plate approximately the size of his palm. A microscopic sandwich, its contents indistinguishable, was centered upon the plate's delicate surface. He consumed this item without comment while Elizabeth poured him a dish of black tea, and passed his plate back for more when she handed him his cup. She looked very severely at him, but declined to scold him for his gluttony. He credited Blenhurst's presence for that.

The foursome embarked upon an excruciating round of small talk. Jack did not contribute unless directly addressed. He ate his way steadily through half the sandwiches and about a quarter of the biscuits, watching Celia with a jealous eye. This ruffled her composure not one whit. She seemed completely unaware of his scrutiny, which made him feel more peevish by the minute.

Neither of his parents took tea in the afternoon, but eventually his other three sisters joined them. Their presence, however enlivening, made it even less likely that Jack would discover an answer to the questions now burning in his brain. He excused himself and spent the next several hours hanging about moodily in the library, hoping that Celia would wander in. She did not, and by the time Jack went to dress for dinner he was feeling sulky as a bear.

Will had laid out his dinner clothes. Jack stood over them for a moment, silently marveling at Will's laborious attention to detail, his painstaking care, and his utter lack of taste. The ensemble so prettily laid before him was hideous. That particular shade of puce, when paired with maroon, was, in a word, repulsive. Nevertheless, Jack did not suggest a single change. Without a murmur, he donned everything Will had chosen. He no longer cared much about scaring off his would-be bride—he was just feeling ornery. When he saw the result in the mirror, he was inspired to send Will down to fetch a sprig of holly—with berries—from the greenery he and Celia had gathered. This he fastened to his lapel. As he had hoped, the crimson berries added immensely to the garish effect. He went down to dinner a vision of ugliness.

When he appeared in the drawing room, his mother's upper lip lengthened in disapproval. "Your clothing is ill-chosen, John," she said icily.

Jack feigned surprise. "Is it? No, no, ma'am, I feel

sure you are mistaken. I've always been a well-dressed chap. But a man can't wear the same thing year after year. Must keep up with the fashions, you know, if I choose to live in Town."

"I speak not of the cut, but of the colors."

He twisted comically, trying to squint down his own body. "Blenhurst, do you see anything untoward?"

Blenhurst smiled blandly. "It is a long time since I lived in London," he said diplomatically.

"Elizabeth, I appeal to you."

But Elizabeth looked even more vexed than his mother did. "No, John, you do not—and neither does your outfit," she said tartly.

It was so rare that Elizabeth made any sort of joke, wittingly or unwittingly, that the company was startled into laughter. Elizabeth flushed, first with wrath and then with pleasure, as she belatedly realized that she had said something witty.

"Touché!" said Jack admiringly. "My dependence is upon cousin Celia, then. Celia, what say you? Am I a figure of fun or of fashion?"

He had been hoping to make her laugh, but she was giving him that odd, pitying look again. Much to Jack's regret, Munsil stepped into the room and announced dinner at that moment, sparing her the necessity of replying.

He could not help noticing that Celia herself was very prettily gowned. She was wearing a white silk dinner dress trimmed with jet—not as pleasing as colors would have been, but a great improvement over unrelieved black.

As he placed her hand upon his arm to lead her down to dinner, she smiled at him. He immediately felt the last vestiges of his sulkiness melt away. He had never been one to stay in the sullens for long, and somehow Celia's presence made it difficult to remember what his grievance had been. He only wished he knew whether she was wearing half-mourning in deference to the Christmas season or in honor of Blenhurst's visit. It was impossible to tell.

During dinner, Blenhurst inquired whether he would have the pleasure of seeing their mutual friend, Mr. Conrad, at the festivities this year. Her Grace took that opportunity to inform him, with majestic unconcern, that they were having nothing more than a quiet family gathering. Poor Blenhurst's expression of dismay was apparent to the entire party. He swiftly recovered, but Jack felt sorry for both Blenhurst and Elizabeth. What a cowhanded thing for Mother to do! It wasn't like her to be so clumsy. Inviting Blenhurst as the sole guest to a family party was clearly intended to force his hand. The unfortunate chap looked completely thunderstruck. Elizabeth's cheeks were burning, and she was stirring the food about on her plate as if she had completely lost her appetite.

It occurred to Jack, thoughtfully chewing, that if he were Blenhurst, he would immediately start making up to Celia in an attempt to thwart his hostess. He instantly determined to keep a sharp lookout and head the fellow off if he started in Celia's direction. Purely for Celia's sake, of course. It was his cousinly duty to ensure that her head wasn't turned by the attentions of a chap who was only using her to shield himself from Her Grace's machinations.

This noble resolve cheered him up a bit, as it gave him an excellent excuse to attach himself firmly to Celia's side when the gentlemen joined the ladies after dinner. He found the prospect oddly agreeable. Besides, it was important that he spend as much time as possible in Celia's company—in order to determine what game she was playing. If any.

But despite Her Grace's bald maneuvers, which should have frightened the fellow off, Blenhurst surprised Jack by fixing his attention on Elizabeth from

the moment the gentlemen entered the room. Of
course, he supposed, it was a bit difficult to do anything else. Elizabeth was playing the pianoforte. Her
playing lacked fire, but her skill was superior. Her
dazzling mastery of the keyboard always commanded
the respectful attention of anyone within hearing.

Augusta was turning the pages for her sister. When
Elizabeth finished the piece, everyone murmured applause, and Her Grace called Augusta away. Jack immediately turned his attention to Celia. Blenhurst
walked to the pianoforte.

Elizabeth busied herself in gathering up the pages of
her music. They seemed to have become unaccountably unwieldy.

"It is always a pleasure to hear you play," said Blenhurst quietly.

Two sheets of music suddenly slipped from Elizabeth's grasp. Blenhurst deftly caught them. "Thank
you, Your Grace," Elizabeth managed to say. She
gave a strained little laugh. "So clumsy! I don't know
what is wrong with my fingers tonight."

She made as if to get up from the piano bench, but
Blenhurst moved to stop her. "I hope you do not
mean to run away? It would give me—I'm sure it
would give everyone—great pleasure to hear you play
again." When she hesitated, he offered her a tentative
smile. "I would be happy to turn the pages for you,
if Lady Augusta is otherwise engaged."

Elizabeth bowed and seated herself stiffly on the
bench again. "You are very good," she said unhappily
and began to dig through her music, averting her eyes
from the duke. He stood over her, gravely watching
her as she attempted unsuccessfully to mask her distress. She pulled a piece from the pile, seemingly at
random, and placed it on the music stand. Blenhurst
helpfully reached over and held the corner. She began
to play.

The music rippled forth, complicated and tuneless. Blenhurst followed the closely packed notes on the paper with some difficulty, but turned the pages promptly enough that Elizabeth was able to continue playing without any break. Her fingers stumbled nervously from time to time, however, causing her to bite her lip with vexation. She seemed relieved to reach the end of the piece. Blenhurst joined in the applause, but Elizabeth, clearly eager to depart, pulled the music from his hands and hastily rearranged the pages, rising from the bench and preparing to join the others. Under cover of the hum of conversation that had broken out, Blenhurst leaned toward her and spoke in a low tone.

"Lady Elizabeth, I hope you will be frank with me. Is it my presence that is distressing you? Would you— would you rather I removed myself? I need not stay past tomorrow, if you desire me to go."

Elizabeth gave a tiny gasp. "No," she said, in a strangled voice. Her face was, by this time, almost scarlet. Her eyes met his fleetingly, but then lowered again as she bent over her task, aimlessly stacking and restacking the music. "I am merely—I am—I am *mortified* that you have been—" She broke off then, struggling for composure, and gave another unconvincing little laugh. "Your Grace, I feel we owe you an apology. We have invited you to a party that is no party at all. I beg you to believe that I had nothing to do with it."

"I see."

"You must wish you were anywhere but here." She gave him an unhappy little smile. "I do not blame you in the least."

Blenhurst smiled too, with an effort. "You are mistaken. Your apology is quite unnecessary, in fact. I don't know why it is, but everyone seems to believe that a newly widowed man wishes to be left alone.

Actually, the opposite is true. Especially, I find, at Christmas. I am glad to be anywhere but home."

Elizabeth looked up uncertainly. Her disbelief was palpable. Blenhurst gave a wry chuckle. "I am speaking quite seriously, I assure you. I was dreading Christmas. Your mother's invitation was most welcome."

"You are all courtesy, Your Grace," said Elizabeth tonelessly.

"Nonsense."

But at least the high color had drained from her cheeks. She looked unhappy, but no longer embarrassed. Her gaze grew thoughtful as she searched his eyes and saw only sober truth there.

"You must think I accepted the invitation with unbecoming alacrity," he said, trying to speak lightly.

Elizabeth shrugged, trying to match his unconcern, but it was clear that he had somehow injured her feelings. "Not at all. I suppose it was the only one you received."

It was, of course. He was going to disclaim, but realized that his previous words had already made that clear to her. It was Blenhurst's turn to feel his cheeks reddening.

Chapter 12

"Look at poor old Blenhurst," whispered Jack, leaning toward Celia. "Care to lay any bets regarding his future?"

Celia gave him a look of reproach. "I do not," she said severely, moving slightly farther away on the sofa.

"I daresay you're not the gambling sort." He could not resist winking at her, she looked so prim and disapproving. This brought a little color into her cheeks, but she bit her lip and looked pointedly away, returning her attention to Elizabeth's performance.

Jack grinned. He had made a beeline for Celia the instant the gentlemen had walked into the room and, upon reflection, was much inclined to believe that his maneuver, rather than Blenhurst's inclination, had forced Blenhurst into Elizabeth's orbit. This had completely restored Jack's good humor.

He stretched his long limbs, resting one arm carelessly on the back of the sofa. Celia immediately straightened her posture, placing several inches between her person and the sofa back. She actually looked a little alarmed. Jack leaned over to her again. "What's amiss?" he whispered.

The combination of his arm behind her and his body leaned in brought the two of them extremely close. He caught a whiff of some elusive perfume, warm and strangely stirring. He could see her individual eyelashes as they swept down against the soft curves of

her face, just above her cheekbone. The sight was be-
witching. Then she turned her face to his, and the
lashes swept up, and he was staring into her eyes.
Mesmerizing. He began to feel drugged and reckless.

"Jack, for heaven's sake, take care. You must not
sit so close to me."

"Why not?"

She looked exasperated. How sweet. "Because if
you do, I shall remove myself to that chair over
there." She pointed determinedly at an empty chair.

He could not tear his eyes from her face. He supposed he had a very silly grin on his face, but he
couldn't help it. "Why?"

She moved to go. He pulled back at once, placing
his hand penitently on her arm. "Don't go! I shall
behave myself."

She stayed, but looked both ruffled and wary. There
was something else in her expression, too, something
he couldn't quite put his finger on. Her next question
was very strange indeed.

"Do you always feel worse in the evenings?"

"Worse?" Jack cocked his head, as if he might not
have heard her correctly. "Worse than what? Do I
seem to be in pain?"

Her eyes searched his face, then dropped. "I beg
your pardon. I don't mean to pry."

His brows flew up in genuine astonishment. "Now,
look here—"

"No, no, pray—! I should not have asked." She
looked embarrassed. "Let us talk of something else.
How—how well your sisters play! And Elizabeth better than the rest, I think. It is a pleasure to hear her."

"Yes, it is. But there is something I would rather
hear."

Her expressive eyes widened apprehensively. "Is
there?"

"You know there is. Come now, cousin, confess!

Someone has told you that I suffer from a weak constitution, or a chronic complaint of some sort. I would very much like to know who has slandered me in this ridiculous fashion and what you have been told."

She was so pretty when she blushed. Her eyes darted round the room, and she seemed to draw strength from confirming that they were surrounded by others. She heaved a small sigh and then faced him squarely. "Very well. Since I have spoken out of turn, I suppose I owe you an explanation."

He waited, one eyebrow quizzically lifted, and watched as she struggled to find words. Soon she leaned earnestly forward, pressing her palms together. "Jack," she said, sounding a little breathless, "do you not know that you are—eccentric?"

"Eccentric? Yes, I suppose I am. It's fashionable to be a little eccentric, you know."

She shook her head determinedly. "No, dear cousin, you are more than a little eccentric." She indicated his clothing with a wave of her hand. "I do hate to say this, but your mother is right. This is not a proper costume to wear."

"Oh. That. I can explain—"

"No, pray let me finish. It is not just your clothing, Jack. Your behavior is sometimes rather—odd. And, you know, most gentlemen do not have a keeper."

Jack stared. "A *keeper*?"

Celia nodded pityingly. "Do you not wonder why your family engaged Hadley to look after you?"

"What the deuce—? *I* engaged Hadley," spluttered Jack.

"And you engaged him as . . . what?" asked Celia gently.

"He is my *valet*!"

"I'm very glad you chose him from among the applicants, for you apparently chose well," said Celia soothingly. "But you told me yourself that he *rules you with an iron fist.* He is something more than a valet, Jack. Think! Is not your way of life a little— different—from other gentlemen of your station?"

"Good God!" Jack was so flummoxed he could scarcely believe what he was hearing. "Do you mean—no, it is impossible! You can't believe that I am *mad*?"

But her sweet expression, so fearful and yet so compassionate, spoke volumes.

Suddenly it all fell into place. He remembered the practical joke he had meant to play and realized that he had played it with stunning ineptitude. His inability to keep to the role he had chosen had doubtless made his behavior appear erratic—at best! He had dressed like a buffoon, and then a sensible man, and then a buffoon again—he had behaved like a leering idiot, and then a garden-variety idiot, and then a rudesby, and then a decent chap, and topped it all off by falling into a fit of jealous sulks—deuce take it! His own behavior had turned the tables, and the joke was on him.

Jack burst into laughter. He laughed so long and so hard that the entire room turned to stare, but he could not stop. It was just too killingly funny. He roared. Tears rolled down his cheeks. He dropped his head into his hands and shook with helpless guffaws. And it only made matters worse when Celia jumped up from the sofa, wringing her hands and crying, "Oh, what have I done?"

He could hear his mother irascibly inquiring what was wrong with him and commanding him to stop this foolishness, stop it at once, but that only made him laugh harder. He could hear Blenhurst, with mild jocularity, asking that he let the rest of the company in on the joke, but he could not stop laughing long enough to speak. He could hear Celia vehemently requesting that everyone talk of something else and then begging his family to help him, help him recover—as if he had fallen into some terrible fit. Which, he supposed, he had. But it was well worth it. This was surely a joke that would make him laugh whenever he recalled it, for as long as he lived. He could hardly wait to tell it at Boodle's.

Jack had to leave the room to regain control. As he staggered into the cold passage he heard Celia nervously ask the assembly, "Is it wise, do you think, to let him go off all alone in such a state?" which sent him back into whoops. He leaned against the wall and howled.

Finally his laughter subsided into hiccups. He pulled out his handkerchief and wiped his streaming eyes, still chuckling. "By heaven, that's rich!" he gasped, shaking his head. "Serves me right. Best joke I've heard in years."

He straightened up, tucked his handkerchief back in his pocket, and walked to where a candle flickered on a small table in the hall. A mirror hung above it, and he straightened his cravat, still grinning.

When he reentered the drawing room, however, he appeared sober as a judge. Celia looked anxiously up at him and he gave her a mournful little bow. His father was entertaining the company with some farfetched theory about the root causes of the corn riots, and everyone was pretending to listen, so there was no need for Jack to say anything. He made his way back to the sofa and sat gravely beside Celia, trying to look ashamed. She actually reached over and patted his hand consolingly. This almost made him laugh again, but he managed to keep his countenance. When the conversation became general once more she turned to him at once and apologized, her forehead puckered with concern.

He waved her apology aside and heaved a despondent sigh. "It is hardly your fault, cousin," he assured her, shaking his head. "I owe *you* the apology, I be-

lieve. It must be frightening to see me go off like that.
My family has grown accustomed to it over the years,
but I suppose it is terrible to witness it for the first
time."

"Do you—do you frequently fall into laughing fits?"

His lips twitched. "Yes, I do. Fairly frequently."

Celia looked appalled. "I must tell you frankly,
cousin, that I fault your family to some degree," she
said in a low tone. "It appears to me that they offer
you little sympathy and less help. And I cannot but
notice that you are worse whenever you are around
them."

"They're not an empathetic lot," admitted Jack.
"But mine is an unusually sober and upright family. I
daresay having a lunatic in their midst is a severe cross
to bear."

"Oh, pooh!" said Celia indignantly. "I have not
known you long, but even with your—your uneven
temperament, I had rather spend time with you than
any of the rest."

What a darling she is, thought Jack. "Thank you,"
he said, touched. "The feeling is mutual." She was so
sweet about it, he could not, in good conscience, pro-
long the joke. "But I'm afraid I have a confession to
make, cousin. There really *is* no excuse for my outrageous behavior, because I am not, in fact, mad."

"Certainly not," said Celia brightly. Her smile was
tinged with pity. "You are subject, perhaps, to odd
humors. But I daresay you might feel quite well, or
at least feel well more of the time, with proper care."

Jack choked. "No, you misunderstand me. I mean
that I owe you an apology, because I am not mad
at all."

Celia bit her lip. He saw the anxiety in her eyes
before she looked away, struggling to find something
safe to say. "Well, I shan't tease you about it," she
said at last.

Good God. She didn't believe him. Jack rubbed his chin and stared, flummoxed, at his kind little cousin. If he protested too loudly that he was sane, she would try all the harder to soothe him. What the devil should he do?

The duchess then claimed their attention, requesting that "the children" entertain Blenhurst with a rubber of whist. Jack readily acquiesced, although he would fain have stayed at Celia's side—at least until he convinced her that he was of sound mind. Unfortunately, Celia did not know how to play and had to be excused from participating. It was Jack, Augusta, and Elizabeth who joined Blenhurst in the game.

Jack soon incurred Augusta's wrath by failing to concentrate on his play. His eyes too frequently strayed to where Celia sat, the lamplight causing her rich brown hair to glow with golden highlights, her soft cheek leaned against her palm, and her eyes, wide and dreamy, fixed on . . . Hubbard.

Hubbard?

He actually slewed round in his chair at one point to confirm what he was seeing. It was definitely Hubbard, standing stolidly behind his mother's chair, who was holding Celia rapt and apparently spellbound.

The instant the game broke up and he could gracefully do so, Jack returned to Celia's side and offered her a penny for her thoughts. Celia looked up at him in surprise.

"Quickly, cousin," he admonished her. "They shall call me back to the whist table at any moment, and I will expire of curiosity."

Celia laughed, but looked puzzled. "Why, I don't know that I was thinking anything at all. Certainly nothing worth sharing."

He glanced over at homely Gertrude Hubbard, who was at the other end of the room, engaged in moving the screen to shield the duchess from some of the fire's heat. He could see nothing unusual, and certainly nothing attractive, about her appearance; nothing that might engage Celia's interest. Still, he pasted an admiring look upon his face and exclaimed soulfully, if sotto voce, "What a lovely woman she is, to be sure!"

Celia looked startled. "Who is?"

"Hubbard, of course. I don't blame you for staring; I can scarcely take my eyes off her myself."

Celia's expression became worried and pitying. Blast his wretched tendency to turn everything into a joke! Poor Hubbard's plainness was so extreme, Celia obviously thought his professed admiration was due to madness. "Hubbard is not a beautiful woman," she said carefully. "I would say, rather, that her appearance is uncommon."

"Why, you must be funning. I just watched you stare at her for ten minutes with hardly a blink. Transfixed."

Celia blushed. "Oh! Oh, dear. I was only thinking of sketching her."

"Aha! I see. Well, that's reassuring. I was beginning to worry about *you.*" Jack dropped onto the sofa beside her. "I remember now. You did tell me you had a talent for sketching."

"Did I?" Celia wrinkled her nose. "Gracious, what a silly thing to say. Talent, indeed! It's nothing of the kind, of course."

"Of course," agreed Jack. "Before you abase yourself completely, let me assure you that there is no need. You have already told me that sketching is your *only* talent, so if I fall into the error of admiring you, it will be quite my own fault."

"Well, that's a mercy, at any rate." Celia was still pink and could not seem to meet his eyes. "I'm very fond of sketching, but that does not mean that the sketches themselves are good."

"Have you a sketchbook? I'd very much like to see it."

Celia shook her head with a little gasp. "Oh, no! No—oh, it was wrong of me to even mention it! You will think me such a baby—" She tried to laugh, but her bashfulness was obviously genuine. "So absurd! I am extremely vexed with myself."

"Yes, you ought to have kept it to yourself. What a pity. Now that the cat is out of the bag, I will think myself very hardly used if you refuse to show me your sketchbook."

"Well, I haven't one," said Celia, with spirit. "So there is no use in teasing me to show it to you."

"How can you sketch without a sketchbook?" Jack's eyes narrowed in speculation. "Easily, I suppose. Cousin Celia," he said severely, "I think you are splitting hairs."

She lifted her chin at him. "And what if I am? If I do not wish to show anyone my sketches, that's my prerogative."

"Are you afraid?" asked Jack provocatively.

"Certainly not!"

"I believe you are. What are you afraid of?"

"Nothing! This is ridiculous." She looked down her small nose at him. "I have indicated that I do not wish to show anyone my sketches. It's not at all the thing for you to badger me about it."

"Very well. If you don't mind appearing cowardly—"

"Cowardly! How dare you?"

"—it's really none of my affair."

Celia's eyes flashed. Jack waited, trying to look injured. She tapped her foot as she hesitated, considering.

"I would be happy to send a servant to your chamber," suggested Jack helpfully. He assumed the aspect of a pleading child. "Pleeease?" he wheedled.

That made her laugh. "No," she said at last. "No, really, Jack. I—I just can't." She dropped her eyes shyly and tried to explain. "I know it must sound disobliging, and probably very silly, but my sketches are just—*personal.* They wouldn't mean anything to anyone but me."

This admission naturally made Jack even more curious to see them, but he bowed his head in a graceful acknowledgment of defeat. "In that case, I beg your pardon for teasing you. I shall say no more."

She lifted eyes brimming with gratitude just in time to catch his mischievous grin. He winked, and completed his sentence: "For now."

Chapter 13

Manegold lay in a puddle of sunlight on the hall carpet, toasting his belly. He lifted his head and blinked in greeting when he heard Jack's footsteps approaching, but did not budge from the precious patch of sunshine. Jack chuckled, bending to tousle the warm golden fur.

"Good morning, fuzzball," said Jack. "What a lazy chap you are."

Manegold stretched and smiled his secret cat smile.

"If you can tear yourself away from your sunbath, I'll sneak you a bit of my breakfast. Come on," said Jack invitingly.

Manegold looked at him expectantly, but did not move. Jack snapped his fingers and repeated, "Come on, old thing. You know where the breakfast room is. Come on, then." He took a few steps to indicate the direction, still snapping his fingers encouragingly.

Manegold appeared mildly surprised. Instead of following Jack, he rolled limply over and glanced at the door behind him. He then looked at Jack as if to say, "Don't you mean the library?"

Jack, well acquainted with his pet, answered the unspoken question. "No, I don't mean the library, you great furry moonling. *Breakfast*."

But Manegold seemed determined to correct his master's misguided steps. He staggered sleepily to his

feet and faced the library, his amber gaze riveted to
the doorknob as if confident it would turn at any
moment.

"You want to go *in* the library?" guessed Jack.
"What's in the library? More sun, I suppose." He ful-
filled Manegold's silent prophecy by turning the handle for him and swinging the door open. Manegold
strolled through the aperture, tail straight up in the
universal gesture of kitty gladness.

The library at Delacourt was no stuffy little chamber full of dark furniture, musty books, and pipe
smoke. It was a glorious gallery, high-ceilinged as a
cathedral and full of light. Tall windows ran along its
length, each with a deeply cushioned window seat, and
on the opposite side of the room the shelves crammed
with books were broken up by two pretty fireplaces.
Comfortable chairs and sofas were grouped charm-
ingly before each of the fireplaces, and at either end
of the room were large tables for viewing maps and
such. It was an elegant and impressive room, and a
favorite of both Jack and Manegold. Manegold was
not an avid reader, but he approved of any room that
contained two fireplaces. The library added to these
attractions by featuring pools of sunlight so huge that
even a very large cat could fall blissfully asleep, un-
afraid of waking to find that the sunbeams had moved
on and left him shivering in a shadow.

On this particular morning, one spot combined the
charms of a crackling fire *and* a sunlit hearth rug. Jack
expected Manegold to head for this spot as if shot
from an arrow. He did not, however. There was an
even stronger claim to his attention present.

Celia was curled in one of the window seats, her
gaze unfocused, tapping a pencil thoughtfully against
her lower lip. The winter sunshine poured across her,
making a nimbus of her brown curls and outlining the
curves of her face with a ribbon of light. She made a

very pretty picture. Even the black frock she was wearing looked striking against the colors surrounding her. Jack had only a moment for the sight of her to register before she looked up and saw him. Then, with a startled little cry, she scrambled to gather up the papers and pencils scattered all about her. Manegold bounded to her side and hindered her efforts by clambering affectionately up onto her lap.

"Oh, Manegold, no! Not now," said the harassed Celia, struggling to dislodge her persistent admirer.

While she was thus occupied, Jack nipped in and snatched up her papers. He nobly refrained from peeking, but could not help seeing that they were, as he had hoped, sketches. He held one up, looking quizzical.

"No sketchbook. I see. You work on individual sheets of paper."

Celia looked up at him, her rosy face expressing both laughter and exasperation. "Pray call off your cat, Lord Lynden! It is unconscionable for you to employ an innocent beast in—oh, Manegold, *really*!" This, as the cat collapsed his considerable weight atop the papers still resting on her thigh.

"Manegold, down!" said Jack, with mock severity. He pointed a stern finger at the happy animal. "Down, sirrah! Get down at once! Sit!"

But Manegold, in the way of his species, was oblivious. He purred heedlessly on, gazing joyously at Celia. She gave a little spurt of laughter. "He's not a suggestible creature, is he?"

"You've bewitched him," said Jack accusingly. "He's always obeyed me before."

Celia choked. "Clicking his heels and saluting, no doubt."

She hoisted the limp cat off her lap, with difficulty, and set him on the floor. Since he immediately poised to spring back into her lap, she quickly seized the papers she had rescued from beneath Manegold and rose, shaking out her skirts. Then she held out her hand to Jack. "I'll trouble you for the rest of them now, thank you," she said primly.

"Won't you show me your sketches? At least one or two?"

"I had really rather not."

He must have looked truly crestfallen, for she hesitated, her eyes softening. But then she frowned and shook her head. "They are nothing special," she told him firmly, still holding out her hand.

"They must be special to you," he said quietly, "or you would not guard them so fiercely." He handed them to her as he spoke, being careful not to invade her privacy by actually looking at them.

She took them, but the uncertainty was back in her eyes. She regarded him gravely for a moment, considering. "You think I am being rude."

"No."

"Childish."

"No."

"Cowardly?"

"Not exactly." He smiled. "I do think you are afraid, but I believe you have a right to be afraid. It seems clear to me that you have done all these sketches in private, or shown them only to persons you trust, because you have invested a great deal of your private self in them. You are right to guard them, just as anyone would guard his most secret thoughts and feelings."

Surprise dawned in her eyes. She nodded, and looked down at the papers in her hands. "I did not expect you to understand," she said, so softly he had to strain to catch the words. "I don't generally let people know that I sketch at all, because—well, because when people discover that I sketch, they make a great fuss about it and clamor to see something.

People seem to think it is polite to express interest, as if I were doing it in a bid for attention. But I don't wish to be admired for my sketching. I am not seeking praise or—or approval from strangers. That is not why I do it. I do it because . . ."

Jack found that he was holding his breath, trying to hear her. He was glad when she looked up and he could let his breath go. When she saw how completely he was concentrating on her words, her eyes lit with amusement and she smiled. "The truth is, I don't really know why I sketch."

Jack nodded wisely. "Spoken like a true artist."

Celia laughed, wrinkling her nose. "But I am no such thing!"

"I'll be the judge of that," said Jack firmly, holding out his hand. He was not really expecting her to hand him any of her papers, although he hoped she might. He was surprised, and a little touched, when she responded by placing her hand in his.

"Very well," said Celia shyly. "I will show them to you, if you are really interested."

It was the first time their hands had touched, ungloved. Jack was wholly unprepared for his own reaction. Such a simple, tiny thing—the unexpected touch of her hand to his. Why did it move him so? It was as if an invisible current sprang from her palm. He could feel it flash through his entire body. For a moment the shock of it held him rooted to the spot. But Celia, unnoticing, picked up a flat wooden box from the corner of the window seat and then, tugging gently on his hand, led him to one of the sofas where the light would fall from behind them.

This well-lit sofa happened to be the one with the well-lit hearth rug before it, so Manegold was already there. When Jack and Celia sat side by side on the sofa, the cat seemed torn: should he stay by the fire or join his friends? Celia's opening the box seemed to make his decision easier. He immediately rose and advanced.

"Manegold is fond of pencils," explained Celia, hurriedly pulling out a sheaf of papers and shutting the box again. Manegold sat on his haunches and gave her a look filled with reproach. He then returned to his spot on the hearth rug and lay down, heaving an audible sigh.

Jack was amused. "How many of your pencils has he destroyed by now?"

"Only one or two," Celia assured him. Then she dimpled. "The rest, he simply lost." She set the box on the floor and cast an apprehensive look at Jack, holding the papers protectively against her chest. "I have warned you not to expect too much," she reminded him.

"Yes, indeed you have," he assured her solemnly.

"I have no real training, you know. And I have made these drawings purely for my own amusement. They were not meant for any eyes other than my own."

He could not suppress a grin. "Celia, I promise you, you have lowered my expectations sufficiently. I will now be astonished if your sketches resemble any identifiable object. In fact, I am shaking in my shoes, afraid that I will wound you by failing to recognize the subject of your work."

She blushed. "I am being silly, aren't I? I beg your pardon." Although the color still bloomed in her cheeks, a mischievous smile played with the corners of her mouth. "But you needn't be afraid of injuring my feelings. After all, I shall be here to explain the sketches to you one by one, so even if you are completely bewildered by them you can easily pretend that you are not."

"Yes, that's a relief," remarked Jack. "What is this one, for instance?"

He reached past her to the box and lifted out the piece he knew she had been working on when he came into the room. Contrary to his professed expectation, he had no difficulty in recognizing its subject. He was none too pleased when he saw who it was, however: Blenhurst.

"Oh! That is not finished," said Celia hastily.

Jack wished he knew whether her embarrassment stemmed from the unfinished nature of the sketch or from his having discovered who was on her mind this morning. Since she had left it in the box, he now realized she had not meant to show this one to him.

Odd that one never thinks of oneself as the jealous type, Jack reflected. It comes as an unwelcome surprise to find that one is, after all, capable of jealousy. A most unpleasant emotion, he discovered. Uncomfortable to experience.

After a brief struggle with himself, Jack managed to say, "It's very good."

It was, actually. There was only the outline of Blenhurst's head and a suggestion of the thinning hair—she was clearly drawing from memory and had left the details out. Either that, or she was deliberately flattering the duke by not dwelling on his receding hairline. Jack felt another stab of jealousy rearing its ugly head at the thought, and again fought to hammer it down.

What she had dwelled on was the face, and especially the eyes. The mouth wasn't quite right, nor the shape of the chin, but the eyes were Blenhurst to the life. The expression did not strike Jack as typical of him, however. He pointed to the eyes. "You've made him look sad."

As soon as the words left his mouth, he wished he could recall them. His stupid jealousy had made him criticize the portrait, criticizing *her,* the last thing in the world he meant to do. He immediately turned to her, an apology rushing to his lips, but the words died when he saw how pleased she looked.

"Yes, that is what I was trying to capture," said Celia softly. "It's only in his eyes, the loneliness— here, and here." She touched the paper, pointing to what she had done. "And perhaps a little in the muscles of the face. A certain strain when he smiles. But I haven't had time to draw that properly."

Jack was amazed. He looked back at the half-finished portrait, studying it anew. By George, she was right. That was how Blenhurst had looked yesterday. She had seen and comprehended something Jack had not seen at all, something Blenhurst himself had probably been at great pains to hide. Of course, Celia had only met him yesterday. She had no prior image of the man to superimpose upon what she actually saw and blind her to his sorrow. Still, she had seen the man clearly, in a way that those acquainted with him had not.

He looked at Celia with new respect. This slip of a girl had the ability to look in a stranger's eyes and see directly into his heart. "You have a remarkable gift," said Jack, admiration in his voice.

Color immediately flooded Celia's face. He saw that she was about to stammer out some disclaimer, and forestalled her by firmly placing his hand over hers. "I'm not flattering you, and I'm not speaking of your sketches, so there's no need to color up. I've only seen one so far, and half finished at that. I don't really know if you are a gifted artist, although I suspect you are. I am talking of something else."

Her eyes were huge with doubt. "I don't know what you mean," she said uncertainly.

Jack's eyes twinkled, but his face remained grave. "I think you would stand out in any set of persons, but among our family you are more than remarkable, you are unique. The milk of human kindness does *not* flow through our veins. I never met a Delacourt with a particle of empathy. Yet you seem to have that quality in abundance."

"What nonsense!" said Celia with spirit. "So have you."

Clearly meaning to change the subject, she took the study of Blenhurst from his hand and replaced it in the box. As she did so, she pulled out another piece of paper. "Pray do not tell me that this fellow looks sad, for I drew it while he was purring."

This time, Jack was delighted. "Manegold!" he exclaimed.

"Yes." Celia pulled a comical face, wrinkling her nose. "I shall be careful to give you a hint, you know, as I hand you each sketch. So if I say I drew it while the subject was *purring,* you won't make the mistake of thinking it's a bowl of flowers or a church spire."

"Thank you," said Jack appreciatively. "But I'd have known this chappie anywhere."

The chappie in question, having heard his name called out, good-naturedly rose and ambled over, with the air of one who confers a great favor out of pure affection. He jumped heavily onto Jack's knee. Jack scratched his ears with one hand and nudged Celia with the opposite elbow. "You see?" he pointed out. "Obeys my every command. Even when I don't intend to give one."

"Especially when you don't intend to give one," agreed Celia. "I am somewhat acquainted with this animal, remember."

Jack shrugged, grinning. "He's a cat," he said, as if that explained everything. Which, of course, it did.

Manegold, evidently expressing his opinion of those who interrupted his nap and then gave him something less than their full attention, gently sank his teeth into the corner of the paper Jack held. The technique worked well; it instantly reclaimed the full attention of both Jack and Celia. Jack gave a startled exclamation and pushed his pet unceremoniously off his knee.

"Manegold, you ingrate," scolded Jack. "I'm sorry, Celia."

But Celia was laughing out loud. "Oh, dear!" she gasped. "It's true what they say—no one likes his own portrait."

Jack grinned ruefully and smoothed the corner, which was now stamped with tiny holes where the cat's incisors had pierced it. "That can't be what he meant to imply. This is a beautiful portrait. And a flattering one—why, he doesn't even look fat. I daresay he didn't understand that the artist is supposed to sign the work, not the subject. Shall I put him out in the passage?"

"No, poor thing! He's done no real harm."

The "poor thing" jumped back up and, with a long-suffering sigh, wedged himself between Jack and the arm of the sofa to continue his snooze. Celia dropped the sketch of Manegold back in the box. As she set down the stack of sketches she had been holding, Jack caught his first good look at the one on top. The page contained several quick studies of the same girl. Celia saw the direction of his eyes and silently handed the sheet to him.

He was not so quick to recognize the subject this time. The sweet face, the laughing eyes, and the curls were Celia's, but there was an indefinable something about the expression that told him these were not self-portraits. "Your sister?" he guessed.

She nodded, her entire face softening. "Margery," she said. Her fingers absently, lovingly, traced the edges of the portrait. "Last spring."

Her eyes were dry, but there was a world of sorrow in her voice. Jack ached for her. He looked again at the sketch of the sunny, smiling girl. She looked mischievous and carefree. Even the slant of her eyebrows

was saucy. "You loved her very much," he said. It
was not a question.

"She was my dearest friend."

Without thinking, Jack reached across the small
space between them and put his arm around Celia,
drawing her close. She came to him as naturally and
easily as if she belonged there, and rested her head
against his shoulder. He placed his cheek against her
hair. They sat for a few moments in silence, looking
at the images Celia had captured on the page. Then
Jack lifted his head from her soft curls and, still keeping his arm around her, turned to the next page in the
stack. It was a sketch of a woman in a cap, holding a
fat baby.

"Mama and Benjy," murmured Celia. A little smile
played round her mouth. "This was done about two
years ago, before he grew to be the household terror."

Behind it were studies of her sister Jane, an incom-
plete sketch of her father, which seemed to bother
her—"I do wish I had finished that one"—several
more of Margery, her brother George on horseback,
a more formal sitting of her mother, and a lively drawing of Jane struggling to brush the hair of a slightly
older, and obviously squirming, Benjy. Each sketch
brought words bubbling out of Celia. She told him
some little story about each member of her beloved
family, making him wish he could have known them.
Her home life sounded so different from his own, it
was difficult to grasp that she was speaking of just
another branch of the same family.

"I scarcely ever drew Fanny," said Celia at last.
"She is the one whom Lady Augusta reminds me of,
you know." She sighed. "I am afraid that Fanny and
I were never close, but I suppose we would have outgrown that, if . . ." Her voice trailed off.

"Are all your sketches portraits, then?"

"Most, but not all." She rummaged through the

sheaf of papers and pulled one out, handing it to him. "This is our village church. Papa was the vicar, you remember."

"Yes." Jack studied it. It might have been any one of a hundred English village churches. There was nothing especially distinctive about it, but it looked homely and familiar, and was lovingly drawn. He smiled a little. She was definitely a portrait artist. She had managed to bestow a personality even upon this stack of lifeless stone. "Very pretty."

"It was like a blessing from heaven to hear the bells yesterday," she said softly. "In the wood. It reminded me so strongly of home that, for a moment, I was there."

"I'm glad."

There was a faraway look in her eyes, and she smiled as she gazed at the drawing of the little church. "Papa would ring the bells himself on Christmas Eve. He *said* it was a kindness to the sexton, so that poor Mr. Christian would not have to come out in the cold in the middle of the night. But since he would never let any of the rest of us do it, I think he just enjoyed ringing in Christmas. Papa was extremely fond of Christmas. We all were."

"Did he ring them at midnight, then?"

She nodded, her smile growing. "He would hold a special worship service at eleven o'clock, and end it promptly at midnight so he could ring the bells. It was a lovely service—my favorite of the year. And the church was always packed as full as it could hold."

"It's a wonder that people would turn out for it in the middle of the night."

Mischief danced in her eyes. "Well, if they did not, the bells would wake them at midnight anyway. Papa made sure of that! But no one ever seemed to mind. It was a much-loved tradition in our village."

She smiled at the drawing a moment more, then the

laughter died in her eyes and her features grew grave
again. She tucked the picture away, and it was easy
enough to read her thoughts. Tonight was Christmas
Eve. But Papa was gone, the village church was far
away, and she would never be the vicar's daughter
again. This year, for the first time, there would be no
joyous chorus of midnight bells to ring in Christmas
for Celia.

The stillness of her face hurt Jack's heart.

"Thank you for showing me your sketches," he said
quietly. "They are beautiful."

Shyness immediately seized her, making her duck
her head, but at least she smiled again. "You are the
first person I have shown them to since . . . in quite
a long time."

The tiny hesitation before she corrected her sentence tugged at Jack's heartstrings anew, but she
turned her smiling face up to his and he forgot everything except her nearness and his arm around her. He
even forgot to breathe. She seemed unaware of the
effect she was having on him. Her smile was completely trusting. "It is so pleasant to have a friend,
Jack. I am glad you came home for Christmas."

"So am I," he said hoarsely, wondering what was
the matter with him.

Celia still seemed oblivious to the inexplicable rush
of feelings swamping Jack. She took the sketches from
his nerveless grasp and prosaically stacked them, prat-
tling about the boxes of completed sketches she had
stored beneath her bed. That finally caught his
attention.

"Beneath your bed, did you say? I've heard of hiding one's light under a bushel, but under a *bed*?" He
shook his head, mystified.

"Well, they are private," she explained. "What you
said earlier is perfectly true: my sketches always reveal
my own thoughts and feelings. I daresay they depict

Celia Delacourt more clearly than they ever depict my subjects! I formed the habit years ago of hiding my work. Because, as I have already told you, it's fatal to let anyone know that you sketch. Only look what happened with you! The instant I mentioned it, you pestered me until I bared my soul to you."

She busily stuffed the sketches in the wooden box. Jack noticed one sheet sticking out, where the lid would surely crush it, and deftly pulled it out from among the sheaf. He had thought to merely hand it back so that Celia could place it on top of the stack— but then he saw what it was.

Celia looked up when she felt Jack go suddenly still, and saw what he had in his hand. She gave a half-smothered little scream and reached for the drawing, but Jack swiftly lifted it out of her reach, still staring.

"By Jove!" he breathed. It was another unfinished piece, but unmistakably it was of Jack. She had captured his grin unerringly, and the way one lock of his hair fell across his forehead.

Celia jumped up and snatched at the drawing, but Jack's superior height and reach enabled him to keep it from her. Celia apparently decided that her most dignified course was to feign indifference, but she was blushing furiously. "Very well," she said warningly. "But pray do not *you* bite the corners when you discover you do not like it! It is quite your own fault for peeking. Remember, no one likes his own portrait."

"On the contrary!!" said Jack admiringly. "I'd no idea I was such a handsome fellow."

Since Celia had said, not two minutes earlier, that her sketches revealed her own thoughts and feelings, the significance of his observation struck both of them at once.

An awkward silence fell. Jack looked thoughtfully at Celia. Celia appeared ready to sink through the floor. Suddenly a loud and inelegant rumbling sound

startled them both, breaking the moment—and reminding Jack that his original destination had been
the breakfast room. Now it was Jack's turn to blush.

They both broke into helpless laughter. Jack turned
with mock outrage to scold Manegold for growling,
but Manegold slept peacefully on.

"Cousin Celia," said Jack politely, "may I escort
you to the breakfast room? Without delay?"

"Thank you, cousin," said Celia demurely. "I will
be pleased to accompany you. Immediately."

Chapter 14

Her Grace actually rose when Celia entered the morning room and extended her hand, smiling. Celia was startled by this sudden cordiality, but the mystery was solved at once when the duchess spoke.

"I have perceived that you are making an effort to entertain John, as I bade you," she said approvingly. "I am glad to see that my confidence in you was not misplaced."

Celia felt her hackles rising. The duchess clearly expected meek thanks and a humble request for further instructions. Her days of subservience to this wretched woman were over, however. "I am making an effort to entertain Jack because I like him," she said firmly.

"Excellent," said the duchess absently. "I have decided it is time to show you a little more of what I do here, and how I spend my days. The management of a large household calls for a great deal of skill. Many a young bride has come to her new station in life ill-prepared and soon found herself under the thumb of her own upper servants. Believe me, it is fatal to rely upon the housekeeper or the butler to show you how to go on. Once you have placed too much power in their hands, you will never truly be mistress of your own establishment."

During this well-rehearsed speech, the duchess had moved smoothly to a stack of ledgers and papers sitting ominously on her escritoire. Celia felt she must interrupt now, or run the risk of succumbing anew to Her Grace's domination.

"But, Aunt Gladys, I shall never be mistress of a large establishment," she protested. The desperate note in her voice sounded weak and silly, even in her own ears.

The duchess fixed her with a look that would have wilted Celia a few days ago. "Do not be missish, Celia. It puts me out of all patience. Attend, if you please! We shall start with something fairly easy. This is the latest menu sent up by Monsieur Andre. I have already sent him my corrections, but pray look it over and tell me whether you see anything wrong."

Celia took it, her hand trembling a little—heavens, it was difficult to oppose such a strong will!—and glanced at it. "It is in French," she said faintly.

"Naturally."

"I—I speak very little French."

The duchess appeared taken aback. Her features stiffened with displeasure. "Can it be possible?" she exclaimed. "Every well-bred woman speaks French."

Celia lifted her chin. Her eyes flashed. "That may be. However, I do not."

Her Grace's face immediately contorted with anguish. Her reaction seemed wildly out of proportion to the cause. Celia watched, in frightened surprise, as the duchess silently pounded her fist, again and again, into the padded top of a nearby sofa. She finally sank onto the sofa, her breathing uneven.

There was something wrong, something beneath the surface of Her Grace's behavior. Every instinct told Celia that Her Grace was struggling to hide something. Illness, or injury, or—

"You must learn French, of course," ordered the duchess, white-lipped. She pressed her hand to her side, and then to her forehead for a moment. "I cannot teach you. It is too much," she said in a querulous tone. Her voice still sounded breathless and faint. "I shall hire someone."

Celia's puzzled frown vanished. "But this is nonsensical!" she exclaimed, distracted by her own sparking anger. "I have no interest in improving my French. Am I to learn a new language merely to enable me to correct a menu? For heaven's sake, madam, if I am ever in a position to hire servants, I shall simply hire servants who speak English!"

The duchess glared balefully at her. "All the best chefs are French."

"Then I shall make do with the second best! Really, dear ma'am, this is absurd."

At this, Her Grace's eyes flashed fire. "You will *not* hire second-best servants for Delacourt!"

"No, indeed. I shall not hire servants of any sort for Delacourt."

"Why do you persist in defying me? Do not argue with me any longer! I am teaching you how to become worthy of this place, you ungrateful little ninny-hammer!"

Celia felt her fingers curling into fists. She hid her hands in the folds of her skirt and squeezed them tight, trying to vent a little of the steam she felt rising in her. Still, her voice was a little unsteady when she spoke. "Aunt Gladys, you are trying to make a silk purse out of a sow's ear. It can't be done."

The duchess's smile was unpleasant. She pressed her hand against her abdomen again, almost as if Celia's words were making her ill. "I own, I have been suffering second thoughts of late. I have recently been wishing you were a little more biddable, and a little less obstreperous! But I never leave a project half done. Come! We are wasting valuable time."

"We are, indeed," said Celia evenly. "Let us waste no more. I have changed my mind, Your Grace. I will not acquiesce in this scheme of yours to bully poor Jack into marrying me."

The duchess's brows snapped together. She seemed almost to be struggling for breath. "What—did you—just say—to me?" she asked, in a ghastly voice.

Celia felt her knees begin to tremble beneath her. She clutched the back of a nearby chair for support and forced herself to speak calmly. "I believe you heard me, madam. I will not help you. I will not help you do this terrible thing."

In the painful silence that followed Celia's announcement, color slowly returned to the duchess's face. She rose from her place on the sofa and towered over Celia like a vengeful goddess.

"I begin to believe it *is* a terrible thing," she said, in a voice of angry amazement. "How dare you challenge me? How dare you defy my will? How dare you accuse me of *bullying* my son? He is a man grown!"

"Yes, he is," flashed Celia, standing her ground. "No thanks to you, I fear! You have made him unwell with your browbeating and your ill-humor—why, you may have even created the very malady that causes you to despise him! But it is *you* who are despicable, not Jack! You are at fault, madam—you are grievously at fault."

Celia found it necessary to dash the tears from her eyes with a shaking hand. The duchess was staring at her, wrath and incredulity writ large across her face, but Celia plunged on, her voice growing stronger as her conviction grew.

"And now you seek to use *me*—to dominate and control me and then marry me to your unfortunate son, so that you might achieve final mastery over us both! You believe he is unworthy of any higher marriage, do you not? You would not have chosen me for him otherwise. You think him *incapable* of securing the affections of a rational woman! It is unjust. You underestimate him. He is as kindhearted as he is handsome, and there is not a woman in the world who would not give—" She broke off, her voice wholly suspended in tears, and gave a defiant sniff. "In short, you do him a grave disservice, ma'am, in trying to match him with me! There is no reason why he should not marry as high as even *you* could wish."

"You little fool!" snapped Her Grace. "Of course he is capable of marrying well. It is through his own choice that he has not! But *you*—I confess, I do not understand you! Had I glimpsed this side of your character beforehand, I would never have brought you here. You are impertinent—willful—unmannerly—I have been grossly deceived in you! But my eyes have been opened this day. You are nothing but a bumpkin, incapable of rising to the heights I had planned for you."

Celia was too angry to consider before she spoke. "I am not incapable, ma'am! I am unwilling. I shall not do your bidding. I *shall* not."

For half a heartbeat, Celia was certain that the duchess would slap her. She even braced herself for the blow, but it did not come. Her Grace regained control over herself, although a murderous fury, terrible to behold, still burned in her ice-blue eyes. "Very well," said Her Grace, in a clipped, toneless voice.

She walked, with graceful movements, to her escritoire and sat, picking up a pen. "I am withdrawing my support, Celia. You need come to me no longer. I will teach you nothing more. I no longer desire you to marry my son. In fact, I will do whatever I can to prevent it. You will never marry a man of rank." Her voice quivered with contempt. "Some ignorant hayseed will be good enough for you."

She dipped her pen briskly in the ink and began to write, still speaking. "Christmas is upon us now, so your departure must be postponed until after the New Year. But go you shall. I will not have you in my house. It pains me to look at you."

Despite Celia's anger, the duchess's words hurt. "Yes, Your Grace," she said stiffly.

The duchess looked up from her task. Her face was utterly calm. It was chilling to see her indifference after the terrible row they had just had and the ugly words she had just said. Celia could scarcely believe the evidence of her eyes. It was incredible that such violent emotions could be quelled so quickly.

But perhaps they could not. Her Grace's smile was eerily bland, her voice pleasant and gentle, but what she said was, "Get out of my sight."

Celia fled, almost running down the passage to her chamber. When she arrived, however, she found housemaids busily tidying it. No sanctuary there. She stayed only long enough to don a hooded pelisse, then snatched up a pair of warm gloves and headed for the back of the palace, down the marble stairs, and out the nearest door. It happened to lead to the water garden. She took a deep draught of the fresh, cold air, and expelled it in a quavering sigh. She then closed her eyes and leaned for a moment against the limestone lintel, waiting for the hammering of her heart to subside.

She would have to leave Delacourt, the duchess had said. Fear licked through her at the thought. It was unconscionable for that wicked woman to tell her this was going to be her home and then renege on the promise—but, after all, Celia reminded herself, she had meant to leave anyway. It was just that she had not yet thought of anywhere she could go. It was all very well to tell herself how glad she would be to live with the Hinshaws, but the Hinshaws had not offered. In fact, it was Dr. Hinshaw who had written to the Duchess of Arnsford and begged her to take Celia away. That was hardly a good omen.

And Celia had formed the intention of leaving before she had come to know Jack. Knowing Jack had altered everything.

Celia opened her eyes and looked forlornly out across the water garden. All the fountains had been turned off for the winter. They looked strange and sad with their bubbling and motion stilled, the stone women holding jars from which nothing poured, the stone dolphins leaping through empty space instead of spray. All those naked cherubs standing in puddles of ice made one shiver in sympathy. She had been looking forward to seeing it in spring, when it would come alive, but it appeared now that she never would. She would doubtless never see Delacourt again once she had left it. Her grandfather had not, after he left— and he had been born here, had grown up here, and had had every right to call it home.

She walked down to the terrace of fountains and looked over the view it gave of the wood and the lake. The snow had, for the most part, melted, and her boots crunched on muddy ice wherever the path was shaded. The stark beauty of the wintry landscape looked bleak to her now. Clouds were moving in, and a stinging wind made her eyes water. It was a fit counterpoint to her mood.

If she wasn't careful, she would slip into maudlin self-pity. That would never do. Celia deliberately stiffened her spine, lifted her chin, and turned to walk back toward the palace. She must be strong, she told herself. For her own sake, but also for Jack's.

She was determined to help him. Whatever strange affliction burdened him, he was not past help. She was sure of it. Why, he appeared perfectly normal more often than not—at least when he was around her. She rather fancied herself a good influence on him.

What would happen to Jack when Her Grace sent her away? Would he suffer a relapse? The idea made her smack her fist into her palm in angry frustration. There was something about Jack, poor man, that made her feel fiercely protective. It seemed there was little she could do for him, but whatever she could do, she would.

Anger gnawed at her as she considered the depth of the duchess's betrayal. How could she hold her wonderful son in such contempt? How could she treat him so? Celia could scarcely credit that any woman, let alone his own mother, could believe Jack Delacourt incapable of forming an alliance suitable to his rank. Jack, of all people! It was staggering. Why, he was the most attractive man Celia had ever met. There were women who would marry a man of his rank and fortune were he ugly, or stupid, or cruel—or all three! Jack was none of these things. And yet his mother had been ready to shackle him to a girl whose only claim to nobility was her surname.

Celia could only suppose that she had not seen the worst of his illness. There must have been some outburst in the past, some frightful exhibition that had convinced Her Grace that Jack was unfit for the marriage mart. This was a depressing thought. And yet, Celia reminded herself, whatever attack Jack may have suffered might have been brought on by nothing more than Her Grace's malevolent influence. In fact, to Celia this seemed not only possible, but probable!

The thought only strengthened her resolve to rescue Jack if she could. Although it was hard to think how she might exchange the evil influence of his family for her own beneficial influence. Short of marrying him, that is.

By this time, she had reached the door again. As she dutifully scraped her muddy shoes against the decorative piece of wrought iron placed there for the purpose, she could not help feeling a little wistful. What a pity it was that the duchess had changed her mind about matching her with Jack. But this was a dangerous path, and Celia turned her thoughts hastily from it. She would stand Jack's friend, she told herself firmly. And it was not the part of a friend to join with the duchess in pushing Jack down a road he did not wish to travel. No matter how tempting that road might appear to Celia.

As she let herself sadly into the house, Jack himself appeared on the stairs above. "Hallo, I've found you at last!" he exclaimed, rubbing his hands together boyishly.

Celia smiled, her heart lifting at the very sight of him. "Were you looking for me?"

"Everyone's looking for you," he assured her. His eyes took in her pelisse and rosy cheeks, and he glanced in surprise at the doorway she was closing behind her. "Have you been wandering round the water garden in midwinter?" he asked, shaking his head as if baffled. "And you say *I'm* mad!"

"I wanted fresh air. Why is everyone looking for me?"

A triumphant grin rendered his features even more handsome than usual. He pulled a sprig of holly out from behind his back with the flourish of a conjurer. "Time to deck the halls! Or, rather, hall. I'm afraid we only brought in enough greenery to adorn a fraction of the place—but then, we wanted to leave a portion of the wood still standing. Come, come! Don you now your gay apparel, and let's get on with it."

Celia's eyes brightened as she took the proffered holly sprig. "Oh, thank you for waiting for me! I shall only be a moment."

She almost danced up the stairs to her chamber, unbuttoning her pelisse as she went. She had soon tossed it unceremoniously aside, together with the stout gloves and wet shoes, and changed into a soft round gown of fine black wool. As she tied the ribbons of her dainty black slippers, she wished, for the second time in as many days, that she could set aside mourning and appear attractive.

She bit her lip. Did Christmas give her sufficient excuse to modify her dress? It did, she decided defiantly. She picked up Jack's holly sprig and fastened it in her newly brushed hair. The glossy green leaves and fat red berries seemed to glow against her curls. Blushing for her vanity, yet feeling happier nevertheless, she hurried toward the stairs.

Christmas was working an especially strong magic this year, she reflected. The bleak despair she had felt half an hour ago had vanished with remarkable speed—almost the instant Jack invited her to deck the halls. During the past day or two she had become increasingly aware of a tug of poignant happiness in her heart, a sudden desire to look pretty again, and a strange inability to stay sad for very long.

Yes, it was all because of Christmas, she told herself firmly. It had nothing to do with Jack.

Chapter 15

Jack heard the patter of quick feet behind him and turned to see Celia running lightly down the stairs. The sight of her made him smile. She looked rosy and excited and absurdly youthful—and she had fixed his holly sprig in her hair. For some reason, that pleased him enormously.

She paused while still on the stairs, her eyes traveling round the hall below her, and then treated Jack to a sound he had not heard from her before: merriment. Her laughter suddenly rang out like the pealing of mirthful bells. It was extremely infectious, and Jack could not help grinning.

"What is it?"

Celia waved her arm to indicate the hall. "I just— I just never saw anything quite like it," she blurted, laughing again.

He looked around, mystified, as she came down to join him. "I see nothing amiss."

"Jack, they have *washed* the greenery!"

They had, in fact, done more than that. The servants had removed from the sledge all the branches and sprigs he and Celia had gathered yesterday, washed them, trimmed them, and carried them into the hall. The greenery had then been sorted by species and arranged in tidy stacks. No brown edges, bark dust, globs of sap, or straggling ends marred their perfection. Had it not been for the piney fragrance filling the hall, anyone seeing the perfect boughs would have assumed they were artificial.

Two tables had been brought in as well and covered neatly with snowy linen. Atop one pristine surface lay several pairs of scissors, some wire, some twine, spools of velvet ribbon in various widths, sheets of tissue paper in various colors, and all manner of materials suitable for the making of Christmas decorations. Atop the other, smaller, table were a platter of gingerbread, a platter of sweetmeats, and a teapot in a cozy. Cups, saucers, serviettes, plates, and spoons were prettily arranged near the teapot. A fire crackled briskly in the huge fireplace, there was not an object out of place, and the room generally gave the impression that it had been prepared by genies.

A slow smile crept across his face as Jack tried to picture how absurd it must look to a girl who had never had servants to smooth every task for her. "I suppose it is a little oppressive," he admitted. "Will it take all the fun out of it, to have Christmas so civilized?"

"Certainly not," Celia said promptly. "It merely took me by surprise. For a moment."

"In that case, have a biscuit."

She chuckled. "No, thank you, but pray do not abstain on my account."

"You're a right one, cousin," Jack informed her, helping himself liberally to the gingerbread.

"Where are the others?"

"Blenhurst should arrive at any moment, and Elizabeth with him. Augusta and Caroline have been persuaded to do the dining room, and Winifred is nursing a toothache."

"Poor Winifred," said Celia piously.

Jack winked. "I confess, I think we will do better without her. But I've always been an unfeeling chap. Ah, here come our compatriots now."

The Duke of Blenhurst and Lady Elizabeth Dela-court entered the room together, walking sedately side by side—but at a respectable distance from one an-other. Their demeanor was formal. Certainly no one would mistake them for lovers, thought Jack, disap-pointed. They looked like acquaintances rather than old friends.

On the other hand, Elizabeth had honored the occa-sion by donning a silk dress in a sort of cranberry color, and twisted her hair up in some new way. She looked almost beautiful. Perhaps she meant to make a play for old Blenhurst after all.

Old Blenhurst didn't look half bad himself. He also seemed to have dressed with meticulous care, but Jack was less sure what inference, if any, could be drawn from that. It might be for Elizabeth's benefit, but it might as easily be Celia whom he sought to impress. Celia greeted him with a trifle more pleasure than seemed strictly necessary, and Blenhurst's smile defi-nitely warmed when he saw her. Jack's biscuit turned to ashes in his mouth, and he felt his own smile fade. He swallowed, and tried to pin an amiable expression onto his face before anyone noticed.

"Well, this is all very pleasant," said Blenhurst, looking round him with satisfaction.

"It's perfect," agreed Celia, choking back a giggle.

"Well, let's not stand about eating gingerbread all day," ordered Jack, who was actually the only one eating gingerbread. "This is not a tea party. There's work to be done, comrades! Where shall we begin?"

"Perhaps the ladies have ideas," suggested Blen-hurst. "In my experience, it is usually the fair sex who display artistic ability."

Jack was disgusted by this mawkish observation, but Elizabeth appeared pleased. "You are gallant, Eu-gene," she said archly.

Jack pricked up his ears at that; had his sister and

Blenhurst progressed to first names? He was inclined to think that a hopeful sign. Some of his cheerfulness returned. He turned at once to Celia.

"If it's artistic ability that's wanted, I fancy we should rely upon cousin Celia," he said, ignoring the stiffness that immediately afflicted his sister when everyone's attention veered to Celia. "What say you, cousin? Have you a plan?"

"Well," said Celia, looking very serious, "I think our efforts would best be spent on the double staircase."

They turned as one to study the staircase. It was a beautiful creation, sweeping down from the gallery in two graceful curves, one on either side of the hall.

Elizabeth laughed affectedly. "Heavens! Do you really think the grand staircase can be improved upon?"

Her tone implied indulgent amusement at the very idea. Celia blushed and dropped her eyes, and Jack had to bite his tongue to keep from saying something pretty sharp to his snob of a sister. "It can certainly be made to look more Christmasy," he avowed, looking daggers at Elizabeth. An idea seized him. "I say, why don't we team up? Celia and I will take one side of the staircase, and you two take the other."

"Very well," said Blenhurst equably. It was impossible to tell if he was disappointed or pleased to be assigned willy-nilly to Elizabeth.

And what did Celia think? Jack searched her face with covert anxiety, trying to discern whether she had hoped to be paired with Blenhurst. Not a clue did he discover. He wished she would show some sort of emotion, whether of pleasure or dismay, at the idea that she must spend the next half hour or so solely in Jack's company. She did not, however. She looked maddeningly serene. Perfectly indifferent, in fact.

Jack cursed himself for his shortsightedness. Had he

suggested that they team up and then waited to see how matters fell out naturally, he might have learned something worth knowing.

Of course, it struck him as a bit confusing that it mattered to him one way or the other. Very odd. It would have been a bore to be paired with Elizabeth, but that should have been Elizabeth's lookout, not his. Being paired with Blenhurst might have been time well spent; he could have used the time to paint the chap a glowing portrait of his sister. Drop him a hint or two. So why was it so important to him that he be teamed *not* with Elizabeth and *not* with Blenhurst, but with Celia and only Celia?

His ruminations were cut short when he was called upon to lift a stack of evergreen boughs and carry them to the banister that he and Celia would decorate. Since not only Jack but also Blenhurst had deferred to her artistic judgment, Celia had been placed nominally in command. Elizabeth looked pretty sour at this arrangement but was managing to swallow her spleen rather than appear shrewish.

The plan proposed was that the men would place evergreen boughs along the banisters and the ladies would follow with twine, scissors, and red ribbon, securing the boughs with the twine once the men had placed them and then tying a swath of wide red ribbon over the twine to hide it. Since the plan was Celia's, Elizabeth and Blenhurst would watch how she and Jack did it before beginning, in an effort to ensure that the two sides of the staircase would match.

Jack carried his assigned armload of fragrant boughs to the sweep of stairs to the right, Celia following in his wake, and set them carefully on the third step.

"Very well, ma'am," he said, bowing. "I am at your service."

"Thank you, Lord Lynden," she said demurely. The sparkle was returning to her eyes now that they were beginning the task. She eyed the stack of boughs earnestly, tapping one finger absently against her teeth.

"This one, and this," she said at last, pointing. Jack lifted up the branches she had indicated, smiling at her eagerness. "Do you set them together atop the banister, here—no, a bit lower—we must arrange it so the end of the branch curves down over the end of the banister and hides the newel post. Oh, very pretty!" And Celia quickly wrapped the twine round the center of the branch to hold it tightly in place. Jack held the twine for her while she snipped it with the scissors and tied a knot. She then took a length of red ribbon and tied it deftly over the twine. He watched, fascinated, as Celia tied an elaborate bow. When she frowned in concentration, he noticed, she caught the tip of her tongue between her teeth. Jack found the habit enchanting. Finally she stepped back to display her handiwork to Elizabeth and Blenhurst, who were loitering at the foot of the stairs.

"That's the most beautiful bow I've ever seen," exclaimed Jack admiringly.

Elizabeth looked a bit dismayed when she saw Celia's perfect bow. She gave a nervous little laugh. "I am not certain I can tie a bow quite like that."

Celia's smile was swift and sweet. "Everyone's style differs a bit," she said agreeably. "It won't matter. We can go back later and make them match if we wish."

There was not the slightest implication in Celia's tone that her own artistry might in any way be superior to Elizabeth's—only different. Jack's heart nearly burst with admiration for his little cousin's tact and generosity. Really, she was the dearest thing . . . he had to catch himself up short and remind himself that he was not yet sure of her motives or her honesty. Why was it so hard to keep that dreary fact in mind?

Elizabeth and Blenhurst removed to the opposite

end of the hall to begin on their own branch of the staircase, and Jack had Celia to himself at last. Would she show any emotion now? Would he be able, finally, to determine what she thought? They were standing so close to one another, he could smell the fragrance of soap in her hair. He even fancied he could feel warmth radiating from her skin. Their hands were ungloved, and would touch from time to time when they began their slow ascent, arranging and tying branches as they went. It all struck Jack as extremely intimate. Not only their close proximity, but the very act of uniting in a shared project, creating something beautiful with their four hands. His heart seemed to beat foolishly faster at the prospect. Would Celia feel the least bit nervous, or exhilarated, or shy of him?

If she did, she did not show it.

Jack, observing Celia's placid face and steady hands, began to feel a bit annoyed. Well, if she was going to be so maddeningly composed, he'd be damned if he would let her see how her nearness affected him. He had one advantage, at least, in being able to watch her closely—for the most part, her hands were busy while his were idle. Studying her downcast face, therefore, he tried to engage her in conversation.

"Do you know, cousin, last year our only celebration of Christmas was the actual feast itself? And, of course, worship in the morning. We haven't done any hanging of the green for years."

Celia looked surprised. "Really? How sad. Do you exchange gifts at all?"

"No. We give something to the servants and tenants, of course, on Boxing Day."

She looked up from the knot she was tying and shot him a mischievous glance. "Well, I'm glad to hear that, actually, since I haven't the wherewithal to give anything worth having."

Jack's eyebrows flew up. "Nonsense. What about

your sketches? Those would be well worth having! Next year, we shall give you sufficient warning and you can do all our portraits for Christmas.''

He was pleased with himself for thinking of that. It would be wonderful to know that Celia was preparing some sort of Christmas gift for him. It would give him an excuse to shower her with presents of his own. And since no monetary value could be placed on a portrait sketch, he could spend whatever he liked on her, buy her any number of things—and she could not refuse to accept his largesse, because he could insist that her gift to him was more valuable than all of his put together.

The pleasant daydream was interrupted when he noticed Celia's silence. A shadow seemed to have fallen across her face. "Oh, I see," he said ruefully. "You don't want my family to know about your sketching. But surely they are your family now, too? Buck up, Celia! I believe I can safely promise you that they would all be pleased to sit for their portraits—only think how it ministers to one's vanity!" He grinned. "And that same vanity will ensure that they will never, ever, make a fuss over you, no matter how brilliant the results. So you see, you have nothing to fear."

But Celia looked even more grave than before. She did smile at him, but the smile did not reach her eyes. "Let us enjoy this Christmas before looking to the next, shall we? Anything can happen between now and then." She paused, looking down at her hands as they snipped a thread. "Why, I may not even be here next Christmas," she said lightly.

"What do you mean?" Jack tried to laugh. "Where do you plan to go?"

Celia looked as if she wished she had not spoken. "Oh, nowhere!" she said quickly. "Nowhere at all." Her smile was definitely strained, and her eyes failed

to meet his. "I daresay I shall be here at Delacourt.
After all, where else would I go?"

But now that she was saying what *should* be the
truth, Jack had the uneasy feeling that she believed it
to be an untruth. He frowned. An unpleasant suspicion tugged at the edges of his mind. He glanced at
Blenhurst across the room, soberly assisting Elizabeth
as she struggled with her spool of ribbon. Did Celia
expect—or at least hope—to marry next year? Is that
why she would not be spending next Christmas at Delacourt? He could think of no other reason why she
would leave. She certainly had, as she herself had
pointed out, no other home.

Jack tried to remember what his mother had said.
Was she taking Celia with her to London for the Season? He rather thought not. It would be unlike her to
do anything so foolish—or so generous—as to frank
Celia's come-out while she still had four unmarried
daughters on her hands. Besides, she meant to blud-
geon Celia into marrying *him*.

But perhaps Celia did not realize that. For all his
Mother's assertion that she had told Celia of her plans,
perhaps Celia meant to get out from under the obligation somehow. The surest way, of course, would be to
meet and marry someone else.

Ah, but if that were Celia's plan, she didn't need a
London Season, did she? The Duke of Blenhurst
would suit the purpose admirably. Dukes were few
and far between, and normally such a matrimonial
prize would never look twice at an unpretentious girl
in deep mourning. But Celia had noticed His Grace's
loneliness. She might very well have gauged the situation correctly; Blenhurst could be vulnerable.

Jack felt a deep and thunderous scowl gathering on
his features as he listened, in stony silence, to the gentle flow of Celia's conversation. She had regained her
composure and was chatting inconsequentially of

Christmas in general, of how pleasant it was to maintain traditions, and of—incredibly—the weather. The *weather*! That sent a real pang through Jack. It was unbearable. She might be conversing with anyone. A complete stranger.

It was a bit of a shock to realize that he was, actually, a stranger to her. Or very nearly. Good God, how had she become so important to him in such a short time? Why did it hurt when she behaved toward him as any young lady of three days' acquaintance would?

Jack maintained his unhelpful silence as he backed slowly up the stairs, handing evergreen boughs to Celia as they were needed, pressing his finger onto the crossed twine so she could pull it taut, holding the ends of the ribbon while she tied her impossibly perfect bows. He would listen to her polite blatherings for as long as he could tolerate them, he promised himself, and then, if she did not put an end to this nonsense, by George, he would. He had never been good at guessing games, and the stakes of this particular game had somehow become too high.

Chapter 16

On the other side of the room, the Duke of Blenhurst was also having to listen to superficial conversation, and liking it no better than Lord Lynden did. His grave courtesy, so ingrained in him that it was second nature, enabled him to listen politely and respond appropriately, however, even while his thoughts were busy elsewhere. He knew Elizabeth was as well trained as he was, so whether she paid any more attention to their discussion of inanities than he did was anyone's guess.

He lifted and placed the evergreen boughs, smiled and chatted, and watched his companion as she did the same.

She was a striking female, he thought. Tall and slender and graceful, with a white skin and dark hair that made her stand out in any crowd. There was a cool elegance about her that had always appealed to him. It was the sort of beauty that would age well, too. It was in her bones, like the beauty of a statue. Her pedigree was faultless, her fortune substantial, and her behavior consistently above reproach. She was, in fact, the quintessential woman of breeding. A man would be proud indeed to win her.

He admired her. And they were very alike, of course; they had everything in common. Lady Elizabeth Delacourt was an obvious choice, a perfect match—she always had been that.

Three years ago, that had not been enough. Now it was. Now, he would settle for a woman he admired and understood. He would settle for suitability. A perfect match was what he wanted. A perfect wife who would provide him with a perfect heir. During the Season, he and Elizabeth would be the perfect couple, the envy of the *ton*. During the rest of the year, they would retire to their perfect estate and lead a well-ordered, calm, and perfect life surrounded by their perfect children.

Esther's face floated briefly in his memory, imperfect and precious. He pushed her painful image away. It did no good to think of his lost love. Comparisons were useless. Besides, the two women were as different as night from day. And that was a good thing. That was a very good thing. It would be terrible to live with anyone who reminded him of Esther, and yet was not Esther. He could imagine no worse torture.

Elizabeth did not remind him of Esther at all.

She accidentally dropped the spool of ribbon, interrupting his reverie, and it bounced merrily down the steps behind them. Since she was in the act of wrapping it round the banister when she dropped it, the spool unraveled ribbon as it went, and when it hit the marble floor it raced eagerly away, trailing a wide stripe of Christmas red all across the hall.

Blenhurst immediately gave chase. This caught the attention of Lord Lynden and Miss Delacourt, who cheered and applauded, so when he caught up the spool he held it aloft like a prize he had caught, then bowed with mock solemnity. However, when he began rewinding the rebellious ribbon onto its spool, he noticed that Elizabeth was not amused. She stood stiffly where he had left her, holding her end of the ribbon. Her cheeks were bright pink, and her face had taken on that pinched, vexed expression she wore from time to time. She looked mortified.

Blenhurst grew thoughtful. By the time he had wound the ribbon up to where Elizabeth stood, her angry flush had diminished. Still, she did not meet his eyes as she took the spool from him.

"Thank you," she said woodenly. "So clumsy of me! I beg your pardon."

He touched her hand, causing her to raise startled eyes to his. He smiled rather whimsically at her. "There is no need to beg my pardon, you know." The flush instantly returned to her cheeks. "Ah," he said quietly. "You *don't* know. I wondered if that might be so."

She gave a completely artificial laugh. "You are all consideration, Eugene."

"I am nothing of the kind. But—forgive me if I speak too plainly—I have noticed that you are rather strict with yourself, Elizabeth. More so now than when I knew you previously, I think. I wonder why that is?"

She looked dumbfounded, as if she could not believe that he would do anything so rude, so unprecedented, as to confront her with a personal remark. "Strict with myself?" she repeated, with a polite, puzzled smile. "I—I don't know what you mean."

She was obviously waiting for the explanation that would reveal that his remark had not been personal at all. He had to fight a craven impulse to give her what she expected—but he had, in fact, meant the remark personally. And having taken the risk, he would not retreat into empty platitudes again.

"You seem, to me, to set impossibly high standards for yourself," he said carefully. "And you become vexed when you display any imperfection, however slight. This constant vigilance makes it difficult for you to have fun, I think."

She actually looked frightened. They were entering uncharted waters now, and she knew it. "Fun? Why—that is for children."

"Perhaps I expressed myself poorly. Surely you don't believe that enjoyment of life is suitable only for children?"

He watched her closely. This was the most personal conversation they had ever had, and he suspected it was the most personal conversation Elizabeth had had with any man. It was important to know whether she would allow his approach or whether she would immediately retreat and freeze him out.

It was an obvious struggle for her. He had caught her off-guard with his directness, just as he had last night during those few moments in the drawing room. She looked to be at a complete loss. He understood very well the rigid training she was battling; he had received the same training. Her first instinct must surely have been to withdraw, offer him a well-bred reproof, and keep him at a distance. Three years ago, he was sure, that was exactly what she would have done.

Today, however, something was giving her pause. He had never before glimpsed uncertainty or indecision in the precise and self-assured Lady Elizabeth Delacourt. But there they were, in every line of her tense shoulders and troubled face. He spoke again, before she could regain her balance.

"Elizabeth, in all the years I have known you, I cannot recall a single instance where you have displayed any genuine pleasure. So far as I know, there is no activity you enjoy for its own sake, and no person you truly care for. I think that very hard—very hard indeed. And self-inflicted, I believe."

She turned away from him, instinctively trying to hide her face, but he caught at her elbow and prevented her escape. She stilled, not trying to break his light grip and not protesting it. He must speak now, he sensed, or never. He pressed urgently on, watching her averted face.

"You think me uncomfortably frank. But I have learned something in the years we have spent apart, Elizabeth. I have learned that frankness is necessary between persons who desire any sort of intimacy—whether of marriage or friendship. In fact, intimacy is not achievable without it. And I have also learned that intimacy—whether of marriage or friendship—is a valuable thing, well worth a little risk. Worth even a little embarrassment."

She finally raised her eyes to his again. They were filled with a sort of desperate wariness, as if she were struggling to overcome her ingrained doubt and suspicion.

He offered her an encouraging smile. "You are right to pause. Frankness is a dangerous thing," he said softly. "If you snub me now, for example, I shall feel extraordinarily silly."

An unwilling smile tugged at her mouth. "I will not snub you, I hope. But I do not know what to say."

"Tell me whether I am near the mark. Is it true? Do you become vexed with yourself over trifles?"

She frowned, seeming to speak with an effort. "Perhaps I do. I have no sense of humor, you know."

He nodded. "I have observed that, I think. My own sense of the ridiculous is not particularly keen, but I have taken pains to develop it. It does add to one's appreciation of life, to have a good laugh now and then."

"I thought one either had it or did not. Is it possible to develop a sense of humor?"

"Oh, I think so." He smiled faintly. "One must be willing to appear foolish, of course."

She made a little moue of distaste, but he was delighted to hear a glimmer of actual humor in her voice when she said, "Then it is no wonder I have not developed my own. I abhor looking foolish."

He chuckled and handed her the scissors. "Well, it

might be sufficient to only laugh at the foolishness of others. But I warn you, if you laugh at others and never at yourself, you will not have many friends."

Her eyes were on her hands as they wrestled with the bow she was tying. "I have never had many friends," she said lightly. "I shouldn't know what to do with them if I had them."

She finished the bow with a flourish, but he saw that her hands were not quite steady. They stepped up to the next stair and he silently lifted another evergreen bough, holding it in place while she picked up the twine. He had not expected to feel so much sympathy for Elizabeth. It had certainly never occurred to him that there was anything pitiable about her self-sufficiency. But her admission that she had never had many friends was striking. He now realized that he could not remember any woman ever naming Elizabeth among her friends and he had never heard Elizabeth mention a friend of her own.

He said nothing while she knotted the twine, knowing she would drop something or tremble if he forced her to feel any emotion, and she would then hate herself for betraying weakness. He would not inflict that on her. He waited until she had finished, then took the twine and scissors from her. When he failed to hand her the ribbon, she looked up at him as he knew she would, and he was able to look steadily into her face. Then he spoke.

"Elizabeth, I count myself your friend."

He saw pleasure in her eyes, but fear as well. She smiled, but it was a rather tentative smile. "Thank you—Eugene." It was still difficult for her to remember to call him by his first name. "I count myself yours."

Her hand rested on the banister, on the knot she had just tied. He covered her hand with his own. "I hope to become something more than your friend. I think you know that. Would that be acceptable to you?"

That was definitely fear he saw in her eyes now. Fear, and pain. And a strange mixture of relief and joy that made her look almost fierce. But she swiftly veiled her eyes and gave a brittle laugh. Her voice sounded strained when she said, "I think we have had this conversation before."

"No, we have not. Not this one." He took a deep breath. "If we talked of friendship before, and you believed that I meant to offer you marriage, I apologize. I truly regret any—misunderstanding. I suppose I was not clear."

She looked very unhappy, but she did not remove her hand from beneath his. "No," she said in a low voice. "You were not."

"I was incapable of speaking clearly to you then. I did not know, myself, what I intended. I am clearer in my mind now, however, and I do intend to offer you marriage, Elizabeth. If you can forgive me. If you will have me."

Now she removed her hand. She stood before him, pale and agitated, and said something he thought he would never hear from her bloodless lips: "You do not love me."

Blenhurst rocked back on his heels, staring at her. His first instinct was to lie, but the lie died when he saw how much it had cost Elizabeth to say such words to him. He would not repay her honesty with some facile assurance that he did not mean. "No," he said unsteadily. "I suppose I do not love you, in the way I think you mean. But I never thought—that is—"

"You did not think it was important to me."

"Frankly, no. I did not."

"Well, you were right. It isn't." Paler than ever, she stood very straight, her hands clenched in the silken folds of her skirt. "But I think it is important to you."

Pain stirred in his heart as Esther's dear image danced in his memory. "It is important," he said hoarsely. "Love is the most important thing on earth."

"Is it? I do not even know what you mean by it," said Elizabeth, in a thread of a voice. "I do not know if I am capable of it. I have been taught to hold such feelings in contempt. I have never inspired love in any man's heart. I have never felt it in my own. I would like above all things to marry you, and I would do my utmost to be the wife you require. But I would have you know, before you take some irretrievable step, that I may disappoint you." She looked desperately unhappy now. "That I will *probably* disappoint you."

It was the first time he had ever seen her appear vulnerable, and something like tenderness swelled his heart. "Thank you for your generous warning, but I do not think you will disappoint me," he said softly. "We shall start with mutual respect. With friendship. I think you can offer me that, can you not?"

Her relief was palpable. "Yes, I can."

"That is all I hoped for. But we may feel differently in future, you know." He smiled into her eyes and felt a tiny, but genuine, flutter of happiness. It seemed to be mutual, for she looked almost as surprised as he felt. "I hope *you* will not be disappointed, Elizabeth, if we discover that we love each other someday," he whispered, and took her hand in his.

Elizabeth's hand felt as cold and smooth as marble—but softer. She was much softer than she appeared.

And she blushed! Would wonders never cease? He felt her cold fingers curl hesitantly around his and knew, without a shadow of a doubt, that however cold her hand was at the moment, he was capable of warming it.

Chapter 17

The woodsy scent of the Christmas greenery grew stronger as the stacks of evergreen boughs were spread along the banisters. The hall was filled with their heady fragrance. Celia and Jack had reached the topmost stair and were fastening the last of the evergreen branches. Before tying the bow, Celia stopped and looked behind her, inhaling deeply. For the first time in the past twenty minutes, her air of artificial politeness dropped and her face lit with real pleasure.

"Oh, I do love Christmas!" she exclaimed.

Jack sniffed the air. It was redolent of pine, with pleasant undertones of tea and wood smoke, gingerbread and furniture polish. The gay red bows along the evergreen-decked banisters were not only pretty, they changed the entire appearance of Delacourt's formal foyer, making it appear more welcoming than Jack had ever seen it. "It's wonderful," he agreed. "Like bringing the outdoors in. And I must tell you, cousin, the room has never looked so well."

Just then, on the other side of the hall, Elizabeth dropped her ribbon. The wooden spool clattered and bounced down the stairs behind her.

"View halloo!" shouted Jack, pointing, and Blenhurst took off after it like a hound after a hare. Celia burst out laughing.

The duke quickly caught up with the spool and held it aloft like a prize. Celia and Jack applauded. "Well done, sir!" cried Celia. The duke bowed and started back toward Elizabeth, who was waiting for him halfway up the stairs.

The moment of spontaneity had broken the spell of constraint. Celia was relaxed and smiling again, although she looked a bit guilty when she glanced at Elizabeth and Blenhurst.

"Oh, dear! They are only halfway up the stairs," she whispered. "I should have worked more slowly."

"Why?"

"I dislike appearing more highly skilled than your sister. I ought not. Especially when it is so important to her to impress her—friend."

Some knot in Jack's chest suddenly loosened. He grinned. "Rubbish. If it is so important to Elizabeth to appear the most highly accomplished woman in the room, all she need do is sit at the pianoforte."

"That is true." Celia's smile was full of mischief. "Or, better yet, seat me at the instrument. Three minutes ought to suffice."

"Do you not play? I thought all genteel young women played the pianoforte."

She wrinkled her nose at him. "I daresay they may. How unkind of you, cousin, to remind me of my humble origins."

"Humble, my eye! Your origins are the same as mine."

Celia looked very prim. "I am a poor man's daughter. You, Lord Lynden, are the Duke of Arnsford's heir. Or haven't they told you?"

"They have, but information of that sort makes little impression on my addled brain. Leaks through it just like water through a sieve."

She was standing one step lower than he, and had to tilt her head to look at him. Her eyes were full of laughter. "You told me last night that there was nothing wrong with your brain."

"Why, so I did!" he exclaimed, shaking his head in mock exasperation. "You see what I mean? Can't keep two thoughts to rub together."

Her eyes went suddenly round with doubt, and she bit her lip. It had obviously occurred to her that it was unkind to laugh at a lunatic. He smiled. What a darling she was. "If you are wondering whether to laugh or not, I assure you that I am joking."

"We ought not to joke about your—health."

"My health is perfectly sound, thank you."

Something kindled in her eyes then, and she squared her small chin. "You know, Jack, I think you *will* be well one day. I mean to help you if I can."

He was touched. "Thank you, Celia," he said gravely, then smiled. "It's almost enough to make me wish there were something wrong. It would give me so much pleasure to let you fix it."

She actually laughed with happiness at his simple statement. There was something about her—her somber black frock speaking of sorrow and loss, and the absurd sprig of holly in her hair singing defiantly of joy—that caught at Jack's heart. She seemed to embody all the sweetness in the world. He was suddenly swamped with a fierce desire to protect her and shelter her, to lift her from her grief and stand like a shield between her and all future pain.

The rush of emotions choked him and he stood, speechless and aching, staring into the velvet depths of Celia's eyes. Her pleased smile faded, and her eyes widened in puzzled wonder as she gazed back at him.

"What is it?" she asked.

But he could not reply. He knew at once what it was, of course. He had lost his heart.

Against all reason, and somehow breaking the curse of the Delacourt second sons, he had fallen irrevocably in love with the very girl his mother had chosen for him. But there was no room in his heart for irony;

it was already full. He loved her. It didn't matter that she was his mother's pet. It didn't matter that he would pay through the nose when he returned to London and had to tell his friends that they had won their bets. It didn't even matter that Celia thought he was a madman.

Well, perhaps that last one mattered a little. He had to admit, it was awkward that she thought he was daft. But time would mend that—he hoped.

He reached impulsively to cover her small hand with his. "Will you do me one small favor?"

"Anything in my power," she replied promptly.

"Meet me here, right at this spot, just before midnight."

She cocked her head to one side, puzzled. "Tonight?"

"Yes. You and I care more for Christmas than anyone else in the household. We'll see it in together."

Her smile was sweet. "I can think of no one with whom I would rather greet Christmas."

"Then you'll be here?"

"Yes."

The short December day was drawing to a close. The Duchess of Arnsford sat by the fire in the small drawing room at the entrance of her apartments and watched the sky darken to purple as the dying light gilded the edges of the windowpanes. She was weary to the bone. She had had to take laudanum for her pain again today. It coursed and curled through her, making her feel sluggish and dreamy.

Mr. Willard had just left. He was a discreet soul. She had no fear that he would betray her secret, not even to her husband. He had expressed his shock and his sorrow, and then had gotten on with the business she had called him to perform. An excellent solicitor, Mr. Willard. And since he had once lost a child to the ministrations of some quack, he perfectly understood her horror of physicians. He wasted no time in stupidly urging her to consult this specialist or that, but simply bowed and sharpened his pen. Good man.

It was an exhausting way to spend the afternoon, wrestling with the provisions of one's last bequests, but there was something satisfying about it as well. It was pleasant to know that she had set in order everything that she could. The bulk of her fortune belonged to her husband, of course, and was not hers to control, but what monies she did control would now pass in an orderly fashion to their most deserving recipient.

The edges of her mouth quirked in an unholy smile. She wished she could be there to see it. Her family would be baffled, and possibly enraged. But Mr. Willard had assured her there was nothing they could do. It was a great deal of money, but little enough reward for a lifetime of devoted service.

As if summoned by her thoughts, Hubbard glided into the room, moving to the fireplace to poke the flames higher. *You'll be a rich woman one day, Gertrude,* thought the duchess. *I hope it brings you more joy than it has brought me.*

She leaned her head back, resting it against her chair, and followed Hubbard's familiar movements with her eyes. Her thoughts drifted here and there. A tiny revelation occurred to her—an insight that she had never had before. The laudanum robbed it of its power to startle her, but still, it seemed worth commenting upon.

"Do you know, Hubbard," said Her Grace drowsily, "the only thing I have ever truly cared for is Delacourt."

Hubbard did not look up from her task. "You have been its best steward, madam," she said matter-of-factly. "You have made it a showplace."

The duchess thought back over the years, remembering the improvements and changes she had instigated. She smiled a little. "I ran it well."

"You still run it well, Your Grace."

"Not long now," the duchess murmured. "Not much longer."

Hubbard straightened, her tall, angular form throwing a long shadow across the carpet. "Shall I draw the curtains?" she asked. Her flat voice had taken on the gruff tone she used to mask emotion. "It grows cold."

"Yes. So it does." The duchess turned her head slightly and watched as Hubbard moved with deft strength to pull the heavy draperies across the tall windows. She suddenly remembered what day it was. "Christmas Eve," she said aloud.

"Yes, ma'am." Hubbard sent Her Grace a searching glance. Her gruff voice roughened further. "I hope you are not overdoing it, Your Grace. Taking on too much, I mean, what with training Miss Delacourt and all. Is there anything more I can do to help you?"

A spasm of pain twisted the duchess's features. "No, Hubbard. I'm afraid not." She lifted her head and frowned at the fire. There was no sense in hiding anything from Hubbard. Still, it cost her something to form the words. "She won't do," she said at last.

Hubbard paused. "She—? Do you mean Miss Delacourt, Your Grace?"

"Yes, unfortunately. I was mistaken. She's a poor choice; completely unsuitable."

Hubbard clucked her tongue sorrowfully. "Ah, Your Grace, I'm that sorry. We had to take her on a bit hasty-like, but I was hoping she would give satisfaction. For your sake."

"Thank you, Hubbard." Her Grace gave a faint sigh. "Well. There's nothing to be done. I had to try; time was short. But now it's shorter still."

Hubbard's sympathy was palpable, although unspoken. Worry sharpened the strange planes of her face. "What will you do, ma'am? I know how much it means to you, finding the right bride for his lordship."

"Yes." The wry smile twisted the duchess's features again. "But, as I say, I have lately realized that finding the right bride for John is secondary. What is primary is finding the right mistress for Delacourt." She moved restlessly, feeling another stab of pain at the thought of her own powerlessness. But she wasn't powerless, she reminded herself. Not while she had breath in her body. "I must ensure that Delacourt passes to worthy hands, to someone who will care for it as I have. Someone who will understand the responsibility and honor it."

"But, Your Grace—" Hubbard hesitated, twisting her hands in her apron. "It will pass, in the course of time, to Lord Lynden's bride. If Miss Delacourt isn't suitable, you can't have her marrying Lord Lynden, can you?"

"No," said the duchess sharply. "Absolutely not. Out of the question. I shall pass Delacourt to Elizabeth."

Hubbard's homely face registered surprise, but she caught herself before blurting out an observation improper to her station. The duchess held up her hand, dreamily watching the firelight burn and sparkle in the jewels that adorned her fingers.

"You are thinking that I have invited Blenhurst here, hoping that he would offer marriage to Elizabeth," she remarked. "Quite right. But I have changed my mind. I think there is little chance that he will do so—after all, he never did before—but, indeed, I must now do what I can to *ensure* that he will not. If John is to remain unwed, Elizabeth must remain unwed."

Hubbard's face creased in a concerned frown. "You take too much upon yourself, Your Grace. You'll wear yourself out, worriting about the fate of everyone around you. There's only so much a mortal body can do." Hubbard's respectful tone robbed her words of insolence. Anticipating the duchess's needs with her usual uncanny efficiency, she crossed to the duchess's chair and moved a footstool closer. "Madam. You know I would never cross you."

The duchess nodded her thanks and placed her feet upon the stool. "Certainly, Hubbard. I know that."

Hubbard folded her arms and said shortly, "I will do what I can to help you. But some things are not within your control. And you'll be easier in your mind if you accept that."

The duchess dropped her head back against the chair again and gazed hazily into the fire. How tired she was. "But I *am* easy in my mind. It's a simple plan," she murmured. "All for the best. Simple plans are best. I have given it a deal of thought today, and my mind is quite made up. Elizabeth shall remain a spinster. She will run Delacourt exactly as I have run it, first for her father and then for her brother. She will enjoy being the lady of the manor. And I know she is more than a capable successor. She is perfect in every way—temperament, ability, training. I am completely satisfied that I have hit, at last, on the correct solution. Elizabeth will be chatelaine of Delacourt."

A quick rap sounded on the door, followed by the hasty entrance of Elizabeth herself. "Mama!" she cried, in a voice of suppressed excitement, and dropped into a curtsey. Her eyes were bright with something that looked very much like happiness, and her cheeks were uncharacteristically pink.

Even through the fog of laudanum, a sense of foreboding gripped the duchess. "What is it, daughter?"

"Good news," replied Elizabeth, exultation in her voice. "Blenhurst is even now with my father. Madam, he has offered for me!" She flew forward in an access of glee and lightly kissed her mother's cheek.

A powerful gust of rage and chagrin swept through Her Grace. She stared up at Elizabeth, feeling the color drain from her face. And then, for the first time in her life, the Duchess of Arnsford fainted.

Chapter 18

At twenty minutes before midnight, Celia buttoned herself into a velvet pelisse. It would be cold in the hall.

The entire family had gone to bed early. She and Jack would be the only ones to see Christmas in. That made her feel rather sad. But then, she had expected to feel a bit depressed tonight. It was sweet of Jack to offer to stay up and help her welcome Christmas.

It had been a strange Christmas Eve. There had been no sense of pleasurable anticipation, no family preparations for Christmas. Part of the reason was that, just as Liz Floyd had told her, Christmas was not celebrated in the great houses of England as it was among the common people. And although there was to be a traditional feast tomorrow, a feast naturally meant less in a house where one dined well every day. Besides that, whatever preparations were being made were being made by the servants, not the family. There might very well be a bustle and a fragrance in the kitchens, but the kitchens were far away. The duchess's sudden indisposition had also thrown a pall over the proceedings—she had been too unwell to come down to dinner. Hubbard had assured everyone that there was no cause for alarm, but it would have been strange to make merry in Her Grace's absence, even if the company had felt so inclined.

In fact, this Christmas Eve would have been a night

much like any other night—if not for the betrothal of
Lady Elizabeth and the Duke of Blenhurst. They had
entered the drawing room before dinner arm in arm,
escorted by Elizabeth's papa, who was beaming and
rubbing his hands together like a delighted schoolboy.
Celia, Jack, Augusta, Caroline, and Winifred had all
looked up, startled. Jack had been the first to realize
the significance of the tableau. He had rushed forward
to wring Blenhurst's hand and clap him on the back,
and the entire room had immediately broken into excited exclamations. The girls had all flown to surround
Elizabeth. It was the first moment of spontaneous joy
Celia had witnessed since she came to Delacourt.
Well, in that sense, perhaps the family had had one
Christmasy moment after all.

She turned up the collar on her pelisse and ran her
fingers through her curls, frowning a little. What had
Jack meant, she wondered, by observing her so closely
this evening? It had been very difficult for her to behave normally. She felt just like a—a cauldron full of
boiling soup. Smooth and blank on the outside, but
with all sorts of commotion bubbling and knocking
about inside. Too many feelings. Too much to think
about. So much, in fact, that her only course was to
try not to think at all.

A quarter to twelve. She picked up her candle and
crept out to the passage, then tiptoed down its dark
and silent length to where it opened out onto the gallery. Light bloomed somewhere below, casting a
warm, faint glow on the curving double staircase. The
scent of pine filled the air. Celia felt her spirits lift
immediately; the familiar fragrance of Christmas made
her smile in spite of herself. She tiptoed to the railing
and peeped over it down into the hall.

The light was coming from the fireplace. Jack, or
someone, had lit a fire—nothing like a Yule log, of
course, but a cheery little fire that crackled and leaped
and did its best to warm and brighten the austere foyer.

Suddenly she felt a prickling awareness that she was not alone, and immediately heard Jack whisper, "Hist!" just behind her. She jumped.

"Jack, you wretch! I nearly dropped my candle."

"Sorry." But his grin was unrepentant. He placed one finger in front of his lips to signal silence and gently pulled her toward the top of the staircase. The touch of his hand on hers gave Celia the oddest sensation—cold and hot and breathless. For the first time, it occurred to her that there was something a bit scandalous about meeting her cousin alone in the dark.

"Where are we going?"

"Just to the top of the stairs. That's where I asked you to meet me, remember?"

She managed a tiny laugh. "I hope you don't mean to throw me down them."

"I don't, actually. I try never to shock the servants. Only think how unpleasant for them, to find your lifeless corpse at the foot of the stairs on Christmas morning! I daresay Munsil, at least, would give notice."

"Yes, Munsil is uncommonly fond of me."

They had reached the top of the stairs, but Jack kept his hand on her arm, steadying her. The candle wavered a bit in her hand as she looked up into his face. His eyes appeared very dark in the half-light, and he was smiling softly in a way that intensified her sense of danger—but she was not afraid at all that he would harm her. She was afraid of something else, but could not think, somehow, what she was afraid of, or why.

He cocked an eyebrow at her. "You're very trusting, aren't you, to meet a madman all alone at midnight?"

She tried to match his light and teasing tone. "I wouldn't meet just any madman. Only you."

"Celia." He took the candle from her nerveless grasp and pulled her slightly closer. "I have a confession to make," he whispered. He reached behind her to set the candle on the newel post, and for a moment she felt herself pressed against his chest.

For that moment, Celia forgot to breathe. "Wh-what is it?"

His smile was both amused and rueful. "Well, to begin with, I'm the world's worst prankster. At this moment I wish I could pass it off as pure lunacy, but that's the coward's way out. I'm not mad. Really and truly, Celia. I'm not mad."

Compassion flooded her. "Oh, Jack." She longed to touch him again; it was an effort to keep her hands at her side. "Only a madman would think of calling that a *confession.*"

"Ah, but it is! For if I am not mad—and I am not—there is really no excuse for my behavior. None whatsoever. So, you see, I owe you an apology. And I *am* sorry, Celia. Sorrier than I can say."

She studied his face. He seemed very serious. "I'm not sure I understand you," she said uncertainly.

"I'll try to explain. But, as I just told you, there is really no excuse I can offer." Jack sighed. "Bear with me, cousin; this is very difficult for me to own. But, you see, I thought you were some mercenary little toad my mother had dug up to bully me into marrying. She's tried that sort of thing before. And I got wind of your being here—or, at least, I suspected that you were—and I didn't know you—and—well—I'm afraid my friends in London egged me on by making silly bets—" He broke off. Even in the semidarkness, she could tell he had turned beet red. He looked extremely embarrassed. "The long and the short of it is, I arrived here with these plans already set."

"What plans?"

"To behave as repulsively as I could—trying to frighten you off, you know. I don't know why you thought I was *mad*—I was just trying to be an ass."

Her eyes widened in bewilderment. "But Lady Augusta *told* me you were mad."

Now he looked genuinely astonished. "The devil she did! *Augusta?* Why on earth—" Then he seemed to remember, casting his mind back over the scene of his arrival. A slow smile gathered on his face, and he started to chuckle. "Well, I've no one to blame for that but myself, have I? What a comedy of errors!"

"Ssh! You'll wake everyone if you laugh out loud. Jack, honestly—truly—are you not mad? Not at *all*?" Celia searched his face anxiously, trying to make sense of what she saw there. She was suddenly aware that she was clinging to the lapels of his jacket and that his arms had gone round her waist in a sustaining clasp—to keep her from falling down the stairs, she told herself. No need to feel embarrassed. No reason to feel all shaky inside.

"Not a whit," he promised her solemnly. "So, you see, I have behaved abominably. But despite the shocking hoax I have played, I hope you will consider the other consequence of my confession."

Celia blinked dazedly at him. She was still struggling to come to grips with the idea that Jack's outrageous behavior had been deliberate. "Consequence? I don't quite follow you." She was sure she ought to feel angry, but she was too puzzled to be angry.

All hint of laughter had vanished from his expression. He gazed intently at her face, seeming to study her. "If I am not mad, I am *nearly* as great a prize as the Duke of Blenhurst." Celia knew at once that the offhand way he said it was meant to disguise the fact that he was in deadly earnest.

"Prize? What do you mean?"

"Why, a sane marquess is a better catch than a mad one," he said lightly. "And although my title is a notch lower than Blenhurst's at the moment, I think a girl might do worse than to marry me. I daresay you have been disappointed that Elizabeth snagged His Grace—"

His meaning suddenly struck her like a bucket of ice water. Celia gasped, wrenching herself out of his arms with a suddenness that almost made her stumble. "Jack, I ought to slap you!" she spluttered. "How *dare* you insinuate—oh! Are you *joking*? No, I see that you are not! Of all the absurd, ludicrous—"

Relief and delight transfigured Jack's face. "Sorry!" he said quickly. "I don't mean to insult you—"

"Well, you have done!"

"How so? Blenhurst is quite a fine fellow, don't you think?"

"I daresay! He may be a paragon; it is not my concern! Good heavens, as if I would ever be called upon to form an opinion of one so far above me! And as for what you are hinting—what I think you mean— oh! Of all the *preposterous* notions—"

Jack's brows drew together in a momentary frown. "Above you? No such thing. You are yourself the granddaughter of a duke."

"*Great*-granddaughter—and that is neither here nor there! How could you think such a thing of me?" She covered her face with her hands, mortified. "What made you think it?"

Jack's hands came up to cover hers. He gently tugged her hands away and held them in his own. She turned her face away from him, still agitated. "I'll tell you what made me think it," he said quietly. "Jealousy, pure and simple."

That brought her eyes back to his, but her feathers were still ruffled. "Jealousy? You were *jealous* of Blenhurst?" She shook her head at him in baffled amazement. "Jack, you *are* mad!"

His face lit with laughter, but there was something else in his expression, something she had not seen before. His arms tightened round her. "Perhaps I am," he whispered. "At the moment."

He bent his head and Celia instinctively closed her eyes, suddenly dizzy. She felt his lips graze her forehead. It was the lightest possible caress, but it made her shiver. Her face must be very close to his; she could smell his shaving soap. Oh, what was the matter with her? Her anger had vanished, forgotten. She could neither move nor speak. She simply clung to him, confused and breathless, unable to make sense of anything. He pulled her close against him, and her arms went round him as if of their own volition.

"So you aren't prowling about Delacourt in search of a husband?" he murmured.

She choked. "I never *prowled* in my life," she told his waistcoat.

"A poor choice of words," he agreed.

"Pray rid yourself of the notion that I came here for any other reason than to oblige your mother," begged Celia, trying to maintain some semblance of dignity despite the fact that her face was pressed against Jack's coat buttons. "She invited me, and I accepted."

"Ah. She didn't say *why* she invited you?"

A pause ensued. Celia found it necessary to remove her cheek from Jack's chest. She leaned back against his arms and looked into his face, troubled. She saw by his gravity that he knew full well why his mother had invited her.

No wonder he had thought her interested in Blenhurst. He thought she needed to marry. Well, it was a logical solution to her difficulties, wasn't it? He thought she had been eager to assist the duchess in her schemes. Perhaps he even believed the idea had been her own! The thought seemed to drain the color from Celia's cheeks.

"Your mother knew I needed a home, and she offered me one. Do you think it remarkable that I accepted?"

"Not at all." But Jack's expression was guarded.

"She did not mention your name until well after my arrival."

Some of the reserve left Jack's demeanor, and he heaved a tiny sigh of relief. "Thank God. We are going to be frank with one another after all."

"Certainly we are."

"Excellent. You need not tell me the entire tale at once. Let us skip to the point where my crafty parent did, in fact, mention my name. I take it she then revealed her fell designs. What, cousin Celia, was your reaction? Dismay? Or delight?"

Celia felt the color return to her face in a rush. "Well—a little of both, I am afraid." She was blushing again. "Pray recall that, at *that* moment, I did not realize you were mad."

Jack gave a crack of laughter. "True! You had not met me." His grin was warm with affection, and she could not help smiling back. Her smile seemed to ignite something in the back of his eyes, and the lighthearted nature of the moment subtly shifted.

He still had her hands, Celia realized. She tried rather halfheartedly to pull them out of his grasp, but at the end of the maneuver she somehow ended up back in his arms. How did that happen? she wondered dazedly.

He cradled her, pressing his cheek to the top of her head. "You haven't asked me why I wanted you to meet me here," he whispered into her hair.

"To—to see Christmas in," she said faintly.

"Yes, but why here?"

"Because of the evergreen, I thought." Oh, this was so foolish. She ought not to hug him like this. Celia pulled out of his arms and stepped back, hugging herself to keep from committing any further idiocies. Why was he smiling at her that way?

"Look up," he said.

She did. He had hung mistletoe in the arch over

their heads. Her eyes barely had time to register this fact before he took shameless advantage of her up-turned face and kissed her.

It was a swift kiss, and gentle, but Celia jumped back as if it had burned her. She pressed her hands to her cheeks and stared at him, eyes wide with shock. It was just as if the scales had fallen from her eyes and she could suddenly see, with blinding clarity, what a fool she had been. It was too much; she could not sort out her emotions amid the jumble of confusing images whirling in her brain.

She had hidden her attraction to Jack behind the safe and comfortable screen of compassion, believing him to be a pitiable creature—but Jack was *not* mad. In that case, she was forced to face the things he made her feel. Her feelings for cousin Jack, she realized in dismay, were not cousinly at all. And some secret corner of her self had known that all along.

What a crazy thing to do, to creep out and meet him at dead of night! She had been *hoping* he would kiss her—and she hadn't even realized it. Well, her secret wish had come true. And now she was ashamed of herself for wishing it.

"Why did you do that?" she whispered, blushing painfully. "It was not—cousinly."

"What I feel for you is not cousinly," he said softly. His voice was not quite steady. He took her hand in his and held it, as if afraid she would run from him otherwise. "Celia," he said urgently, "I shouldn't pounce on you like this, I know—you have not had time to accustom yourself to the notion, and you barely know me—"

"That's not it," she said, trying to free her hand. He did not let go, however.

"I've behaved like a prime idiot the entire time you *have* known me—"

"That's not it, either! Jack—"

"I don't ask you to give me an answer tonight. I'm sure you cannot. Or, rather, you can't give me the answer I wish to hear. But if you would just give me a chance—"

"Jack, for pity's sake—"

"Oh, Celia, please. Please." He was pulling her into his arms again. She was too weak, too confused, to resist. "Don't say no," he whispered. "Please don't say no." It sounded like a prayer. And then he kissed her again.

And she did not, in fact, say no.

This kiss was completely different from the first one he had given her. It was ardent and aching and filled with passion, and Celia felt herself responding to it with a passion that matched his. She fancied she could hear their hearts pounding amid the thunderous rush of feelings thrilling through her. Her very ears were ringing with it, almost like—bells.

Why, it *was* bells.

She tore her mouth away from his and opened her eyes, disoriented. He was smiling down at her, a smile that was both tender and foolish. "Merry Christmas, Celia," he murmured, touching her cheek softly.

He bent to kiss her again, but she placed her palms against his chest and held him at bay for a moment, too amazed, too surprised even to kiss him—although a second ago she had believed that nothing could have distracted her from that agreeable occupation.

He grinned at her expression. It must have been a sight. The sound of bells filled the air from all directions—the dinner gong was sounding in the dining room, the single bell in the belfry of the palace's chapel was tolling with its hoarse clang, handbells were tinkling from several rooms nearby, and someone was shaking sleigh bells outside the front door. Several someones. The sleigh bells were louder than all the rest.

"What—how—" she stammered.

"It's midnight. It's Christmas. I wanted you to have bells," he said simply.

Celia's heart, full to overflowing, welled in her eyes. Memories of Christmases past, lost to her forever and unbearably sweet, suddenly touched the present—but the present was also unbearably sweet, and the present was hers to keep. The love she had lost and the love she had found caused past and present to blur together, and the future beckoned with the promise of new joy. The terrible weight of fear, fear she had carried for so many months that she had become inured to its constant presence, fell from her like a stone. She would never be homeless again. Her father's voice tolled in her memory, reading from a beloved Book: *Perfect love casteth out fear.* Celia burst into tears.

"Oh, Jack!" She buried her face in his waistcoat. His arms came around her, strong and comforting. "I don't care if you're mad as a hatter. You are the k-kindest and b-best man in the world."

He kissed her again, of course, promptly and thoroughly. By the time he finished, the bells had fallen silent. "I've arranged for a wassail bowl in the servants' quarters," he said, a little unsteadily. "And music. I'm sure we would be welcome, if you'd care to go."

"Fraternizing with the staff? Your mother would not approve," murmured Celia.

And then she remembered. Her eyes flew open wide. "Oh, Jack—I almost forgot." She clung to his lapels again, looking anxiously up at him. "She—she no longer wishes us to marry. The duchess, I mean. She will do what she can to *prevent* it, she said."

"What!" He looked stunned. "Are you sure?"

Celia nodded, ashamed. "I should have told you. She has—she has withdrawn her support. We had the most frightful row. She has ordered me to vacate Delacourt as soon after the New Year as I can."

A slow smile spread across Jack's features. "Perfect," he exclaimed.

"Perfect?"

"Yes! I thought something was not quite right about all this. But you have set my mind at rest. You have removed my last lingering doubt, in fact. If *she* opposes the match, I know we will be happy! Marry me, Celia."

She cocked her head to one side, not sure she had heard him correctly. "But, Jack, your mother—"

"Oh, hang my mother! Will you marry me, or won't you?"

Celia bit her lip. "I *ought* not," she said, distressed. "Your family will not like it. And truly, Jack, when I think of all the grand ladies you might marry—"

"Nonsense. This is England, my dear girl. I am only allowed to marry one lady."

"Yes, but it shouldn't be me!"

"It will be you," he promised. "You, and no other." His arms tightened round her in a way calculated to turn her breathless. "If you tell me you are indifferent to me after all the liberties you have just allowed me to take, you will give me the most shocking opinion of your character."

She blushed and ducked her head to hide her smile. "Well," she admitted, "I am not *indifferent* to you, precisely—"

It was some time before Celia was allowed to finish her sentence, and by the time she was able, she had forgotten what she was going to say.

The Duchess of Arnsford tossed and muttered on her pillow, troubled by feverish dreams. It seemed to her that Delacourt was burning. Everything she had tended and protected for so many years was going up in flames while she stood helplessly by, watching as everything she cared for was destroyed.

She hovered for a moment beneath the surface of awakening, the nightmare still clutching at her as she tried to escape it. Then she fought it off, breaking into consciousness. "Fire," she murmured, her voice slurred with laudanum and sleep. And then, more strongly, "Fire!"

With a gasp, she sat upright and struggled to throw off the heavy bedclothes that were smothering her. But Hubbard was there, looming up out of the darkness like a guardian angel. Hubbard's strong hands gripped her arms.

"Ssh, now, madam," said Hubbard soothingly. "There's nothing amiss. You're dreaming."

The duchess stared dazedly at Hubbard's features, all but invisible in the near dark. The leaping, dancing flames of her nightmare receded, resolving themselves into the dying embers of the fire glowing faintly in the grate. It was not Delacourt that burned, but only the familiar torment gnawing at her vitals. She was awake. But the alarm she had heard in her dream still sounded.

"No fire," she said numbly. "There is no fire."

"No, madam."

"What is that sound?"

"Bells, madam."

"Why—why are bells ringing if there is no fire?"

"It's Christmas. Do go back to sleep, dear ma'am. There is nothing to worry you." Hubbard reached behind to plump up her pillows.

"Christmas," repeated the duchess incredulously. Pain stabbed her, hard, jerking her out of the mists of her drugged dream. Anger came with the pain as she realized she had been frightened out of her sleep by some idiot ringing bells in the middle of the night. "We have never rung bells at Delacourt for Christmas. Who gave such an order? Why was I not informed?"

Even as she spoke, the bells died away as if sensing

her displeasure. Hubbard did not immediately answer, however, but tossed and punched the pillows with swift efficiency, seemingly focused on the task at hand.

"I ought to have told you," Hubbard admitted at last, settling the pillows behind the duchess. "But I did hope you would sleep through it. I never dreamed a few bells would kick up such a racket! Fit to wake the dead, it was. There, now. Do lie down again, ma'am, and we'll see if we can make you comfortable."

But the duchess still sat upright, straining her eyes in the dimness to make out Hubbard's expression. She had the oddest notion that Hubbard was keeping something from her. She smiled thinly. "What! Am I no longer mistress of Delacourt? Who dared to give such an order without consulting me?"

" 'Twas Lord Lynden," said Hubbard gruffly. "So don't be thinking you are not mistress here! 'Twas only one of Lord Lynden's notions."

Annoyance and relief flashed through the duchess. "John," she said crossly. "I might have guessed as much." She settled back against the pillows, shivering as the pain settled back with her.

Hubbard's sharp eyes missed nothing. "Shall I poke up the fire, then?"

She was not cold, but nodded, not trusting her voice until she mastered the pain once more. It was always worse at night. She would lie awake, now, until dawn. It mattered little; sleep brought no refreshment these days.

Her eyes followed Hubbard as she crossed to the grate and wielded the poker. The light grew, outlining Hubbard's homely features, plain night rail and cap, and the thick gray braid that hung down her back. There was something about her folded lips and tense shoulders that sent a frisson of suspicion through the duchess.

"I wonder what possessed John to order bells for

Christmas," Her Grace mused aloud. She watched Hubbard as she spoke. "And without a word to me! It seems odd. Did he think I would forbid it?"

"You weren't well," said Hubbard shortly. "I fancy the notion seized him just this evening."

"Ah." The duchess's hands clenched on the edge of her counterpane. "To celebrate his sister's betrothal, no doubt. A pretty thought."

She had been unable to keep the bitterness from her voice, and Hubbard looked up, her brows knitting. She straightened, then, and stood with her hands clasped loosely before her. "No, Your Grace. Or, at least, that wasn't all of it." Her words sounded rough with suppressed emotion.

Fear licked through the duchess, but she kept her voice pleasant and steady. "What is the rest of it, Hubbard? I think you had better tell me."

Hubbard walked to the bed and sat on the edge of it, facing the duchess. The very fact that she would take such a liberty told Her Grace how strongly moved her henchwoman was. Hubbard stared intently at her, her expression unreadable. "I'll tell you, if you're wishful to know. But I'm afraid you won't like it."

"Tell me," said Her Grace.

"Very well; I will. I'd rather you hear it from me, when all's said and done." Hubbard sighed and looked away. "Lord Lynden fancies Miss Delacourt. Everyone on the staff has seen it and remarked on it; if you hadn't been keeping to your rooms lately, you'd have seen it, too. I was thinking you'd be pleased, until I heard what you had to say about her. Now, I know you won't be. But when his lordship asked that everyone on the staff—everyone who cared to, that is—find a bell and ring it at midnight, as close to the grand staircase as might be, but out of sight—and said it was a surprise for Miss Delacourt, so on no account to let her know about it—why, what were we to think? In order to keep the secret, we had to know he was meeting Miss Delacourt on the grand staircase at midnight." Hubbard stole an uneasy glance at the duchess, who was sitting as motionless as if she had been turned to stone. "And one of the housemaids saw Lord Lynden tiptoe out this evening and hang mistletoe over it. With his own hands."

A tiny sound escaped the duchess. Hubbard's face went almost fierce with compassion. "It's not difficult to add two and two, is it, dear ma'am? Especially since he ordered up a Christmas party, with music and dancing, to begin directly after, in the servants' hall."

Gladys Delacourt, now convinced she was the last true Duchess of Arnsford, buried her face in her hands. So this was what a Pyrrhic victory felt like. She had schemed and worked and striven to bring all this about, and her accomplishments had turned to ashes even as she triumphed. Elizabeth would marry Blenhurst, a match she had tried for years to promote. And John would marry Celia—a project to which she had turned her hand only lately but that was, nevertheless, the most important project of all. Dead Sea fruit, all of it. A complete disaster.

A sudden hitching sensation seized her diaphragm. It had been so long since she had either laughed or sobbed, she was not sure which of the two was overcoming her. A little of both, she supposed. It was shameful to lose control in this way, but she could no more suppress it than she could hold back the tide. She began to utter a queer little barking sound behind her hands, over and over.

She felt Hubbard's weight leave the bed. "Madam!" cried Hubbard, sounding frightened. "Your Grace! Oh, lud, I oughtn't to have told you. It could have waited for morning. Dear ma'am, how can I help you? Oh, 'tis cruel, to see you so distressed! What afflicts you? Is it the old pain, or a new one?"

The duchess shook her head weakly. Agony ripped through her, and still she laughed. Or sobbed. She emerged from behind her hands, however, and managed to smile at poor Hubbard.

"A new one, dear Gertrude," she said. "I believe they call it 'irony.' "

In the hush that followed midnight, Celia sat beside Jack on the top step of the curving staircase, surrounded by fragrant greenery. Music sounded faintly from the servants' hall. The tail of a gay red bow trailed across her skirt. This surely was going to be the best Christmas of her life.

She leaned her head against Jack's shoulder and played with the ribbon absently, a foolish little smile wavering across her face. "I don't deserve to be so happy."

"Yes, you do."

"No one does. I am happier right now than any mortal deserves to be."

"I mean to keep you this happy if I can. Always."

"I couldn't bear it. I should expire from joy." She nuzzled his arm. "Jack?"

"Yes, love."

"What shall we do, exactly?"

"I shall send a notice to the London papers. And send for Hadley, you'll be glad to know. He'll arrive with the rest of my wardrobe. You won't recognize me once he's done with me."

"Oh, dear. I do hope you are wrong about that." She chuckled. "But—you'll stay here, then? At Delacourt?"

His arm tightened around her. "Yes. I'll not leave you to fight the dragons alone. We shall have the banns read right here in the village, starting the day after tomorrow."

She relaxed dreamily against him. "Oh, how lovely."

"You're still in mourning, so we can't have a large wedding. No sense in waiting for the Season and dragging you off to London for a round of betrothal parties and all that. Unless you'd prefer it—?"

"No," she said quickly. "No. There will be time for all that later."

"Yes. Marry me soon, Celia." He whispered it close to her ear, and his warm breath made her shiver happily. "Let's not give anyone time to say us nay."

A tiny pang of guilt creased her forehead. "We cannot escape that, I fear. Your mother will be livid."

"I daresay it will do her good."

"I hope so." Celia smiled, but there was still a hint of worry in her eyes. "She says I do not have the makings of a duchess in me. She believes I am completely hopeless. That however earnestly I might try, I will forever fall short of the standards she has set."

Celia pulled back against Jack's encircling arm, looking anxiously up at him. "She's right, you know. I am pert and opinionated and familiar with the servants and—and I have no accomplishments—I don't play the pianoforte, and I don't play the harp, and I can't speak French—and, oh, Jack, I'm afraid I will never be anything but what I am!"

Jack grinned the lopsided grin she loved. "Thank God," he said fervently.

Read on for excerpts from some other delightful Christmas Regency romances from Signet.

Available at www.penguin.com or wherever books are sold.

FATHER CHRISTMAS

Barbara Metzger

The Duke of Ware needed an heir. Like a school-yard taunt, the gruesome refrain floated in his mind, bobbing to the surface on a current of brandy. Usually a temperate man, His Grace was just a shade on the go. It was going to take more than a shade to get him to go to Almack's.

"Hell and blast!" Leland Warrington, fifth and at this point possibly last Duke of Ware, consulted his watch again. Ten o'clock, and everyone knew Almack's patronesses barred its doors at eleven. Not even London's premiere *parti,* wealth, title, and looks notwithstanding, could gain admittance after the witching hour. "Blasted witches," Ware cursed once more, slamming his glass down on the table that stood so conveniently near his so-comfortable leather arm-chair at White's. "Damnation."

His companion snapped up straighter in his facing seat. "What's that? The wine gone off?" The Honorable Crosby Fanshaw sipped cautiously at his own drink. "Seems fine to me." He called for another bottle.

Fondly known as Crow for his anything-but-somber style of dress, the baronet was a studied contrast to his longtime friend. The duke was the one wearing the stark black and white of Weston's finest evening wear, spread over broad shoulders and well-muscled thighs, while Crow Fanshaw's spindly frame was draped in magenta pantaloons, saffron waistcoat, lime green wasp-waisted coat. The duke looked away. Fanshaw would never get into Almack's in that outfit. Then again, Fanshaw didn't need to get into Almack's.

"No, it's not the wine, Crow. It's a wife. I need one."

The baronet slipped one manicured finger under his elaborate neckcloth to loosen the noose conjured up by the very thought of matrimony. He shuddered. "Devilish things, wives."

"I'll drink to that," Ware said, and did. "But I need one nevertheless if I'm to beget the next duke."

"Ah." Crow nodded sagely, careful not to disturb his pomaded curls. "Noblesse oblige and all that. The sacred duty of the peerage: to beget more little aristocratic blue bloods to carry on the name. I thank heaven m'brother holds the title. Let Virgil worry about the succession and estates."

"With you as heir, he'd need to." Crow Fanshaw wouldn't know a mangel-wurzel from manure, and they both knew it.

The baronet didn't take offense. "What, ruin m'boots in dirt? M'valet would give notice, then where would I be? 'Sides, Virgil's managing to fill his nursery nicely, two boys and a girl. Then there are m'sister's parcel of brats if he needs extras. I'm safe." He raised his glass in a toast. "Condolences, old friend."

Ware frowned, lowering thick dark brows over his hazel eyes. Easy for Crow to laugh, his very soul wasn't engraved with the Ware family motto: *Semper servimus.* We serve forever. Forever, dash it, the duke unnecessarily reminded himself. His heritage, everything he was born and bred to be and to believe, demanded an heir. Posterity demanded it, all those acres and people dependent upon him demanded it, Aunt Eudora demanded it! God, King, and Country, that's what the Wares served, she insisted. Well, Leland made his donations to the church, he took his tedious seat in Parliament, and he served as a diplomat when the Foreign Office needed him. That was not enough. The Bible said be fruitful and multiply, quoted his childless aunt. The King, bless his mad soul, needed more loyal peers to advise and direct his outrageous progeny. And the entire country, according to Eudora Warrington, would go to rack and ruin without a bunch of little Warringtons trained to manage Ware's vast estates and investments. At the very least, her annuity might be in danger.

Leland checked his watch again. Ten-ten. He felt as if he were going to the tooth-drawer, dreading the moment yet wishing it were over. "What time do you have, Crow?"

Crosby fumbled at the various chains crisscrossing his narrow chest. "I say, you must have an important appointment, the way you keep eyeing your timepiece. Which is it, that new red-haired dancer at the opera or the dashing widow you had up in your phaeton yesterday?" While the duke sat glaring, Fanshaw pulled out his quizzing glass, then a seal with his family crest before finally retrieving his watch fob. "Fifteen minutes past the hour."

Ware groaned. "Almack's" was all he could manage to say. It was enough.

Fanshaw dropped his watch and grabbed up the looking glass by its gem-studded handle, tangling ribbons and chains as he surveyed his friend for signs of dementia. "I thought you said Almack's."

"I did. I told you, I need an heir."

"But Almack's, Lee? Gads, you must be dicked in the nob. Castaway, that's it." He pushed the bottle out of the duke's reach.

"Not nearly enough," His Grace replied, pulling the decanter back and refilling his glass. "I promised Aunt Eudora I'd look over the latest crop of dewy-eyed debs."

Crosby downed a glass in commiseration. "I understand about the heir and all, but there must be an easier way, by Jupiter. I mean, m'brother's girl is making her come-out this year. She's got spots. And her friends giggle. Think on it, man, they are, what? Seventeen? Eighteen? And you're thirty-one!"

"Thirty-two," His Grace growled, "as my aunt keeps reminding me."

"Even worse. What in the world do you have in common with one of those empty-headed infants?"

"What do I have in common with that redhead from the opera? She's only eighteen, and the only problem you have with that is she's in my bed, not yours."

"But she's a ladybird! You don't have to talk to them, not like a wife!"

The duke stood as if to go. "Trust me, I don't intend to have anything more to do with this female I'll marry than it takes to get me a son."

"If a son is all you want, why don't you just adopt one? Be easier in the long run, more comfortable, too. M'sister's got a surplus. I'm sure she'd be glad to get rid of one or two, the way she's always trying to pawn them off on m'mother so she can go to some house party or other."

The duke ignored his friend's suggestion that the next Duke of Ware be anything less than a Warrington, but he did sit down. "That's another thing: No son of mine is going to be raised up by nannies and tutors and underpaid schoolmasters."

"Why not? That's the way we were brought up, and we didn't turn out half bad, did we?"

Leland picked a bit of imaginary fluff off his superfine sleeve. Not half bad? Not half good, either, he reflected. Crow was an amiable fribble, while he himself was a libertine, a pleasure-seeker, an ornament of society. Oh, he was a conscientious landowner, for a mostly absentee landlord, and he did manage to appear at the House for important votes. Otherwise his

own entertainment—women, gaming, sporting—was
his primary goal. There was nothing of value in his
life. He intended to do better by his son. "I mean
to be a good father to the boy, a guide, a teacher,
a friend."

"A Bedlamite, that's what. Try being a friend to
some runny-nosed brat with scraped knees and a
pocketful of worms." Crosby shivered. "I know just
the ticket to cure you of such bubble-brained notions:
Why don't you come down to Fanshaw Hall with me
for the holidays? Virgil'd be happy to have you for
the cards and hunting, and m'sister-in-law would be
in alt to have such a nonpareil as houseguest. That
niece who's being fired off this season will be there,
so you can see how hopeless young chits are, all airs
and affectations one minute, tears and tantrums the
next. Why, if you can get Rosalie to talk of anything
but gewgaws and gossip, I'll eat my hat. Best of all,
m'sister will be at the Hall with her nursery brood.
No, best of all is if the entire horde gets the mumps
and stays home. But, 'struth, you'd change your tune
about this fatherhood gammon if you just spent a day
with the little savages."

Ware smiled. "I don't mean to insult your family,
but your sister's ill-behaved brats only prove my point
that this whole child-rearing thing could be improved
upon with a little careful study."

"Trust me, Lee, infants ain't like those new farming
machines you can read up on. Come down and see.
At least I can promise you a good wine cellar at the
Hall."

The duke shook his head. "Thank you, Crow, but
I have to refuse. You see, I really am tired of spending
the holidays with other people's families."

"What I see is you've been bitten bad by this new
bug of yours. Carrying on the line. Littering the coun-
tryside with butterstamps. Next thing you know, you'll

be pushing a pram instead of racing a phaeton. I'll miss you, Lee." He flicked a lacy handkerchief from his sleeve and dabbed at his eyes while the duke grinned at the performance. Fanshaw's next words changed that grin into so fierce a scowl that a lesser man, or a less loyal friend, would have been tempted to bolt: "Don't mean to be indelicate, but you know getting leg-shackled isn't any guarantee of getting heirs."

"Of course I know that, blast it! I ought to, I've already been married." The duke finished his drink. "Twice." He tossed back another glassful to emphasize the point. "And all for nothing."

Fanshaw wasn't one to let a friend drink alone, even if his words were getting slurred and his thoughts muddled. He refilled his own glass. Twice. "Not for nothing. Got a handsome dowry both times."

"Which I didn't need," His Grace muttered into his drink.

"And got the matchmaking mamas off your back until you learned to depress their ambitions with one of your famous setdowns."

"Which if I'd learned earlier, I wouldn't be in this hobble today."

The duke's first marriage had been a love match: He was in love with the season's reigning Toast, Carissa was in love with his wealth and title. Her mother made sure he never saw past the Diamond's beauty to the cold, rock-hard shrew beneath who didn't want to be his wife, she wanted to be a duchess. There wasn't one extravagance she didn't indulge, not one risqué pleasure she didn't gratify, not one mad romp she didn't join. Until she broke her beautiful neck in a curricle race.

Ware's second marriage was one of convenience, except that it wasn't. He carefully selected a quiet, retiring sort of girl whose pale loveliness was as different from Carissa's flamboyance as night from day. *Her* noble parents had managed to conceal, while they were dickering over the settlements, that Lady Floris was a sickly child, that her waiflike appeal had more to do with a weak constitution than any gentle beauty. Floris was content to stay in the shadows after their wedding, until she became a shadow. Then she faded away altogether. Ware was twice a widower, never a father. To his knowledge, he'd never even sired a bastard on one of his mistresses, but he didn't want to think about the implications of that.

"What time do you have?"

Crosby peered owl-eyed at his watch, blinked, then turned it right side up. "Ten-thirty. Time for another drink." He raised his glass, spilling only a drop on the froth of lace at his shirt-sleeve. "To your bride."

Leland couldn't do it. The wine would turn to vinegar on his tongue. Instead, he proposed a toast of his own. "To my cousin Tony, the bastard to blame for this whole deuced coil."

Crosby drank, but reflected, "If he was a bastard, then it wouldn't have mattered if the nodcock went and got himself killed. He couldn't have been your heir anyway."

His Grace waved that aside with one elegant if unsteady hand. "Tony was a true Warrington all right, my father's only brother's only son. My heir. So *he* got to go fight against Boney when the War Office turned me down."

"Protective of their dukes, those chaps."

"And *he* got to be a hero, the lucky clunch."

"Uh, not to be overparticular, but live heroes are lucky, dead ones ain't."

Leland went on as though his friend hadn't spoken: "And he was a fertile hero to boot. Old Tony didn't have to worry about shuffling off this mortal coil without a trace. He left twins, twin boys, no less, the bounder, and he didn't even have a title to bequeath them or an acre of land!"

"Twin boys, you say? Tony's get? There's your answer, Lee, not some flibbertigibbet young miss. Go gather the sprigs and have the raising of 'em your way if that's what you want to do. With any luck they'll be out of nappies and you can send 'em off to school as soon as you get tired of 'em. Should take about a month, I'd guess."

Ware frowned. "I can't go snabble my cousin's sons, Crow. Tony's widow just brought them back to her parents' house from the Peninsula."

Fanshaw thought on it a minute, chewing his lower lip. "Then marry that chit, I say. You get your heirs with Warrington blood, your brats to try to make into proper English gentlemen, and a proven breeder into the bargain. 'Sides, she can't be an antidote; Tony Warrington had taste."

The duke merely looked down his slightly aquiline nose and stood up to leave. "She's a local vicar's daughter."

"Good enough to be Mrs. Major Warrington, eh, but not the Duchess of Ware?" The baronet nodded, not noticing that his starched shirtpoints disarranged his artful curls. "Then you'd best toddle off to King Street, where the *ton* displays its merchandise. Unless . . ."

Ware turned back like a drowning man hearing the splash of a tossed rope. "Unless . . . ?"

"Unless you ask the widow for just one of the bantlings. She might just go for it. I mean, how many men are going to take on a wife with *two* tokens of her dead husband's devotion to support? There's not much space in any vicarage I know of, and you said yourself Tony didn't leave much behind for them to live on. 'Sides, you can appeal to her sense of fairness. She has two sons and you have none."

Leland removed the bottle and glass from his friend's vicinity on his way out of the room. "You have definitely had too much to drink, my tulip. Your wits have gone begging for dry land."

And the Duke of Ware still needed an heir.

Heaving breasts, fluttering eyelashes, gushing simpers, blushing whimpers—and those were the hopeful mamas. The daughters were worse. Aunt Eudora could ice-skate in Hades before her nephew returned to Almack's.

Ware had thought he'd observe the crop of debutantes from a discreet, unobtrusive distance. Sally Jersey thought differently. With pointed fingernails fastened to his wrist like the talons of a raptor, she dragged her quarry from brazen belle to arrogant heiress to wilting wallflower. At the end of each painful, endless dance, when he had, perforce, to return his partner to her chaperone, there was *la* Jersey waiting in prey with the next willing sacrificial virgin.

The Duke of Ware needed some air.

He told the porter at the door he was going to blow a cloud, but he didn't care if the fellow let him back in or not. Leland didn't smoke. He never had, but he thought he might take it up now. Perhaps the foul odor, yellowed fingers, and stained teeth could discourage some of these harpies, but he doubted it.

Despite the damp chill in the air, the duke was not alone on the outer steps of the marriage mart. At first all he could see in the gloomy night was the glow from a sulphurous cigar. Then another, younger gentleman stepped out of the fog.

"Is that you, Ware? Here at Almack's? I cannot believe it," exclaimed Nigel, the scion of the House of Ellerby which, according to rumors, was more than a tad dilapidated. Hence the young baron's appearance at Almack's, Leland concluded. "Dash it, I wish

I'd been in on the bet." Which propensity to gamble likely accounted for the Ellerbys' crumbling coffers.

"Bet? What bet?"

"The one that got you to Almack's, Duke. By Zeus, it must have been a famous wager! Who challenged you? How long must you stay before you can collect? How much—"

"There was no wager," Ware quietly inserted into the youth's enthusiastic litany.

The cigar dropped from Ellerby's fingers. His mouth fell open. "No wager? You mean . . . ?"

"I came on my own. As a favor to my aunt, if you must know."

Ellerby added two plus two and, to the duke's surprise, came up with the correct, dismaying answer. "B'gad, wait till the sharks smell fresh blood in the water." He jerked his head, weak chin and all, toward the stately portals behind them.

Leland grimaced. "Too late, they've already got the scent."

"Lud, there will be females swooning in your arms and chits falling off horses on your doorstep. I'd get out of town if I were you. Then again, word gets out you're in the market for a new bride, you won't be safe anywhere. With all those holiday house parties coming up, you'll be showered with invitations."

The duke could only agree. That was the way of the world.

"Please, Your Grace," Ellerby whined, "don't accept Lady Carstaire's invite. I'll be seated below the salt if you accept."

No slowtop either, Leland nodded toward the closed doors. "Tell me which one is Miss Carstaire, so I can sidestep the introduction."

"She's the one in puce tulle with mouse brown sausage curls and a squint." At Ware's look of disbelief, the lordling added, "And ten thousand pounds a year."

"I think I can manage not to succumb to the lady's charms," Ware commented dryly, then had to listen to the coxcomb's gratitude.

"And I'll give you fair warning, Duke, if you do accept for any of those house parties, lock your door and never go anywhere alone. The misses and their mamas will be quicker to yell 'compromise' than you can say 'Jack Rabbit.' "

Leland gravely thanked Lord Ellerby for the advice, hoping the baron wasn't such an expert on compromising situations from trying to nab a rich wife the cad's way. Fortune-hunting was bad enough. He wished him good luck with Miss Carstaire, but declined Ellerby's suggestion that they return inside together. His Grace had had enough. And no, he assured the baron, he was not going to accept any of the holiday invitations. The Duke of Ware was going to spend Christmas right where he belonged, at Ware Hold in Warefield, Warwickshire, with his own family: one elderly aunt, two infant cousins.

Before going to bed that night, Leland had another brandy to ease the headache he already had. He sat down to write his agent in Warefield to notify the household of his plans, then he started to write to Tony's widow, inviting her to the castle. Before he got too far past the salutation, however, Crow Fanshaw's final, foxed suggestion kept echoing in his mind: The Duke of Ware should get a fair share.

Sugarplum Surprises

Elisabeth Fairchild

Bath, 1819

Fanny Fowler, an accredited beauty, one of Bath's *bon ton*, slated to be the most feted bride of the Christmas Season, was not in her best looks when she burst through the door of Madame Nicolette's millinery shop, on a very wet December afternoon right before closing. The violent jingle of the bell drew the attention of everyone present. And yet, so red and puffy were Fanny's eyes, so mottled her fair complexion, so rain-soaked her golden tresses, she was almost unrecognizable.

"Madame Nicolette!" she gasped, noble chin wobbling, sylvan voice uneven. Bloodshot blue eyes streamed tears that sparkled upon swollen cheeks almost as much as the raindrops that trickled from her guinea gold hair. "It is all over. Finished."

Madame Nicolette's elaborate lace-edged mobcap tipped at an angle, along with Madame's head. The heavily rouged spots on her heavily powdered cheeks added unusual emphasis to the puzzled purse of her mouth. She spoke in hasty French to her assistant, Marie, shooing her, and the only customer in the shop, into the dressing room.

Then, clasping the trembling hand of this, her best customer, she led her to a quiet corner, near the plate glass window that overlooked the busy, weather-drenched corner of Milsom and Green Streets.

"Fini, cheri?" she asked gently, taking in the looming impression of the Fowler coach waiting without, the horses sleek with rain, their harness decked with jingling bells to celebrate the season. Gay Christmas ribbon tied to the coach lamps danced in the wind.

"The wedding is canceled!" Fanny wailed, no attempt made to lower her voice. "He has jilted me. Says that nothing could induce him to marry me now. Ever."

The distraught young woman fell upon the matronly shoulder, weeping copiously. Madame Nicolette, green eyes widening in alarm, patted the girl's back. *"Vraiment!* The cad. *Abominable* behavior. Why should he do this?"

"Because I told the truth when I could have lied." Fanny gazed past Madame with a sudden look of fury. "I should have lied. Might so easily have lied. Any other female would have lied."

She burst into tears again, and wept without interruption, face buried in the handkerchief in her hands, shoulders heaving.

Madame offered up her own handkerchief, for Fanny's was completely sodden. "What of the *trousseau*?" Madame asked, for of course this was the matter that concerned her most.

Fanny wept the harder, which brought a look of concern to Madame's eyes, far greater than that generated by all previous tears.

"Papa . . ." Fanny choked out. "Papa is in an awful temper. He refuses to p-p-pay." This last bit came out in a most dreadful wail, and while Madame continued to croon comfortingly and pat the young woman's back, her lips thinned, and her brows settled in a grim line.

"And your *fiancé*? Surely he will *defray* expenses."

"Perhaps." Fanny made every effort to collect herself. "I do not know," she said with a sniff. "All I know is that he intends to leave Bath tomorrow morning. Now, I must go. Papa waits."

"Allow me to escort you to the coach." Madame solicitously followed her to the door.

"But it is raining." Fanny wielded both sodden handkerchiefs in limp protest. "And Papa is in such a mood."

Madame insisted, and so the two women ran together to the coach, under cover of Madame's large black umbrella, and Madame greeted Lord Fowler, his wife, and younger daughter standing beneath her dripping shield just outside the fulsome gutter. "An infamous turn of events," she called to them.

"Blasted nuisance," my lord shouted from the coach. "Frippery female has gone and lost herself a duke, do you hear!"

"Fourth Duke of Chandrose, and Fourth Marquess of Carnevon." Lady Fowler's voice could barely be heard above the pelter of the rain that soaked Madame's hem, but as the door was swung wider to allow Fanny entrance, her voice came clearer. "A fortune slips through her fingers."

"Silly chit," her father shouted as Fanny climbed in, cringing. "I credited you with far too much sense."

Fanny's sister kept her head bowed, her eyes darting in a frightened manner from parent to parent.

Fanny resorted to her handkerchief as she plopped down into her seat.

"Do you know what she has done to alienate him?" Lord Fowler demanded of Madame Nicolette as if she should know, as if he were the only one in Bath who was not privy to his daughter's thinking.

Madame shook her head, and gave a very French shrug as she leaned into the doorway of the coach. "My dear *monsieur, madam,* I sympathize most completely in this trying *moment,* and while I understand you have no wish to pay for the *trousseau* that has

taken six months work to assemble, the *trousseau* Miss
Fanny will not be wearing, I wonder, will you be so
good—"

Lord Fowler sat forward abruptly, chest thrust forth,
shaking his walking stick at her with ferocity, the sway
of his jowls echoing the movement. "Not a penny will
I spend on this stupid girl. Not one penny, do you
hear? More than a hundred thousand pounds a year
she might have had with His Grace. Not a farthing's
worth shall she have now." Like a Christmas turkey
he looked, his face gone very red, his eyes bulging,
his extra set of chins wobbling.

"I comprehend your ire, my lord," Madame per-
sisted calmly. "But surely you intend to offer some
compensation for my efforts, my material?"

His lordship's face took on a plum pudding hue.
"Not a single grote. Do you understand? Not one.
Make the duke pay." He thumped the silver head of
his cane against the ceiling, the whole coach shaking.
"Jilting my daughter." Thump. "Disgracing the family
name." Thump. "Two weeks before the wedding,
mind you." Thump-thump. "Bloody cheek."

With that, he thumped his cane so briskly it broke
clean through the leather top so that rain leaked in
upon his head, and in a strangled voice, the veins at
his temples bulging, he ordered his coachman, "Drive
on, damn you. Drive on. Can you not hear me
thumping down here?"

The horses leapt into motion with an inappropri-
ately cheerful jingle, and Madame Nicolette Fieullet
leapt back from the wheels.

"Fiddlesticks," she muttered in very English annoyance as the coach churned up dirty water from the
gutter in a hem-drenching wave. She took shelter in
the shop's doorway to shake the rain from her
umbrella.

The wreath on the door seemed suddenly too merry,

the jingle of the door's bell a mockery. *Christmas.*
Dear Lord. Christmas meant balls and assemblies, and
dresses ordered at the last minute, and she must have
fabric and lace and trim at the ready. But how was
she to pay for Christmas supplies now that so much
of her capital was tied up in Fanny's *trousseau*?

"*Madame!* You are soaked," her assistant, Marie,
cried out as she entered.

"*Oui. Je suis tout trempe.*" Madame kept her skirt
high, that she might not drip, her voice low, that their
customer might not hear. "You will give Mrs. Bower
my excuses while I change?"

Marie followed her, a worried look in her deep
brown eyes. "Is it true, Madame? He refuses to pay?"

"*Oui.*"

"*Mon dieu!* The material arrives tomorrow. However will we pay?"

"I shall think of something. Do not torment yourself." Madame sounded confident. She looked completely self-assured, until she locked herself in the
back room, pressed her back to the door, and sinking
to the floor, wept piteously at the sight of Fanny's
finished dresses.

More than a dozen beautiful garments had been
made up to Miss Fowler's specific measurements, in
peacock colors to flatter Fanny's sky blue eyes and
guinea gold hair. Thousands of careful stitches, hundreds of careful cuts, and darts. How many times had
she pricked her fingers in the making of them? How
many times had she ripped seams that they might fit
Fanny's form more perfectly? It was heartbreaking
just to look at them. Tears burned in Madame's eyes.
Her breath caught in her throat.

The masterpieces were, of course, the wedding
dress, and two ball gowns, one in the colors of Christmas, an evergreen satin bodice, vandyke trimmed in
gold satin cord, Spanish slashed sleeves that had taken

several days to sew, a deeply gored skirt of deeper green velvet, with a magnificent border of gold quilling, and twisted rolls of satin cord that had taken weeks' worth of stitching.

"Fanny must have something entirely unique," her mother had insisted, "something worthy of a duchess."

The results were exquisite. Madame's best work yet. They were the sort of dresses every young woman dreamed of. Head-turning dresses, and yet in the best of taste, the perfect foil for youth and beauty. They were the sort of dresses she had once worn herself in her younger days. Gowns to catch a man's eye without raising a mother's eyebrows. Gowns to lift a young woman's spirits and self-esteem as she donned them. She had hoped these dresses would be the making of her name, of her reputation.

Now they were worthless, completely worthless. Indeed, a terrible drain upon her purse.

Defeat weighed heavy upon Madame's shoulders. Tears burned in her eyes. Sobs pressed hard against her chest, her gut, the back of her throat. What to do? Panic rose, intensifying her feelings of anger and regret.

She had believed the future secure, the holiday fruitful, her worries behind her at last.

But no! Life surprised her most mean-spiritedly, at Christmastime, always at Christmas time.

The tears would not remain confined to her eyes. It had been long since she had allowed them to fall. They broke forth now in an unstoppable deluge.

She clutched her hand over her mouth, stifling her sobs, choking on them. But they would not be stopped. Disappointment surged from the innermost depths of her in a knee-weakening wave. She was a child again, unable to contain her emotions. She thought of her mother, lying pale and wan in her bed, the familiar swell of her stomach deflated, the strength of her voice almost gone.

"My dear Jane," mother had whispered, cupping the crown of Jane's head, stroking the silk of her hair. She could still feel the weight of that hand, the heat. "I had thought to bring you a baby brother for Chr-Christmas." Her mother's voice had caught, trembled. She had given Jane's hand a weak squeeze, her hand hot, so very hot. "But life never unfolds as one expects, pet."

Jane had been frightened by her mother's tone, by the strangled noises of distress her father made from the doorway. She had not understood it was the last time she would have to speak to Mama. She had patted the feverish hand, then held it to her cheek and said, "Do not cry, Mother. If you have lost my little brother, Papa will buy you another for Christmas. Won't you, Papa?"

Her father had made choking noises and stumbled from the room.

"Jane!" Miss Godwin, her governess, had sounded cross as she snatched her up from the side of the bed.

But Jane had clung to her mother's fingers, the strength of her grasp lifting her mother's arm from the bed. Something was wrong, terribly wrong.

Her mother's clasp was as desperate as hers. "Cherish what is, my pet, not what you imagined," she said, the words urgent, the look in her eyes unforgettable. And as Miss Godwin had gently pried their hands apart, she had said with an even greater urgency, "Promise me, Jane, my love. Promise me you will not allow regret to swallow you whole."

Jane had nodded, not knowing what she promised, looking back over Miss Godwin's shoulder with a five-year-old's conviction, no comprehension of the words. Promising was easy. Honoring that promise was not.

"Look for the silver surprises, my love, in the plum pudding at Christmas, and know that I put them there for you." Her mother's words were almost drowned out by the muffled desperation of her father's cries.

He sat, bent over in the dressing room, a balled hand-kerchief stuffed in his mouth. His shoulders had shaken in a manner she had never before witnessed.

"Is Papa all right?" she had asked Miss Godwin, all concern.

Miss Godwin had made comforting noises and carried little Jane off to bed, her own cheeks wet with silent tears, her shoulders shaking like Papa's, as hard as Jane Nichol's shook now as she rocked back and forth, her fist pressed to her mouth.

The wet hem of her skirt had soaked her petticoats. Her legs were cold.

"Oh, Mother," she whispered as she stood to wring out the wet. "What silver surprise am I missing? 'Tis all soggy pudding, this."

The rack of clothes mocked her silently. They were dry, and perfect, a reminder of her past in so many ways, and yet she must remember they promised to throw her carefully constructed present into chaos.

Jane turned to the old mirror that had been tucked into the corner behind the door. Clouded at the edges, it had been removed from the dressing room, replaced by a newer, less timeworn cheval. The buxom, brightly dressed woman that stared back was still a stranger to her, not the picture of herself she carried in her head. Her frizzled brown wig was even more frizzled from exposure to the rain. Her oval spectacles were speckled with raindrops. The careful veneer of face powder and rouge was much besmeared by her tears.

Jane had to laugh, a tragic, pitiful gust of a laugh, as she took off the horn-rimmed spectacles that so completely dominated her face, and wiped at the streaked powder with the damp sleeve of her gown, exposing smooth, youthful flesh, complexion quite at odds with the sad horsehair wig and matronly mobcap.

A sight—a proper sight she was. She could not face customers looking like this. She needed a fresh powdering—dry clothes.

The wedding dress caught her eye, the ball gowns and walking dresses, morning and evening gowns, the capes, and pelisses, and negligees. Dry clothes. Beautiful dry clothes, so beautiful any young lady would be tempted to wear them.

The silver surprise of it made her smile as laughter filled her chest and shook the weight from her shoulders.

She rose to examine her choices with a devil-may-care tilt to her head, a daring idea taking hold—a silver surprise of an idea. She laughed again, and fingered the fall of satin flowers at the sleeve of the second ball gown.

A light rap came at the door, and Marie called out, "Madame, Mrs. Bower has gone. Shall I lock up?"

"*S'il vous plait.* Do not wait for me, Marie. I have a bit of work to do." Jane fell into the French accent she affected without blinking, without thinking. It came so naturally now, the pretense.

Time to stop pretending, if only for an evening. What a relief it would be. What a joy.

She needed joy. It was a Season of joy, was it not?

She peeled off the dreadful wig and undid the ties on her dress. The false bosom fell away, the padded hips. She felt lighter, smaller—herself again. A different silhouette looked back at her from the mirror—a tear-streaked face, and swollen eyes. She ruffled her fingers through flattened flaxen tresses, exhaled heavily, and straightened her back with a rising sense of resolution.

Lord Fowler had left her with good advice if nothing else. His words still rang in her ears.

"The duke must pay!"

And so he must. It was a necessary solution. She needed the money desperately, and she would not allow His Grace to leave Bath before he had given it to her.